CLAWS
FOR
ALARM

T. C. LoTempio

BERKLEY PRIME CRIME, NEW YORK

BERKLEY
PRIME
CRIME

An imprint of Penguin Random House LLC
375 Hudson Street, New York, New York 10014

CLAWS FOR ALARM

A Berkley Prime Crime Book / published by arrangement with the author

ISBN: 978-0-425-27021-9

PUBLISHING HISTORY
Berkley Prime Crime mass-market edition / November 2015

PRINTED IN THE UNITED STATES OF AMERICA

10 9 8 7 6 5 4 3 2 1

Cover illustration by Mary Ann Lasher.
Cover design by George Long.
Interior text design by Kristin del Rosario.

This is a work of fiction. Names, characters, places, and incidents either are the product of
the author's imagination or are used fictitiously, and any resemblance to actual persons,
living or dead, business establishments, events, or locales is entirely coincidental.

PUBLISHER'S NOTE: The recipes contained in this book are to be followed exactly
as written. The publisher is not responsible for your specific health or allergy needs
that may require medical supervision. The publisher is not responsible for any
adverse reactions to the recipes contained in this book.

Penguin
Random
House

For Larry Marshall and Mary Lou Ricciardi
Always in my heart

ACKNOWLEDGMENTS

Once again I would like to thank my fabulous agent, Josh Getzler, and his assistant, Danielle Burby, for their encouragement, hand-holding, and prompt answering of all my questions and concerns even when they're trivial! I would like to thank Faith Black for believing in Nick and Nora from the start. I would also like to thank my new editor, Kristine Swartz, for stepping in to take over Nick and Nora and for all her help and encouragement, and the entire editorial staff at Berkley Prime Crime for the fabulous job they do. A special thanks to the fabulous copyediting team, who managed to keep this manuscript on track, and a big shout out to Mary Ann Lasher for another fabulous cover. (Although ROCCO thinks Nick's a bit too thin—but that's a discussion for another day!)

I would also like to thank all the fabulous authors that I have come in contact with through the years via ROCCO's blog. I've learned so much from all of you! Special thanks to Carole Nelson Douglas, who's always there with a word of encouragement. (And Midnight Louie, too!) A huge thank-you to Emily Hall and Laura Roth, who graciously consented to beta-read CLAWS for me! Your comments were much appreciated.

ACKNOWLEDGMENTS

Finally, an author owes a lot to their readers, and I would like to thank each and every person who bought and read *Meow If It's Murder*, and who follow ROCCO's blog. Your support means the world to me, and I hope you are looking forward to the future adventures of Nick and Nora as much as I am!

PROLOGUE

When he pulled out of the circular driveway of his beautiful English Tudor home that morning, Professor Thaddeus C. Pitt had no idea he was in the last hours of his life.

A robust man in his late fifties, he could easily pass for ten years younger. His thick, curly hair was still a striking jet-black, with nary a gray strand in sight. His health was quite good—it had been ages since he'd seen the inside of a hospital—and for that he credited his sensible diet, sparing consumption of alcohol, and the Gold Crown membership at his health club. Money had rarely been a problem for him: He'd amassed a considerable fortune over the years, partly due to his own talent as an artist and, in the later years after the arthritis had made it impossible to continue painting, through his art acquisitions. It was well known he had one of the largest collections of rare paintings and sculptures on the West Coast. Why, only last month Donald Trump and Sylvester Stallone had offered him millions for the rare Cezanne he'd recently acquired. It had given him enormous pleasure to turn them down cold.

He liked having things other people wanted.

One thing he was certain several people wanted was the young, beautiful, blond wife he'd acquired a few years ago. Giselle couldn't tell a Cezanne from a Renoir, had not the faintest idea who Leonardo da Vinci was ("Isn't he the guy who was in that *Wolf of Wall Street* movie?"), but her other—ahem—attributes more than made up for her lack of polish. Yes, he was a lucky man indeed.

He pushed his wire-rimmed glasses up on the bridge of his aquiline-shaped nose and cast a wary eye at the stack of student portfolios left to grade that teetered on the edge of his cherrywood desk, threatening to spill over onto the thick shag carpeting. Even though teaching was a profession foisted upon him because he could no longer hold a brush in his hand for more than ten minutes, he had to admit to a certain satisfaction from nurturing his more talented students, inspiring them on to bigger and better things. The less talented ones—well, most of them, he feared—appreciated neither his candor nor his bluntness. Only the passage of time would most likely heal the wounds his words, perhaps cruel in tone but not cruelly meant, inflicted.

He leaned back in his chair. The glove leather felt like butter against his skin, and he let out a sigh of contentment as he reached for the top folder. He'd done half already, given them back in today's class. Not one student had gotten higher than a C—and none of them deserved any higher, in his opinion. Several of them had expressed their displeasure both verbally and visually, and his blasé attitude at their fury only served to add fuel to their fire, which he could only hope and pray might manifest itself in future works. One student in particular had not taken his criticism well at all—although if he were to be perfectly honest, Lacey Charles wasn't quite as hopeless as the others. Her portrait work was quite good, actually, but even so, she was certainly no Anne Rowe or William Branson. Lacey's problem was, surprisingly, a lack of confidence. All she needed was a fire lit under her—that was why he'd told her to come to his office after her last class today.

One thing he was very, very good at was lighting fires.

His eye fell on the photo of Giselle in the silver frame square in the center of his desk, reminding him he still had yet to answer her about going to that damned fund-raiser. He leaned back in his chair, trying to think of a worthy excuse, and as he did so his gaze fell upon an object tucked on the shelf on the far wall. He abruptly straightened in his chair and reached for his phone, brows drawn together as he punched in a number. The frown deepened as voice mail kicked in, and when the beep sounded, he said, "It's me. You didn't call as you were supposed to. Avoiding me won't change anything. As I told you this morning, I've discovered the flaw—the dirty little secret of what you sold me, and since I don't take lightly to abuse of art in any form, unless this matter is resolved—and quickly—I'll be forced to take further action. Oh, and for the record, I don't bluff."

That done, he rose, stretched, and made his way over to the well-stocked bar at the other end of his office. He poured himself a glass of port and stood in front of the bay window, sipping and looking out at the dimly lit street below. After a few minutes he began to feel groggy. He put his hand to his head, rubbed at his temples.

You're getting old, Thaddeus, my man. You can't drink like you used to.

He held the glass aloft, swirled the liquid, and took another sip. He held the glass out, frowned. Was it his imagination, or did the liquid seem a tad cloudy?

Impossible. I drank from this decanter only last night and everything was fine, just fine.

His knees started to wobble, and the wineglass slid from his hand, landing on the carpet with a soft *thud*. The room seemed to spin crazily, and his vision blurred. His dimming gaze fixed on the bottle of wine as the shudder ripped through his body.

Good God. I've been drugged.

His legs went out from under him, and he fell upon the soft carpet, his head lolling to one side like a broken doll's. So dulled were his senses that he was oblivious to the creak of the office door as it opened, or the soft footfalls that signified the presence of an intruder. Pitt never felt the sharp blade of the knife as it entered his body and pierced his heart. He let out one long, shuddering gasp as his lungs started to bleed into his chest cavity, and his last conscious thought as the life slowly ebbed out of him was that, even had he been a praying man, no amount of it could help him now . . .

ONE

"*C*hérie, I don't think you have a choice. You have to get rid of him."

I brushed an errant auburn curl out of my eyes and squinted at my friend. "There's always a choice," I said. "But I guess you're right. He's got to go."

"*Ow-owrr!*"

We both burst out laughing as the large black-and-white cat rose from his post in front of my refrigerator, stretched his forepaws out in front of him, and then sat back on his haunches, regarding the two of us with catly disdain. He lifted one large paw and waved it imperiously in the air. "*Ow-owrr,*" he said again.

"Relax. Not you, Nick," I said. I reached out and tapped at the large blackboard that hung just to the left of the store counter. "Brad Pitt. See?" I pointed to the list of specials on the blackboard and the *Brad Pitt All-American Hero* that was wedged in between the *Jennifer Aniston Garden Salad* and the *Angelina Jolie Tuna Club*. "Chantal's right. Some die-hard Aniston or Jolie fan will be sure to complain."

My BFF, Chantal Gillard, knelt down beside the stocky cat and petted him on the white streak behind his left ear. "Ah, Nicky, do not worry," she crooned. I stifled a grin. Chantal loved to speak in an affected French accent, so it came out sounding like, *Ah, Neekey, do naht worree.* "Nora would never get rid of you. Where else would she find such a charming store mascot—and where would I find as handsome a model?"

At the word *model*, Nick's eyes flew open. He got up, turned, and marched, his tail straight up, back to his post in front of the refrigerator where he squatted, his back to us.

"*Mon Dieu*," Chantal said. "And here I thought he enjoyed modeling my collars."

Chantal and her brother, Remy Gillard, co-ran Poppies, the local flower store. Chantal had also turned a portion of the store into a combination New Age store slash tearoom, where she also read tarot cards (my friend has psychic abilities), and recently she'd branched out into a new venture: homemade jewelry. This included a line of pet collars, for which she'd drafted Nick as a model—a chore the feline wasn't particularly fond of.

I chuckled as I picked up the eraser. "Nick would probably rather solve mysteries than model collars—after all, his former owner was a PI. It's in his blood."

Nick's ears perked up and he let out a soft meow.

"It's in yours, too, Nora Charles," my friend said, waggling her finger. "You can't turn your back on a good mystery, either—as the Grainger case proved."

"Maybe not," I admitted. "But Cruz is a quiet little town. How many mysteries can it have?"

"You'd be surprised," said a deep voice behind us.

We both started. We'd been so deep in our conversation neither one of us had heard the shop door open. The newcomer walked over to my counter and leaned his elbows on it. Lance Reynolds was six-four, built like a sumo wrestler, and the guy who escorted me to my senior prom in high school, even though everyone knows he's always carried a torch for my younger sister, Lacey. After getting a degree in business from UCLA he tried accounting for a while, but it soon became evident that being a nine-to-fiver wearing a suit and tie was most definitely NOT up his alley. His brother, Phil, felt pretty much the same, so the two of them pooled their resources and opened the Poker Face, a quaint tavern about a block away from my shop, Hot Bread. Now he grinned at me and said, "You've got a mystery right here, under your very nose." He inclined his head toward where Nick squatted. "The mystery of the missing owner." He paused. "Or have you succeeded in finding him?"

I shook my head. "No—but then again, I haven't tried all that hard."

My tubby tuxedo formerly belonged to a PI, also named Nick—Nick Atkins. Feline Nick is a cat of many and varied talents, some of which may or may not have been taught to him by his former owner, which also include a flair for detective work. The story of how our association began is a long one (recounted elsewhere, for those who are interested— even for those who are not) that ended with my routing out a hired hit man and preventing two more deaths in the process—and with Nick saving my hide from the aforementioned murderer.

"Nora couldn't care less if Atkins ever turns up," Chantal said with feeling. "She's gotten quite attached to Nicky—as have I." Chantal slipped her oversized tote bag over her shoulder and blew the cat a kiss. "I have to get going for my shift at Poppies, but tomorrow, Nicky, I will bring along those new collars. You will love them."

Nick put both paws over his face and let out a soft *grr*, then wiggled his portly body underneath the table at the rear of the kitchen. Once Chantal had disappeared out the door Lance turned to me and chuckled. "I swear, sometimes I think that cat's part human."

"Yeah, well, you're not the only one. So—what can I get you? A nice *Thin Man Tuna Melt*? Or maybe you'd like to try out the *Brad Pitt All-American Hero*? Baloney, ham, American cheddar, tomato, hot peppers, and shredded lettuce with mayo and oil and vinegar on a long roll."

"Yum." He made smacking sounds with his tongue. "I'll take two to go. Phil and I have a long evening ahead of us, and we need something to see us through." He pulled a face. "Annual audit. I'm hoping Phil has all the receipts labeled this time. You have no idea what we went through last year. For an ex-accountant he's horribly disorganized."

I bit back a chuckle. Neither Lance nor his brother were particularly organized.

Lance leaned across my counter and rested his chin in his hands, watching as I removed two long rolls from the breadbasket, sliced them, then spread them liberally with mayo. "So," he asked casually, "heard from Lacey lately?"

I shook my head as I pulled the Virginia ham out of the glass case. "Not for a few weeks. This is midterm time at that art school she's attending. Aunt Prudence said that she's been so immersed in her work, she's hardly seen her, either."

Lance chuckled. "Immersed in work, eh? Now there's a phrase I'd never have associated with your sister."

"Me, either." I arranged the ham on the bread, wiped off the slicer, and turned back to the case for the baloney. "She has had her share of jobs over the years. and I, for one, hope this passion of hers continues. I was beginning to wonder if she'd ever find anything she liked to do for more than five seconds." I finished slicing the baloney, arranged it on top of the ham, then returned to the case for the cheddar. "Mom always used to worry that Lacey would just shuffle aimlessly through life."

Lance's lips twigged upward. "Your sister never shuffled a day in her life. Barreled right through is more like it. She'd never get caught dead shuffling."

I spread cheddar over the cold cuts, added lettuce, tomato, salt and pepper, a splash of oil and vinegar, and a generous helping of hot peppers to both sandwiches, then started to wrap them in wax paper. "You're probably right. I've thought about driving out there one afternoon—you know, pay Aunt Prudence a visit and see how she's doing—but if I know my sister, she'd just resent it. She's always accused me of not having faith in her, of always checking up on her. She was particularly vocal about it after Mom died."

Lance laughed. "Well, she's not wrong, is she?"

I carried the wrapped sandwiches over to the register and returned Lance's grin. "No, I suppose not. This is the first time, though, in years that I can actually say my sister and

I have gotten along—she's actually been civil to me on the last few phone calls. I really don't want to jeopardize it right now. Besides, I have a lot on my own plate."

"Louis said the article you did on the Grainger case was a big hit."

"He told me." Louis Blondell was the editor of *Noir*, an online true crime magazine I'd started writing articles for. Louis had recently offered me my own column, which I was seriously considering. "He'd love it if I did one like that for him every month."

"Well, you could. That'd be right up your alley."

"Sure—but to do it right takes careful research, for which one needs time, which I don't have lots of right now, not if I intend to revamp and make a go of Mom's business." I gave my head a brisk shake, letting the auburn curls fall in ringlets across my cheeks. "Damn—why wasn't I born rich instead of beautiful?"

Lance tamped down a smile. "We all have our crosses to bear."

I gave Lance his change, walked him out, then locked the door, turned the sign to CLOSED, and pulled down the shade. As I turned around, Nick's head popped out from underneath the damask tablecloth. A few seconds later the front paws followed. I caught a glimpse of a square object underneath his paws and frowned.

"Hey, you. What have you got there?"

I made a dive for him; he wiggled back underneath the table. I squatted on the floor and raised the tablecloth up to peer underneath. Nick lay pressed up against the wall, curled in a tight ball, with what looked like a beat-up leather notebook clutched in his claws. The book was open, and he had one paw thrown possessively over the page, his sharp teeth nibbling at the paper's edge.

"Nick, what are you doing? Give me that? If you're hungry I made lobster salad yesterday."

Without really thinking I reached out and grasped the edge of the book. Nick could have easily scratched me but good with those talons of his—but he didn't. Instead he rolled rather meekly on his side and allowed me to drag the book out. I picked it up and took it over to the counter, where I smoothed the wrinkled, chewed page.

I glanced over my shoulder. Nick's head had popped out from underneath the table, and he was watching me, head cocked to one side, golden eyes wide. I shook my fist at him. "This is one of your former human's journals, Nick. What are you doing with it? And how did you get this? I thought I had these locked upstairs in my desk."

The eyes blinked once, twice. His ears flicked forward.

A little sigh escaped my lips. Oh yes, I should know better. Locked drawers, doors—they all meant nothing to this portly tuxedo cat. He could have taught Harry Houdini a few tricks, and for all I knew, he well might have.

"You rascal. You've got your own method of communication, don't you?" I grumbled. I leaned over to inspect the chewed page more closely. It was an account of Nick Atkins's investigation of one Bronson A. Pichard—and a very colorful account, at that. I shot my gaze back to the cat. "So, Nick, tell me: What's the attraction here? Why this particular page? Are you trying to tell me something?"

Nick's ears flicked and he began to purr.

Tucking the notebook under one arm, I hurried up the stairs to my apartment and made a beeline for my desk and my trusty Rolodex. I found the number I wanted, grabbed my cell, and a few minutes later heard a familiar voice:

"Sampson Atkins Investigations. Oliver Sampson here."

"Well, I see you haven't dissolved the partnership yet."

"No—at least not officially, anyway. All in due time, I suppose." I could feel his smile over the wire. "Well, well, Nora Charles. What a nice surprise. How are you, and how is my missing partner's cat? Little Nick is behaving himself, I hope. Or has he gotten you involved in another murder case?"

"I'm not sure," I answered truthfully. "He managed to get his paws on one of Nick's journals, and one page in particular— notes on a Bronson A. Pichard."

"Oh," Ollie said, and then grew very quiet. "Pichard, eh?" he said at last. "Now there's a blast from the past. That guy was creepy."

"Creepy? In what way?"

"Nothing I could put my finger on, I only saw him once or twice but – maybe it was those eyes of his. They were two different colors. One blue, one brown. Gave him a sinister appearance. Anyway, that investigation was quite an undertaking. Pichard's wife hired Nick to get some dirt for her for their divorce."

"And did he?"

Ollie cleared his throat. "Did he ever. Isobel ended up with practically everything. Pichard lost his business, most of his holdings and money, and—he blamed Nick."

I felt heat sear my cheeks. "I just love guys like that," I said with feeling. "They cheat, but they're the injured party."

"There's a bit more to the story," Ollie said. "Pichard owned an art gallery that specialized in rare paintings and sculptures. He did well at first among the San Francisco high society, but then his prices started to get out of control. Plus, there were some rumblings that he, ah, misrepresented authenticity on quite a few pieces—real expensive ones. Nothing was ever proven, but his reputation went downhill fast." I frowned. "He suspected Nick of tipping off the authorities."

"Did he?"

A pause and then, "What do you think?"

I sighed. "I think Pichard sounds like a man with a grudge and a very big axe to wield—or a gun. If he isn't responsible for Nick's disappearance himself, he might know something about it."

"Ordinarily I'd tend to agree, but Pichard's been off the radar for years. He's disappeared even more effectively than Nick has. The last address I have on file for him is over five years old. Mandrake the Magician's got nothing on him."

"Haven't you heard?" I couldn't keep the smile out of my voice. "I'm pretty good at finding people who do just that. Now, what about Pichard's ex-wife? Got any info on her?"

"Nothing current. Isobel moved to Italy two years ago. She wouldn't be of any help anyway. Wanted nothing to do with Pichard once the ink was dry on the divorce papers. Listen, Nora," Ollie sighed. "I'd sure like to know what happened to Nick, but digging around about Pichard—that just seems like asking for trouble. Besides, lately I've been thinking . . . maybe Nick *wanted* to disappear."

I sat up straighter. "You think he vanished on purpose?"

"Who knows? I'm just saying it's a possibility. Nick knows many ways to make himself scarce." Ollie paused and then added, "Sometimes it's best to let sleeping dogs lie."

"Maybe so, but I've never been one to do what's best."

He sighed heavily. "Okay. I can see your mind is made up. But don't say I didn't warn you. And if you need help—any help at all—you call me, y'hear?"

"I hear. And thanks."

I put down the phone and nibbled at my lower lip. Almost as if he knew I'd been thinking about him, Nick appeared, jumping into my lap with surprising ease for a cat of his girth. I rubbed the sensitive area behind his ears and whispered into his ruff, "You'd like to know what happened to your former master too, wouldn't you?"

Nick raised his sleek black head. "*Er-ewl,*" he mewled as his little (debatable point) kitty claws moved up and down, kneading my lap.

"That's what I thought." I picked up the piece of paper on which I'd written the address Ollie'd given me. "St. Leo isn't far away—as a matter of fact it's only about two miles from Aunt Prudence's house. We could conceivably kill two birds with one stone, say, tomorrow afternoon?"

His steady rumble made me smile. I gave his head a quick pat. "I thought you'd agree." I reached for my cell phone. "Maybe I'd better warn Aunt Prudence we're going to be stopping by, though. So she can prepare my sister."

Nick's eyes popped wide, and he leaned back on his haunches, pawed at the air.

I laughed. "Yes, she might find you charming, and then again . . . with Lacey, you can never tell. We—we've never gotten along all that well. I'm sure she'll like you, though." I leaned over to stroke his head, and I didn't imagine the cat smile he gave me. As I reached for my cell with my other hand, it started to ring. I snatched it up, glanced at the number, and then hit the button. "Aunt Prudence. You must be psychic. I was just going to call you."

"Oh, Nora, I'm so glad I got you." My aunt's voice was a high-pitched wail of distress. "The most awful thing has happened.

"Your sister's been arrested—for murder."

TWO

I was so startled at my aunt's declaration that for a minute, I couldn't speak. Finally, I stammered, "M-murder? What—are you sure?"

"Of course I'm sure," my aunt sniffed. "I was standing right in my own living room when it happened."

I tugged at an errant curl, trying to process the information my aunt had just pummeled me with. "But are you sure they arrested her? Maybe they just took her in for questioning."

"When that detective came in and read Lacey her rights, he said outright he was arresting her for the murder of Thaddeus Pitt."

"Thaddeus Pitt?" It was my turn to sound incredulous. "The Thaddeus Pitt? The one who owns the art school Lacey's going to?"

"Yes, yes, he's the one. That's what's going to make this so complicated. I mean, the man is a legend here. Why it's like—like murdering Santa Claus." She sucked in a sharp breath. "You know all this is very traumatizing to me, Nora. I realize it must seem old hat to you, what with your background and all, but I've never actually seen anyone arrested before, let alone a beloved family member. And for MURDER!"

My temples started to pound, and I pinched the bridge of my nose between my thumb and forefinger. "They've got to have some sort of evidence," I said. "They can't charge anyone without reasonable cause. Unless there's some specific reason they feel a murder charge would stick, she should just be considered a person of interest."

There was a slight hesitation, and then my aunt said slowly, "Would standing over the body holding the murder weapon be enough to make a murder charge—how did you say it—stick?"

"WHAT?" This got worse with each successive sentence. "Are you telling me she fled the scene? That's not good, Aunt Prudence. Flight is considered evidence of guilt."

"*Fled* is such a strong term, Nora. Your sister wasn't thinking clearly. She's never been good under pressure—you know she's not coolheaded and collected like you are, dear. She intended to go down to the police station, once she'd calmed down, but by then that detective came to arrest her."

I squinched my eyes shut. It was true, my sister had done some pretty outrageous things in the past, but I also doubted her capable of murder, whether it was premeditated or in the heat of passion. However, law enforcement would surely view her being caught with the body and then fleeing the scene in a not-so-favorable light.

My aunt was still moaning into the phone. "Oh, it's such an awful mess. Irene—that's Irene MacGillicuddy—you remember her? My childhood friend? Well, maybe not. Anyway, she's staying here at my house—hers is being fumigated, long story—anyway, I don't know what I'd have done if Irene hadn't been here. She told me I should call you right away."

I bit down on my lower lip so hard I tasted blood. Prudence's habit of drawing out details hadn't diminished over the years, that was for sure. "Yes, it's good you did. Now, did you also call a lawyer?"

"I called Herbie Jenkins—he's taken care of my affairs for years, but he only does family law, and Monroe Schlessinger only does real estate. They did make some recommendations, but—" She uttered a long, drawn-out sigh. "No one in the family's ever been accused of murder before. I just don't know what to do, or who to hire. Oh, it's such a *mess*." The last was another long, drawn-out wail.

I made up my mind. "Okay, Aunt Prudence, you just sit tight. Hot Bread's closed now, so I'm going to make a few calls, see if I can track down a lawyer." I glanced at my watch. "It's not too late—maybe there's still something that can be done today."

"Oh, thank you, dear." My aunt's tone brightened considerably at my announcement. "I knew we could count on you. You were always the levelheaded one in the family." Aunt Prudence took a quick breath and then continued, "It's true, I don't know many of the details, but I know my niece. Lacey might have panicked and done some foolish things, but she's not a killer. Why, she has trouble offing a spider. How could she murder a *person*?"

* * *

Once I'd calmed my aunt down as best I could under the circumstances, I immediately called Daniel Corleone. I got his answering machine, so I left a message, hitting the highlights and asking him to dig up any information he could on Pitt's murder.

Daniel Corleone is an FBI agent whose acquaintance I'd made during my previous adventure. Our professional relationship had a rocky beginning, for sure, but we'd also both felt a mutual attraction to each other in spite of it. Following the successful completion of that case, he'd accepted a position heading up an FBI satellite office in Carmel. He shared the office with a DOJ (that's Department of Justice, for those not in the know) agent, Rick Barnes, for whom I suspected Chantal harbored quite a crush. Over the past few weeks Daniel and I had been "getting to know" each other over some casual lunches. As of yet, our relationship hadn't gotten past the friendly stop-by-for-a-quick-lunch level, but after my last relationship (which had turned very, very sour . . . another long story), taking it slow seemed a good idea to me.

Since I've never been a particularly patient person, and since I had no clue how long it would be before Daniel might call back, I dragged out my trusty laptop and proceeded to search for some mention of Pitt's murder, which proved to be no easy feat. There were loads of articles on Pitt—on his contributions to the town of Carmel, his academic prowess, his school. Likening him to Santa Claus was putting it mildly. A male Mother Teresa would be more apropos. Hardly a mention, though, of his untimely end; apparently the Carmel police were trying to keep the incident on the down low. I finally found one mention in the *Carmel Herald*:

LOCAL CELEBRITY FOUND
STABBED TO DEATH

Professor found dead in office

Professor Thaddeus Pitt, 58, renowned artist and the founder of the Pitt Institute located in nearby St. Leo, was found stabbed to death Wednesday evening in his office at the school on Peachtree Drive.

Pitt's body was discovered around ten thirty Wednesday evening. Police were called to the scene shortly thereafter. The cause of death appears to be a stab wound directly to the heart. An autopsy will be held to accurately determine the cause and exact time of death.

A California native, Pitt was raised in both California and Texas. He displayed artistic ability at an early age and was admitted into the prestigious Otis College of Art and Design at age 16. He gained fame for both his Impressionistic drawings and portraits of famous people such as Marilyn Monroe and Pope John Paul XXIII. His work hangs in museums such as the Guggenheim, the Smithsonian, and the Metropolitan Museum of Art. Although he himself has not painted for the last fifteen years, Pitt's school, started twelve years ago, has produced many fine artists, all of whom mourn his untimely passing.

Even though a possible suspect has been taken into custody, the police declined further comment at this time, other than to say the incident remains under investigation.

At least, I thought thankfully, Lacey's name was withheld—for the time being. I drummed my fingers on the edge of my desk. I needed more details, and I also needed to find a good criminal lawyer. I'd known tons in Chicago, but here . . . As I debated the situation my phone rang. I glanced at the number, then immediately picked it up.

"Daniel, hi. Thank you for calling back so quickly."

"Well, I'm FBI, remember? Speed is our middle name." His tone sobered. "How are you holding up, Nora? This must have been quite a shock for you."

"Well, Lacey is the last person I'd ever expect to be accused of murder—then again I haven't really been in touch with her in a long, long, time. I keep thinking how my mother would have reacted." I swallowed over the sudden lump in my throat. "So, were you able to find out any details?"

"The way the St. Leo detective explained it, the night guard heard a scream and went to investigate. He found your sister standing over Pitt's body, knife clutched in her hand. The guard's a pretty old guy, and when he went to grab your sister's arm, she pushed him out of the way and got the hell out of there. She kept her face averted, so he couldn't really see it—but Lacey's name was in Pitt's appointment book, and she fit the guard's general description."

"Fantastic," I sighed. "Whatever possessed her to touch that knife? She used to watch those crime shows with Mom. She should have known better."

"True. When you combine that with fleeing the scene and what transpired earlier in the day, it provided enough reasonable cause to book her for murder one."

I felt a chill snake up my spine. "What happened earlier in the day?"

"Apparently the grade Pitt gave your sister didn't sit too well with her. They had a, quote unquote, heated exchange. That's why they were meeting. She was supposed to show him some of her sketches for extra credit—so he'd pass her."

"Great. So, I guess she's in jail?"

I pushed my hand through my hair. No one knew better than I just how vicious Lacey could get in the heat of an argument. Our mother had always said her tongue was like a battle weapon—a sharp-edged sword. Still, I had the distinct impression Daniel was holding something back. Before I could call him on it he added, "She's being held at St. Leo County Jail. And more bad news—I hear the DA thinks this is pretty open and shut."

"Well," I sighed, "this cinches it. She's going to need a good criminal lawyer. Too bad Perry Mason's a fictional character. What I need right now is a reasonable facsimile thereof."

"I just might be able to help you. My friend Peter Dobbs was an FBI agent, but he left it all behind to go to law school. He's been working the past year as a public defender in San Francisco, and just last month he opened his own law firm in St. Leo. He interned for a year at the DA's office, too, working for his uncle—Helmut Dobbs."

I let out a low whistle. You had to be living under a rock not to at least be aware of Helmut Dobbs's reputation. As the DA of Los Angeles County he'd put some pretty high-profile criminals away. "Your friend has a good pedigree. Do you think he'd be willing to take the case?"

"He's not only willing; he's at the jail with your sister as we speak. He told me to tell you to meet him there tomorrow morning at seven thirty a.m. sharp. He'll get you in to see her before the arraignment."

I let out a sigh of relief. "If you were here right now, I'd give you a great big kiss."

"Hold on to that thought. By the way, I'm going to be in-communicado for a few days, but I'll check back with you as soon as I can."

Disappointment arrowed through me. "New case?" I asked, and then added, "You don't have to say. I realize you probably can't talk about it anyway."

"Thanks for understanding. Now, you're sure you're going to be all right?"

Aha! The million-dollar question. "I have to be. Lacey needs me to think clearly, because all this has to be one huge mistake." I paused. "Unless there's something you're not telling me?"

There was a moment of silence and then Daniel said, "Well, you'll find out tomorrow anyway. When I told you there was a heated exchange I was being kind.

"When Pitt gave her that grade, she flipped out and threatened to kill him—in front of about thirty witnesses."

THREE

Once I'd hung up with Daniel I called Chantal to fill her in and ask if she could mind Hot Bread tomorrow. I felt bad asking her—it was Friday, and Fridays were always my busiest day. Lunchtime could get a bit hairy, but Chantal was familiar with the store and most of my regular customers and their preferences. Cooking shouldn't be an issue despite her self-proclaimed lack of prowess in the kitchen—I had detailed descriptions of each and every sandwich on Hot Bread's menu along with step-by-step prep instructions in a Rolodex in the kitchen, plus I'd already prepared two dozen of each special listed and stored them in the large refrigerator. Mollie Travis, the high school junior who worked part-time, would be there to help out, too. I knew she only had one class on Friday, and she was always willing to put in some extra hours. Chantal agreed quickly, assuring me making a sandwich was a lot easier than boiling water (go figure) and to call if I needed anything at all. I thanked her profusely before hanging up to call Aunt Prudence, who was thrilled when I asked her if it would be all right for me to spend the night. It would be a lot easier going to the St. Leo police station from her house than battling rush-hour traffic from here. I filled her in on a few more of the details Daniel had shared with me but left out the part about Lacey threatening to murder Pitt. Prudence was upset enough, and I just couldn't take listening to more of her wailing right now—I had to get my own thoughts in order. As I set down the phone, I heard a loud *"Meow"* from across the room. I glanced over and saw Nick, curled on top of the pet carrier I'd bought last week at the Pet Palace.

"So, what? You want to come with me, eh?" I got up, walked over, and started to scratch him behind his ears. "Well, maybe that's not such a bad idea. I could use a friendly face around me at Aunt Prudence's tonight, and it will spare you from Chantal's clutches. 'Cause if you want to stay here, a little birdie told me modeling more pet collars is on the agenda."

Nick's shoulders hunched in a feline shudder, and I grinned.

"Aunt Prudence won't mind. She's always had a soft spot for animals—any stray in the neighborhood could always count on a helping hand from her."

Nick hopped down from the carrier top and ambled off toward my bedroom, head and tail held high. I gave a soft chuckle and followed him. He lay down on the rug beside my bed and watched with slitted eyes as I hoisted my brand-new hard-backed overnighter out of the closet and laid it on the bed. I tossed underwear, nightshirt, and slippers inside and then crossed to the closet to get something to wear to the jail the next day. When I turned back I saw Nick's rotund bottom wiggling underneath my comforter.

"Hey," I said, dropping the navy blue pantsuit I'd chosen and fisting my hands at my sides. "What are you doing under there, Nick? Did you lose one of your toys?"

"*Er-ewl*," came the plaintive sound. I bent down and peeped underneath the edge of the comforter. Nick lay there, head resting comfortably on his forepaws. As soon as he caught sight of me he began to purr loudly. He shifted his body to one side, and I caught a flash of something white peeping out from beneath his rotund tummy.

"What are you hiding now?" I demanded. I knelt down all the way and reached underneath the bed. I poked my finger at his soft underbelly. "Let me see what you've got."

He rolled over a bit farther at my prodding (none too agreeably, I might add), and I saw that the "hidden treasure" clutched firmly in his shivs was a sheet of notepaper and a faded photograph. I tickled him on his tummy, and he loosened his grip, purring loudly. I snatched up his "treasure" and rose, perching myself on the edge of the bed. Nick rolled over and narrowed his eyes.

"Sorry, chum. I know it was a bit sneaky of me, but would you have given 'em up willingly?"

Nick stretched out full length and turned his head.

I chuckled. "I didn't think so." I held the photo up for inspection. It was pretty grainy, but I could make out a dark-haired man in an expensive-looking suit sporting a pair of expensive-looking sunglasses emerging from a building. I set the photo to one side and smoothed out the paper, biting back a gasp as I recognized the cramped handwriting and what was written there.

The left side of the page chronicling Bronson A. Pichard was ragged, with deep slashes that resembled claw marks. I glanced across the room at the low table I'd set the journals on and wasn't surprised to find them knocked in a pile on the floor. Well, that'd teach me to lock things up, although with Nick around, that didn't seem to do much good, either.

He wiggled out from underneath the bed and sat, head up, staring at me. I waved the paper in the air. "Well, Nick, what have we here? Who said it was okay for you to deface your former owner's property?"

He stared at me another minute, then calmly raised his front paw and began licking it.

I folded the paper and crossed the room to tuck it inside my purse. "If this is your way of reminding me about my promise to look up Pichard, I haven't forgotten. I want to follow up any lead I can on your former master's whereabouts, but right now isn't the best of times. I'm a bit distracted by the honey of a mess my sister's gotten herself into. But I'll get to it—don't worry."

Nick's ears flattened back against his skull. I got the distinct impression if he could speak, he would have said something like: *Stupid human. I am a cat, and an extremely talented one. Haven't you figured out I can do whatever I want?*

Apparently not. But I was learning.

I pulled up at Aunt Prudence's a few minutes before nine thirty. She'd moved several times since I last visited her, which had been the year I'd moved to Chicago. I'd never been to this house, and it was too dark now for a real good look, but if the wide latticed porch that went around the front and almost the entire left side was any indication, the place was HUGE.

I glanced over at the ball of black fur in the passenger seat. Nick, unfortunately, had turned out to be a mite too big for the carrier. (Did I say *mite*? I'm being kind again.) Good thing he enjoyed riding shotgun. I sighed and gave his fore-paw a shake. "Wake up, Nick. We're here."

His head came up a bit, and he looked first right, then left, before dropping it back onto his forepaws. I switched off the ignition and tapped my keys against the steering wheel. "Get that tail moving and your rear in gear. I'm not carrying you. And first thing Monday I'm taking that carrier back to the Pet Palace and getting a refund. I can't even exchange it, dammit. That was the biggest one they had."

The porch light flicked on just as I climbed out of the SUV, bathing the surrounding area in a harsh white light, and then a stout figure with short, stylishly cut gray hair, bundled head to foot in a bright purple terrycloth bathrobe, burst out of the front door and made a beeline straight for my car, arms stretched wide.

"Nora! Thank God you're here at last!"

Aunt Prudence is barely five-three, and I'm five-eight in flats, so I dutifully bent over to let her chubby arms envelop me in a bear hug to end all bear hugs. She planted a kiss on my cheek and whispered against it, "Everything will be all right now, I know it. Sharon always said you were the one with the cool head, the one she'd count on if she were in a fix. I remember her exact words: *If ever I get in trouble, Pru, I'd rely on Nora to get me out. When the good Lord passed out common sense, he gave her a double dose.* She said that—yes, she did."

Mention of my mother's name caused my own eyes to mist a bit. I blinked away the moistness and forced a smile to my lips. "You look tired, Aunt Prudence."

"It's been a long day. Irene tried to get me to relax and take a nap, plied me with chamomile tea, but—" Her shoulders lifted in a shrug. "Hard to relax when you're worried about a loved one. I don't know many of the details, but I know Lacey didn't do what they say she did, Nora."

"You don't have to convince me. I know that, Aunt Prudence. Lacey's many things, but a murderer isn't one of them." *No matter what sort of evidence they may have*, I added silently.

She wrung her hands in front of her. "My goodness, I'm not thinking straight. You must be exhausted after that drive. I'll show you to your room, and then we can catch up over a nice cup of coffee." Her gaze shifted to a point somewhere beyond my left shoulder, and she let out a small squeal. "Nora—is that a cat in your car?"

I turned. Nick had his portly bod stretched full length against the windshield. "Um, yeah, that's a cat, all right. Aunt Prudence, meet Nick."

Aunt Prudence continued to stare at Nick, who wriggled off the windshield and hopped onto the driver's seat where he sat, nose pressed against the window, watching us. "He—he's yours? I'm sorry to sound so surprised, it's just—you never expressed much interest in pets. Your mother told me about the chameleon."

My sigh rippled the crisp night air. "It's not like I went down to the shelter and deliberately picked him out. To be frank, he picked me. Just wandered into Hot Bread one day, and now . . . I've grown fond of the little guy."

"Oh, you don't have to tell me, dear. I've had my share of pets over the years—six dogs, four cats, twelve goldfish, two parakeets, and a parrot. I know all about stray animals choosing owners. He looks handsome. Let's get a better look." She waddled over to the passenger side and tapped her fingers against the window. Ever the exhibitionist, Nick lay down on the seat and rolled over on his back, paws in the air, and gave his rotund behind a little wiggle.

"Oh, he's so cute!" Aunt Prudence gushed over her shoulder at me. "I can see how even someone like you not fond of animals would get attached." She flung open the car door and scooped Nick up into her arms, pressing him against her ample bosom. He gave a contented sigh and let his chin rest on her shoulder. The twenty-plus tonnage must have gotten to her, though, because a few moments later she set him down on the ground at my feet. "What do you feed him? He's a big boy."

"Oh, you know, the usual. Friskies, Fancy Feast— sometimes Purina."

Aunt Prudence's eyebrows shot up like two rockets. Nick even gave me a look that said, *Liar.* I gulped and added, "To tell you the truth, he's fonder of human food. I usually let him eat whatever's left over at the end of the day from our specials."

Aunt Prudence clicked her tongue against the roof of her mouth. "That's not good, Nora. No wonder he's so . . . plump. But don't worry"—she waved her hand in the air—"I had the same problem with Gladys. The vet gave me a diet regimen and canned food guaranteed to help your pet maintain a sensible weight. I can give you one or two cans to take home. It will slim him down in no time."

Nick looked at Prudence, then at me, and let out a loud, "*Meow*."

My aunt reached out and chucked him under the chin. "Vocal, isn't he? I think it's cute you named him Nick. I know how you loved those *Thin Man* movies."

I retrieved my overnight bag from the car, and then we followed Aunt Prudence inside. I moved into the foyer and rolled my suitcase over to the base of the staircase, pausing to let my eyes travel around. To my right a corridor led toward a kitchen. The living room was directly in front of me, and off to the left in what appeared to be a study, bookshelves overflowing to capacity with both hardcover and paperback volumes took up one entire wall. I cast a quick glance into the living room and saw nothing in there but a wide three-cushion sofa and a high-backed Queen Anne chair in front of a fireplace. What Prudence's house lacked in furnishings, however, seemed to be more than made up for in trappings. The carpet beneath my feet felt thick and luxurious, and the crown moldings and wall coverings looked expensive.

"I thought Irene would be here to welcome you, but she must have fallen asleep." Aunt Prudence threw me a grin that seemed both rueful and apologetic.

"No worries." I was actually glad the other woman hadn't put in an appearance. I glanced around. "This house seems much bigger than your other one."

"Oh, it is. I take boarders in, you know, but right now I'm in a bit of a dry spell. I'm using the time to have the second floor redone, but I've got a nice big room on the third floor for you and Nick." Her finger jabbed upward. "I hope you don't mind stairs? It's an old house. They're pretty steep."

"No problem." I patted my flat stomach. "I don't mind—it's a good way to keep in shape."

"That it is." She nodded past me. "Think *he* can make it?"

I turned and looked at Nick, sprawled spread-eagle on the carpet, his rotund belly heaving in and out.

"We'll soon find out, won't we?" I sighed.

Twenty-eight steps later I had my suitcase on the twin bed in the room and Nick lay sprawled out on the braided carpet next to the bed. The room wasn't much, but it was homey; it boasted an iron-frame twin bed, a wooden dresser, and a small nightstand. The walls were covered in a paper that was denim blue and cream, and the chenille bedspread was a lighter shade of blue. Uninspiring quarters, to be sure, but at least they were clean. I took out the suit I'd packed to wear to the police station in the morning and hung it in the tiny closet, then pulled out a small bowl and a package of Fancy Feast for Nick. He scampered double time off the rug, turning around and around as I filled the bowl with salmon and chicken bits. I left him happily hunkered down in the corner and went downstairs in search of the promised coffee.

By the time I reached the first floor the aroma of freshly brewed Kona blend assailed my nostrils. I followed the scent straight into the large, homey kitchen I'd glimpsed upon my arrival and stood in the doorway for a better look. Gleaming stainless steel appliances took up almost one entire wall, while the one opposite held shelves overflowing with cereal, canned goods, and other assorted groceries. Light streamed in from the window above the sink and filtered over the large wooden table that stood in the center of the room. To the side of the window was what looked like a large covered cage on a stand. I wondered what was inside then decided I was probably better off not knowing. A sizable orange, white, and black calico cat sat square in the middle of the room, paws folded under its head, eyes closed. Aunt Prudence, in front of a massive double oven range, turned, smiled at me, and saw the cat. She immediately hustled over, scooped it up, and deposited it gently in a fluffy fleece bed lying off to one side of the massive double-door refrigerator. The cat shifted comfortably in the bed, with not a peep or a meow.

"That's Gladys." My aunt smiled fondly at the cat. "She's fourteen but still pretty spry. I'd introduce her to your Nick, but . . . I'm afraid she's not very sociable with other animals."

"That's okay. I'm sure Nick won't mind. To be honest, I haven't had him very long, so I don't know how he interacts with other animals, either."

"Some cats need other feline companionship, while others are perfectly happy being 'only children.' Gladys loves having the run of the house. She's fondest of the kitchen, especially at mealtime, but if Irene ever saw her up on the table . . ." She shot me a quick eye roll. "Irene's not too fond of cats. Doesn't like the fact they can jump most anywhere."

I eased myself into one of the high-backed lemon yellow wooden chairs. "Well, I'll try to keep Nick in my room while we're here."

A light shuffling sound reached my ears. I swiveled my head in the direction of the covered cage. Aunt Prudence saw me and smiled. "That's only Jumanji, my African parrot. He's a complete dear."

"Dear, dear," sounded softly from beneath the cover.

My aunt poured steaming coffee into two mugs and

brought them over to the table. "Do you take your coffee straight, or with milk or cream?"

"Milk's fine."

She bustled over to the stainless steel refrigerator, returning with a small white ceramic pitcher, which she placed on the table in front of me. I poured some milk into the mug and took a long, satisfying sip.

"So," Prudence settled herself in the chair next to me. "How do you like running the sandwich shop? I imagine after palling around with undercover cops and tracking down criminals it must have been quite a change for you."

"Change, change," chirped Jumanji.

I ignored the parrot and turned to my aunt. "It was," I admitted, "but not an unwelcome one. I've always liked to cook, as you know, and I enjoy making up different sandwich combinations for my customers. People love my *Thin Man Tuna Melt*, and the *George Foreman Griller* is also pretty popular. And I've been writing articles in my spare time for an online crime magazine, so . . . I guess you could say I've got the best of both worlds, right now."

"It certainly sounds as if you're happy, carrying on the family tradition. Oh dear, I do hope your business won't suffer, you know, what with you being here and all."

"It won't. After all, it's not as if I'm three thousand miles away. It's less than a twenty-minute drive, and besides, I've got Chantal and a high school girl to watch the store." I squeezed her arm. "We've got more important things to worry about."

"True." Aunt Prudence let out a sigh and cupped her mug with both hands. "To be honest, I don't know how you did it back in Chicago, dealing with crime and criminals, day in and day out. This fiasco with Lacey has me worn down to my last nerve." She lifted the mug to her lips, took a long sip, and then glanced at me over the rim. "It's a mistake, that's what it is. A horrible, horrible mistake."

"Of course it is," said a raspy voice behind us. "Anyone with an ounce of sense can see that girl's not a murderer. If anyone lacks the killer instinct, it's her."

"Murderer," came from the depths of the cage. "Killer."

"Gosh, what's got that parrot all riled up? He's usually not this chatty so late."

I glanced over my shoulder. A tall woman wearing a burgundy quilted housecoat that seemed a size too big on her lean frame moved forward, hand extended. "You must be Nora. I'm Prudence's friend, Irene."

I took a moment to study her. Irene clearly was not what I'd expected. From Aunt Prudence's description, I'd envisioned her childhood friend as an elderly lady with iron gray hair, stoop shouldered, someone who wore a hearing aid, housedress, and apron and fussed over her boarders like a momma hen fussed over her chicks. Well, Irene MacGillicuddy had a hearing aid alright, in her left ear, but that's where that resemblance ended. She was as tall as me, maybe an inch or two taller, built like a linebacker with ramrod-straight posture. Curly coal black hair was piled atop her head, a few loose tendrils framing her oval face. Her skin was clear and unlined. Had I not known her age, I would have pegged her for someone in her late thirties or early forties—she was that well preserved.

I took the proffered hand and shook it. "Yes, I'm Nora. It's nice to finally meet you, Irene."

Sharp black eyes snapped, crinkled up at the corners.

"You, too. I'm only sorry it has to be under such dire circumstances." She lifted her head and sniffed the air. "Is that Maui Kona I smell?"

"Yes. I know it's your favorite." Aunt Prudence jumped up, crossed over to the counter, pulled out another mug, and filled it to the brim with the hot liquid, then returned to the table and set it down. "Have some, dear. We were just discussing . . . the day's events."

Irene pulled out the chair next to me and eased her tall frame into it. She took a sip of the coffee and shook her head. "You made it a bit on the strong side, Prudence. You and that heavy hand of yours," she muttered. "You put six scoops in this—I can taste it. I told you, four is more than enough."

"Of course," my aunt sniffed, "if you like drinking dirty water. Nora needed a good jolt of caffeine."

In his cage, Jumanji tittered loudly.

"Irene," I decided to interrupt in the hopes of forestalling what looked to be a doozy of an argument over coffee strength. "Aunt Prudence told me you were here when they arrested Lacey."

Irene turned her sharp gaze to me. "Yes, I was. It all happened so fast, too. Lacey didn't say a word, she looked calm, but I could tell the poor girl was scared half out of her mind."

"Well, wouldn't you be?" Prudence demanded before I could say anything. "Accused of a crime you didn't commit? Railroaded to jail like a common criminal?"

"Hardly common, Prudence. Murder isn't like robbing a convenience store." She paused and rubbed at her stomach. "My, I'm hungry. Would either of you like some toast?"

We shook our heads. Irene pushed back her chair and walked over to the kitchen counter. She opened a large breadbasket, removed two slices of bread, plunked them into the gleaming four-slice toaster, and pushed a stray tendril out of her eyes. "Let's see. The doorbell rang when I was watching Dr. Oz. I went to answer, and there's this nice-lookin' guy standin' on the stoop. Before I could say a word he whipped out a badge and says he's from Homicide, and is Ms. Lacey Charles home?" She moved her shoulders expressively. "What could I do? I let him inside and told him I'd go and see. Just at that moment she comes walking down the staircase and, let me tell you, she looked just like a doe caught in the headlights. Her eyes were big and round, and she was pale, oh, so pale—I thought she might faint. So I said, 'Lacey, this gentleman is lookin' for you.' And she just nodded, you know, like someone in a trance. So then that detective walks right up to her and he asks, 'Lacey Charles?' and when she nodded, he said, 'You're under arrest for the murder of Professor Thaddeus C. Pitt. You have the right to remain silent,' and he just went on and on, you know, like they do on *CSI*. I kept waiting for him to pull handcuffs out, but he didn't, thank the Lord. Just took her arm, led her out to the car at the curb, and off they went. She didn't protest, didn't let out one peep."

"It's all a giant mistake," Aunt Prudence burst out. "It's got to be. Lacey wouldn't harm a fly, let alone deliberately murder anyone. This is all absurd."

"Mistake," squawked the parrot. "Mistake."

Irene removed the toast, then walked to the refrigerator, took out the butter, and slathered it liberally on the bread before returning to the table. She took a large bite, chewed it thoroughly, and then said, "I don't like to butt into family matters, but you must agree, Prudence, Lacey hasn't been acting like herself lately. She's been in a bit of a funk—a real odd mood." Irene took another bite of toast. Gladys's head lifted and the cat stretched, ambled from the fluffy fleece bed, and seated herself beside Irene's chair. Irene glanced down, saw the cat, and hitched her chair away from the animal closer to my aunt. Then she turned back to me. "She put a lot of pressure on herself, that girl. Why, she was desperate to get an A from that Professor Pitt. She worked late at that studio and then stayed up here till all hours, working on her projects. She put her whole heart and soul into her work, and then when it wasn't appreciated, when he embarrassed her"—she put her hand across her heart and sighed dramatically—"it must have been more than she could bear."

"Oh, really, Irene," my aunt bit out the words. "Just because someone gets in a mood every now and then doesn't make them a murderer."

"Maybe, maybe not. I watched a show once on the Discovery Channel that said anyone could be capable of committing a murder, if they were pushed far enough."

The corners of Aunt Prudence's mouth turned down. "Bullhockey."

"It is not." Irene's jaw jutted forward. "Look how many murders are the result of some stupid argument. Why just yesterday in the police blotter—"

I decided to interrupt this discussion before it escalated into a full-out war. "How do you know he embarrassed her, Irene?"

"I don't," she said bluntly. "I'm just making a logical assumption. From stories Lacey's told since she's been here, and from what I've heard from other people, Pitt could be a real asswipe, especially where art was concerned. If it didn't measure up to his exacting standards . . ." She shrugged. "Asswipe," she repeated.

I threw a quick glance at the clock above the sink and stood up. "Well, I guess I'd better try and get some rest. I've got an early day tomorrow."

Prudence turned to Irene. "Nora managed to contact a criminal lawyer. She's meeting him at the jail tomorrow."

"Well, he'd better be damn good," Irene remarked. "If they do charge her with first-degree murder, it'll take nothing short of a miracle to get her out. She'll either be facing life in the big house or, heaven forbid, the death penalty."

Beside me, Aunt Prudence's sharp intake of breath was unmistakable. "The death penalty! Oh my Lord, you don't think . . ."

"Hey, the evidence against her is pretty strong," Irene cut in. "An eyewitness caught her with the body, remember?"

"Standing over it," my aunt retorted. "Not actually stabbing it."

Irene waved her hand in the air. "Still . . . the DA's already sent four people to death row on a lot less this year. He's on a roll. It's an election year, you know, and word on the street is his goal is to get half a dozen sent up before year's end. Lacey would make number five. Not a bad incentive to nail her as guilty, if you ask me."

I turned to leave, and Jumanji shuffled in his cage.

"Guilty," he warbled. "Guilty, guilty, guilty."

Great.

FOUR

I was up well before anyone else the next morning, made myself a quick cup of coffee, and arrived at St. Leo's Central Station, an imposing building located in the downtown area, a few minutes past 7:30 a.m. As I entered the lobby, a tall, slender, sandy-haired man rose from the bank of chairs and started toward me. He was wearing a navy pin-striped suit that draped nicely on his tall frame, a white button-down shirt, and a navy and yellow striped tie, and was carrying an expensive leather briefcase. He extended his free hand. "Nora Charles? I'm Peter Dobbs." He grinned, slow and easy. "The description Daniel gave me was spot-on. Beautiful redhead, hourglass figure, snapping green eyes, walks with confidence—it fits you to a tee."

Heat seared my cheeks as I shook his hand. "Wow, I'm at a loss. Daniel didn't describe you at all, Mr. Dobbs."

He held up one hand. "It's Peter. Mr. Dobbs is what folks call my father—or my uncle."

He had a manner about him one couldn't help but find appealing, and in spite of the situation I found myself grinning. "Okay, Peter. I don't want to waste any time. What can you tell me about my sister, and when can I see her?"

He put his hand on the small of my back and guided me over to the bank of chairs. Once we were seated, he set his briefcase on the floor between us and said, "As soon as I got off the phone with Daniel I came straight here. She was still being processed, but they let me have a few minutes with her. She appeared to be doing well, under the circumstances. Naturally, she was a bit confused, and a mite indignant as well. I have a few friends on the force, so I used my influence to have them handle her with kid gloves. They kept her here overnight, pending arraignment. If she's denied bail, they'll want to transfer her, but if we can get a quick court date, she'll most likely be kept locally, at County Jail. And believe me, if she's got to stay in jail, far better here than the alternative. Here her cell mates would only be a few vagrants or drunks. Elsewhere . . . you get the idea."

I winced at the thought of my free-spirited sister behind bars no matter where the locale. "What do you think her chances of bail are?"

"Depends on what they decide to charge her with. First-degree offenders rarely are granted bail, and in your sister's case, well, she was caught holding the murder weapon, standing over the body, plus she threatened him in front of witnesses. Second-degree or manslaughter would be a stretch." He ran his hand through his hair, mussing the sides. "In any event, I'm going to argue she be granted bail. I'm sure you'd prefer she not be incarcerated in prison during the trial. Unfortunately, she's appearing before Judge Blaskowitz, and he's a stickler for the letter of the law." He reached into his pocket for a packet of mints, held one out to me. I shook my head, and he popped one in his mouth. "Be warned, though, if Blaskowitz does grant it, it'll be high. Very high."

I set my jaw. "That's okay. I have savings, and I have my shop. I'm sure I can meet it."

He nodded. "Lacey is lucky to have a sister like you."

"I'm sure she'd disagree with that. We really don't get along all that well."

He chuckled. "No sibling gets along one hundred percent of the time with the others. I haven't spoken to my brother or my sister for months." He shoved his hands in his pocket. "You're familiar with the details leading up to her arrest?"

I grimaced. "I know she was found with the body holding the murder weapon. And I know she's supposed to have threatened him in class earlier that day."

"In front of over thirty witnesses," Peter sighed. "She told me she'd made an appointment with him to look at more of her work for extra credit, but she was running late. She got to the office, and the door was slightly ajar. She went in and, at first, didn't see anything, then she noticed a large red stain. She walked around the desk, saw Pitt sprawled beneath, the knife sticking out of his chest, and she just reacted. She bent over, pulled it out of him, and by the time it dawned on her what had actually happened, the guard had entered, yelled at her to drop the weapon. He moved pretty slowly, though, and when he went for the phone she took off." He ran a hand through his hair. "Said she just had to get out of there. She needed to think, to process what had happened. She said she wasn't quite sure what she should do, and by the time she decided to go to the police, well, it was too late."

"Any chance there are other prints besides hers on that knife?"

Peter shrugged. "Homicide hasn't shared those results with me yet. But I wouldn't bet on it."

I pushed hair out of my eyes with the heel of my hand. "It just seems like a setup to me. Her altercation with Pitt made her a perfect patsy for the real murderer."

"I had the same thought," Peter admitted. "Of course, the murderer would have to have known about their late-night meeting." He looked at me for a long moment, then said, "For what it's worth, your sister denies having absolutely anything to do with his death. She said she was mad enough to kill him, but she didn't."

I looked him straight in the eye. "Do you believe her?"

He met my gaze. "Yes. I do."

I let out a heartfelt sigh. "I'm sorry. I had to ask. And I'm glad I did. I'm glad you believe in her, and this isn't just a favor you're doing for a friend."

His lips relaxed into a slow grin. "I've always been fond of Daniel, but there is no number of favors owed that would convince me to take a case I didn't believe in. I'll do everything I can to absolve her, but in order to do that I'll need her help. Let's just say your sister isn't as cooperative as you'd expect a person in her position to be."

"Knowing my sister, I can imagine. You can rest assured, though, I'll do anything I can to help prove her innocence."

His lips twitched upward, and I caught a glimmer of a twinkle in those eyes. "Yes, Daniel mentioned you used to be a top-notch investigative reporter. And that you gave it all up to make sandwiches."

"Not just any sandwiches, either. They're specialty sandwiches, with specialty names. Clear my sister of this murder charge and I'll even name one after you," I promised. "How does the *Peter Dobbs Panini* sound?"

"If it's as good as your *Thin Man Tuna Melt* I'll be flattered. Daniel raved about it." He rose and took my arm. "Now, let's go see your sister."

We walked down a long corridor and through a door marked SECURITY. Inside, we stepped through a metal detector, and I handed my purse over to a female officer. She gave it a thorough going-through and then handed it back, then went through the same procedure with Peter's briefcase. Then we were escorted into a large room that reminded me of a hospital cafeteria. Gray metal tables were arranged in a large square. The chairs were a dull black, and the floor was a black-and-white checked pattern. The only bright spot was the large window along the south wall, which allowed the early-morning sunlight to pour into the room, brightening it up considerably. The officer waved her hand in the direction of the chairs.

"Have a seat. She'll be in shortly. The arraignment is set for ten."

The lieutenant left and Peter leaned in toward me. "Just a word of caution," he said. "I know you'll want to touch your sister, give her a hug and a kiss, but it's best if you don't. This isn't a family visit, remember, and we don't want to alarm the guard with unsolicited behavior. They might think you're passing something to her."

I nodded. "I'll remember."

Several minutes later the door opened and my sister, accompanied by a dour-faced guard, entered. I could see even this brief period of incarceration had taken a toll on my sister. Lacey had on navy pants and a matching shirt. Her hands were manacled, and her eyes were dull and expressionless. Her normally bouncy ash-blond hair hung in limp strands around her pale face and looked as if it could do with a shampoo.

"Hello, Lacey," Peter said. "You remember me—we met last night."

Lacey stared at him blankly, and then her gaze traveled to me. She sucked in her breath and didn't say a word, but her eyes widened and seemed to lose their glassy stare. The guard unlocked the handcuffs and waited until Peter and I were seated before moving to a seat on the other side of the room.

Lacey perched awkwardly in her chair, arms folded tightly across her chest. She kept her gaze down, fixed on the tabletop.

"Lacey," Peter said, "I've brought someone with me who would like to talk to you."

"Lace." My hand started to move across the table, and I had to catch myself midway. I could feel the guard's eyes on me as I drew it back, put it in my lap. "Lace, it's good to see you."

My sister slowly raised her gaze to meet mine. She blinked back tears, hugged herself more tightly. Still she did not say one word.

"Don't you worry," I said, with far more confidence than I felt. "Everything's going to be all right. I know you didn't murder Pitt, and so does Peter. We're going to find out who did."

A tear trickled down her cheek. I pulled a tissue from my jacket pocket and placed it on the table. She picked it up, dabbed at her eyes, then clenched her fist tightly around the tissue before raising her gaze to meet mine. "You shouldn't have come. You shouldn't have wasted your time."

I leaned forward a bit, but not too much, as the guard had her eagle eye trained right on the table. My sister had lost her former sense of bravado. I couldn't recall ever hearing her sound so dejected. "Why do you say that, Lacey? The only way my time would be wasted would be if you did kill him, and you didn't, right?"

Her lips tugged downward. "You don't sound very sure of me. Of course I didn't." Her chin shot up, just a hair. "I might have wanted to, maybe, just for a minute, but . . . He was a pompous, arrogant ass, but I knew that when I signed up for the course. I wanted to study under the best. I never dreamt he was so . . . so malicious, such a bully. His biggest delight was in making people feel small, feel inadequate. Of course, it might just have been his way of igniting one's creative flame, but I thought it sucked. And I told him so."

"Good for you," I murmured. "People who think belittling someone is the way to make them do a better job make my skin crawl."

We were all silent for a few moments, and then Lacey dropped her arms to her sides and sat up a bit straighter in her chair. "I asked him what I could do to improve my grade. I knew I deserved more than that damned C minus. God, all of them did. I was the only one with any guts to ask for extra credit. He said he'd think about it, and I should come to his office after my last class. I told him that I'd definitely be there."

"Okay," I said as she took a breath. "Then what happened?"

"I went back to the studio and worked on my portraits. I had three of them, and I worked on them all day. My last class ended at nine thirty that evening, and I'd forgotten one of my portraits, so I had to go back to my locker—that's why I was late for our meeting. I figured he might think I wasn't going to show and leave, but when I got there I saw the door was ajar. I called out his name, and I thought I heard a sound."

"What sort of sound?" I asked.

She shrugged. "I'm not sure; it was so faint—if I had to guess I'd say it sounded like a faint click, you know, like a drawer being shut. Anyway, I pushed the door all the way open and went in. I called out his name—no answer. At first I thought he'd left, and then . . . I saw that red stain. At first I thought it might be wine—the decanter was off center, and I could swear I smelled it. Pitt was such a fanatic about his wine; he always had a glass or more in the evenings, and he could have spilled some, but . . . there was just so much red. Then when I realized what it was, what happened next . . . well, it's kind of a blur." She scrubbed at her eyes with the palms of her hands. "I walked around the desk and he was lying there, that antique knife of his bulging out of his chest. I don't know what I was thinking. Maybe that if I could get that knife out, he'd start to breathe. I saw all the blood, and yet—I don't know why, I thought maybe I could still save him. So I grabbed the handle with both hands and just pulled it out. For what it's worth, I honestly don't think he'd been dead very long. Next thing I knew the guard was standing in the doorway, yelling at me to put the knife down and step away from the body. All I could think of was I just had to get out of there, to figure out what to do, so when he went for the phone—" Her shoulders lifted in a shrug, and she raised her head. She fixed me with a penetrating stare. "I must say, you certainly got here fast, Nora. How did you hear about this so quickly? Either this was front-page news over in Cruz or Aunt Pru called you," she said flatly. "Of course she did. Who else could get to the bottom of this mystery?"

"That's not true," I began, but my sister cut me off.

"Oh right. You came back home to take over the family business because I couldn't make a go and wanted to sell. As usual. The cool, levelheaded older sister has to step in to save the family legacy from the flighty, impetuous younger sister, the one who has yet to make a success of anything she undertakes."

"Don't flatter yourself," I bit out. "I was considering coming back to Cruz anyway. Let's be honest, here. We really haven't had a serious talk in a long time. You have no idea what's been going on in my life, any more than I have in yours. And it's a shame."

She regarded me thoughtfully for a moment and then said, "Touché. So let's be honest, just like you suggested, *sis*. You always did like to play rescuer, and everything you touch turns to gold while everything I touch turns to crap. Here's yet another opportunity for you to show me up. Why do you think I *didn't* call you?" Her words tumbled out, double time, and now she stopped for a shaky breath. "I didn't kill him. I wish to God I knew who did." Her shoulders heaved up and down, and then her body curled into itself as she began to sob in earnest. I wanted to go to her, put my arms around her, and cradle her, but I knew I couldn't, so I just sat and watched until her sobs slowly subsided and her breath came out in hiccups.

"I'm so sorry you felt you couldn't call on me for help," I said softly. "You have to know I love you."

"No, I'm the one who's sorry," she said at last, pushing hair out of her eyes with the heel of her hand. "We've had our share of differences over the years, but I don't mean to be ungrateful. You got me a lawyer, and came all the way out here—but honest, I think it's a lost cause. I didn't kill him, but the police aren't looking for anyone else. They've got a dummy right here, who got caught with the body and was stupid enough to touch the murder weapon. It's open and shut as far as they're concerned."

"Them, maybe, but not us." I tapped the edge of one nail against the tabletop. "If Pitt was as egocentric as you claim, there must be other students who hated him, too."

"Gosh," Lacey pushed her hand through her hair, "there were lots who felt that way, who hated his guts, but none of 'em would ever come right out and say so—except yours truly." Her brow furrowed, then cleared. "Well, maybe Julia. She was always one to speak her mind."

"Julia?"

"Julia Canton. She's one of his students—was one of his students—and she also does some modeling. Rumor has it she and Pitt have been, ah, seeing a lot of each other lately."

"Seeing a lot of each other? As in dating?"

"If you put any stock in the school rumor mill, which, FYI, is right more often than wrong."

"What a glowing endorsement." I glanced across the table at Peter, who'd whipped a pad and pen from his briefcase and was scribbling down notes. "I thought Pitt was married."

"He was," Peter chimed in. "Been married to his second wife for a little over eight years now." His lips twitched slightly as he added, "I believe the second Mrs. Pitt would be what's known as a 'trophy wife.'"

"Ah." I rubbed my hands together. "And wife number one?"

"Apparently the divorce was amicable in spite of the circumstances. They do have a son, Philip. Boy's got a lot of problems—to be precise, the ponies and Vegas. From what I understand, Pitt has very little to do with the boy, yet he's on surprisingly friendly terms with the wife. Gave her a large settlement when they split, and a generous monthly allowance."

"He dumped her for a younger model, though, right?" I tapped my chin with my forefinger. "Sounds like a guilty conscience to me."

"Assuming Pitt has a conscience, yes. Anyway, since Althea hasn't worked full-time in years, I see no reason why she'd want to see her cash cow dead. Giselle, on the other hand, signed a pre-nup. In a divorce, she'd get virtually nothing, but as the widow"—he paused and finished with a flourish—"she'd get millions."

"If Pitt was planning on racking up a new trophy, she's a good possibility. Money's always a prime motive for murder." I slit my eyes in thought, then turned to Lacey. "Anyone else who wasn't his number one fan?"

Her eyes rolled upward, answer enough for me even without the vocal confirmation. "Geez, where do I begin? He was always picking on Taft Michaels on one thing or another—he's another student and model. And I think Jenna Whitt—she's another student—might have had a disagreement with him recently." Her brow puckered in thought and then she said, "And there's Kurt."

"Kurt?"

"Kurt Wilson. He manages a gallery in Pacific Grove that displays some of the more promising students' work from time to time. I think Pitt bought some pieces recently from Kurt's gallery. Maybe—maybe they could have had a disagreement over that. But I couldn't say for sure."

I laid my hand on Peter's arm. "It would seem there are quite a few other people who could have had a motive for murder. Now why aren't the police looking into them?"

"Why should they? As far as they're concerned, I had means, motive, and opportunity," Lacey cut in. "None of the others threatened to kill him in public and then got caught holding the murder weapon." She scrubbed at her face with both hands and let out a giant sigh. "Mom said it best. I'm my own worst enemy."

I wanted desperately to pat her on the shoulder and restrained myself with effort. "Can you think of anyone who might have heard you making that appointment with Pitt?"

Her lips scrunched up as she thought. "Julia might have been standing nearby; maybe Taft, too. The door was open, and I wasn't exactly quiet. Anyone walking by or standing in the hall near the door could have heard, I guess." She slapped her forehead with her open palm. "I'm sorry, I just can't remember. I was just so *mad*. All my focus was on Pitt and getting him to agree to look at more of my work." She paused and her shoulders slumped dejectedly. "And how much crow I'd probably have to eat for my earlier words, of course."

I leaned a little bit forward, not too far as I caught the guard watching us carefully. "Is there anything else you can think of, Lace? What about the office when you went in? Did anything seem off to you?"

"You mean other than seeing the dead body on the floor, and all that blood?" She let out a giant sigh. "If anything did, it went from my mind the minute I saw that."

"I know finding a body can make other details blur," I said. "Believe me, I know. But if there was anything that seemed a bit out of the ordinary to you, anything at all, try and remember. Sometimes even the smallest detail . . ."

Her eyes squinched up at the corners. "I'm trying, Nora, honestly, I am. Do you think I want to go to prison? I've had plenty of time to rack my brain, believe me. There—there may have been something I noticed at the time, but now, after all that's happened . . . I just can't remember, or focus. My mind's a blank."

"Easy, it's okay," Peter interrupted soothingly. "You're doing fine. We'll get there." He glanced at his watch and snapped his briefcase shut. "It's almost time for the arraignment. The guard will take you over to the courthouse. I'll meet you over there. I'm going to try and get you out on bail, but I can't guarantee anything."

Lacey bit her lower lip. "I'm not getting my hopes up. Besides, even if they offer it, I'm sure I can't afford it."

"You can't, but I can," I interjected. "And if at all possible, I want you out."

She slid me a glance. "You'd do that for me?"

"Of course, silly. We fight like cats and dogs, but you're my sister. We're family, and family sticks together." I saw her eyes start to fill up and said quickly, "Provided you won't skip town and make me lose my investment."

Her lips twisted into a wry half smile. "Heck no. I'd welcome a good night's sleep in my bed—lumpy mattress and all."

Peter picked up his briefcase and rose, signaling to the guard. "Time to go. Stiff upper lip, now."

Lacey's eyes brightened, although the corners of her mouth drooped down. "You're not discouraged? You're going to stick with my case, hopeless though it seems?"

"Are you kidding?" He smiled at her. "You're stuck with me, Lacey Charles. For better or for worse."

She thrust out her hands so the guard could slip the handcuffs on again. "I'd like to say the worst is behind us, but I hate to lie. I haven't had the best luck lately."

After Lacey was led out, Peter turned to me. "Going to the arraignment hearing?"

"Try and stop me. Even if bail's denied I want Lacey to know I'm there every step of the way for her." I smiled at him. "I think she's lucky to have you in her corner, too. Thank you for everything, Peter."

"Save your thanks, Nora. I haven't done anything yet."

"You took a case where the cards look stacked against her, and that's something. This gathering was very helpful. I think I've figured out the key to proving her innocence."

His eyes widened. "You have? What?"

"I'm convinced the real murderer is someone connected to the art school. It's such a perfect setup, it just has to be. And now that we have some other possible suspects, we just have to narrow them down. The key to Lacey's freedom is finding out which of them is the real murderer." I paused. "And to find out fast. Really, really fast."

FIVE

"**S**o, no bail, huh?"

I'd arrived back at Prudence's about twenty minutes ago, to find that she and Irene had gone to the local Pathmark to get some groceries. She'd left me a note, inviting me to stay for dinner. I'd gone up to my room, kicked off my shoes, and, since Nick was snoring peacefully in the corner, dug out my cell and called Chantal. Her psychic senses must have been on overdrive, because *no bail* were the first words she uttered, even before hello.

"No. Peter put up a pretty persuasive argument, but the ADA was more persuasive. She managed to convince the judge otherwise, which, considering the circumstances, wasn't all that hard to do." I flopped down on the edge of the bed and let my leg dangle over the side. "The ADA was determined to get a quick court date, and Peter didn't object. If the case is brought to trial quickly, they can keep her in jail locally; otherwise she'd have been remanded to the women's prison in Chowchilla."

"Ouch," Chantal said. "That does not sound good."

"It's not. The prosecution must feel they've got a strong case for conviction, so unless we can unearth the real murderer, she still may end up there. The police aren't exactly looking elsewhere right now, thanks in part to my sister and her temper."

I kicked off my heels and pulled the list of names out of my jacket pocket. "According to Lacey, there were quite a few people who weren't exactly charter members of the Thaddeus Pitt fan club. I'm betting one of them set her up."

Chantal was very quiet for a moment, then said, "I did a reading, *chérie*. The High Priestess appeared, the guardian of secrets, right next to the Empress, who is known to represent all things traditionally feminine. Tell me, is one of the people you suspect his wife?"

"Funny you should say that. She does seem a good prospect, but there are others that fill that bill as well." I paused. "So—the cards said *cherchez la femme*? Look for the woman?"

"They could be interpreted that way, yes." She hesitated, then added, "There is a bit more. The Lovers card also appeared, in the past position. It usually indicates a past relationship that might have ended badly, or that the person might be of some help in the present."

"Hm," I said. "Lacey thought Pitt might have had someone on the side that could be a possibility."

"Well, that reading was not one of my better ones," Chantal admitted. "My concentration was not the best. I will do a cleanse and attempt another one later. You are coming back tonight?"

"I was, but my aunt wants me to stay for dinner, and under the circumstances, I think I should. So, would you mind doing the breakfast and lunch crowd tomorrow? I probably won't be able to get back to Hot Bread until late Saturday."

"Take your time. Everything is fine here. And give Little Nicky a kiss for me. I miss him. I thought you would leave him here. I have some new collars ready for him to try on."

Since I had her on speaker, Nick's head jerked up at the word *collar*. He bared his fangs with a loud hiss.

We exchanged a few more pleasantries, and then I hung up and pulled my laptop out of my tote. I settled in at the small table near the window and decided now was as good a time as any to start my research on other possible suspects. I plugged Taft Michaels into the search engine, and almost immediately names appeared on the screen. Some were variations on the name: guys with the last or first name of Michaels, a couple of schools with Taft in the title. On the third page I came across Taft Michaels's Facebook. I clicked on it, and the screen shifted to that particular site.

Nick hopped up on the table, startling me. "Well, well," I said. "So, were you dreaming about all those nice collars Chantal's got for you to try on?"

I got a hiss and an indifferent stare in return. I chuckled. "Guess not."

I turned my attention to Taft Michaels's photo. He looked like a younger version of Jon Hamm—coal black hair cut stylishly; wide, twinkling blue eyes; a firm chin; thick lips parted to reveal gleaming perfect teeth. He was bare chested in his FB page photo, and his chest was broad, the muscles clearly defined. My gaze moved to the particulars beneath the photo. Occupation was blank, but the Pitt Institute was listed as his school, and his place of residence was San Fran. Under relationship it merely said "Involved," vague to say the least. Below the page photo was a directory marked "Photos." I clicked on that. Another page marked "Taft's Albums" appeared. There were three: one was labeled "Page Photos," another "Publicity Shots," and a third "New Year's Eve." As I hesitated, Nick's paw shot out, pressing down on the mouse. He must have moved it to the "New Year's Eve" page, because the screen suddenly shifted to reveal about twenty photos, all of which featured Taft drinking and carrying on. Two photos showed him talking to two men. One man had his back to the camera, another was bathed in shadow, so it was impossible to discern who they were, but somehow I doubted either of them was Pitt. In some of the photos he had his arm around a beautiful brunette. The last photo, however, showed him in silhouette, in what appeared to be an elegantly appointed den underneath a portrait of a setting sun, kissing another girl who was most definitely not the brunette. This one was blond, and although most of her face was in shadow, the little that was visible seemed extremely attractive. Most of the photos had captions beneath them—the ones with the women, however, did not.

"Hm," I mused. "It looks like an amateurish attempt to keep something secret, although if he really wanted to do that he shouldn't have made his page public. He's got virtually no controls in place, which means he doesn't care who views his stuff."

Nick let out a loud "*Meow*" of agreement.

This time I typed in Julia Canton's name. When her

Facebook page appeared, I sucked in my breath. No doubt about it, Taft's brunette companion and Julia Canton looked to be one and the same. I took a quick look at her pertinent information, which seemed to mirror Taft's. Apparently they had vagueness in common.

"Well, well. Looks as if Taft and Julia are pretty cozy. Maybe that's the reason for the bad blood between him and Pitt."

I opened Julia's photo page, but there were only two albums: one was her cover photos, of which there were three, each more beautiful than the last. The girl was stunning: long dark brown, almost black hair that fell nearly to her waist, bright blue eyes, dimples at either end of her lips when she smiled. To be honest, it was hard to imagine any guy wanting to be just friends with her, unless he played for the other team, of course. "They both look cut from the same mold. The beautiful people. I see why they're models. It's a wonder they don't do that full-time. I'm sure they'd make much more money than an artist ever could. And why isn't modeling listed as a profession, hm?"

Next I keyed in Kurt Wilson, but nothing came up on Facebook for him. Ditto Twitter and LinkedIn. I managed to find an address and phone number in Pacific Grove for the Wilson Galleries, which I promptly dialed, only to get a recorded message: "You've reached the Wilson Galleries. No one's available at the moment, but your call is important to us. Please leave a message at the tone." I left my name and phone number and hung up.

"Man of mystery is right," I said. "He's got my vote so far. People who like to stay that low-key usually have some deep, dark secret as the reason. Maybe Pitt knew it and was blackmailing him."

As fast as the thought entered my head, I rejected that theory. Blackmailers rarely bit the hand that fed them—or killed it. Besides, it would have been the other way around. If that scenario held water, Pitt would have killed *him*.

I pushed both hands through my mass of curls and jammed my hands in my pocket. My fingers closed around something long and hard, and I remembered that Prudence had given me the key to Lacey's room yesterday, in case there was something in there she might want. I turned the key over in my hand and jerked to my feet. I glanced over at Nick.

"I'm going to check out Lacey's room. Want to come?"

I'd barely pushed open the door when I felt a breeze around my ankles. Nick swept past me into the hallway, a blur of black fur, disappearing around the corner faster than a genie out of its bottle.

"Guess so," I chuckled.

Lacey's room was larger than mine but with the same sparse furnishings. Her neatly made bed, adorned with the same type of blue chenille bedspread, stood in the center. A bottle of Charlie perfume, a few books on art, and the latest issue of *Entertainment Weekly* lay on her dresser. The desk and wooden chair by the window looked like an exact duplicate of the ones in my room. A worn armchair upholstered in a purple floral print was over in the corner, a wooden ottoman in front of it. Right next to the small bathroom was a closet. Instead of a door, the opening was covered with a thick white shower curtain. I walked over and pushed it aside. Lacey's clothing hung there: several pairs of jeans, a few T-shirts, two long-sleeved pin-striped shirts, her one good George Simonton black dress with the scoop neck and lace sleeves that once upon a time had been mine.

I moved toward the desk. On the desktop a bouquet of pens and pencils sat in a worn leather cup, and beside it a frame lay facedown. I picked it up and my breath caught in my throat. I felt moisture well up in the corners of my eyes, and before I could stop it, the sting of wetness graced my cheeks.

The photo showed a smiling, redheaded woman in a checked sundress. Under each arm was tucked a rosy-cheeked child—one with flame red hair and a toothless grin under the right arm; a blond, paler girl with a serious expression under the left. I hadn't seen that photo in years. I'd wondered where it went, and now, to find it in my sister's things . . .

I felt something wet and cold against the back of my hand, and a second later Nick nudged his nose into my palm. I chucked him under the chin, then brushed at my wet cheeks with the back of my hand. "This isn't helping her," I murmured.

I started to slide open the desk drawers. Nothing much was there. The top drawer had a sketch pad in it, and I lifted it out, started leafing through it. The portraits on the pages were good, really good. There was one of Prudence that looked almost as if she were about to speak. On the last page was another familiar face.

"Wow," I shook my head. "She must have copied this

from my graduation photo." I slid Nick a glance. "What do you know, Nick. My sister actually has talent."

"Your sister?"

The sudden voice coupled with the creak of the door behind me made me drop the sketch pad. I whirled and caught a glimpse of short platinum blond hair framing a round face. A pair of hazel eyes framed by thick black lashes peered at me, and then the door swung all the way open.

"Oh goodness. I'm so sorry. I didn't mean to startle you. The nice woman downstairs said that I should just go right on up, but she didn't mention anyone else was here." She cocked her head to one side, studying me. "Yep, you've got to be her sister. I can see the family resemblance right around here." She made a gesture that encompassed the area around her eyes.

"Yes, I'm Nora Charles. And you are?"

"Oh, I'm sorry." Her laugh tittered out. "Jenna Whitt. I study at the Pitt Institute, too. Lacey and I have worked on some projects together."

I took a moment to study her. She was short, maybe five-two, but well built, and she looked as if she spent some time in the gym maintaining that build. She wore a cobalt blue tracksuit unzippered down the front to reveal a bright lime green T-shirt that emphasized her full bosom. She wore thick Nikes on her feet, which explained why I hadn't heard her sooner. I placed her age as mid to late thirties. If I had to give a truthful assessment, she was probably more on the sunny side.

"Nice to meet you, Jenna. I'm afraid, though, my sister isn't here right now."

"Oh, I know." She waved her hand carelessly. I noted the

slight nicotine stains on the tips of her finger and thought it a shame she smoked. It took away from her expensive French-tip manicure. "She's in the slammer. Poor thing. If you ask me they should be giving her a medal, not prosecuting her."

I was a bit surprised at her candor with a perfect stranger and struggled to keep my tone even. "She hasn't been found guilty yet."

Jenna shook her bobbed head. "Oh right. I'm sorry. It's just—now don't get me wrong—I like your sister, she's a nice gal. But you've got to admit it'd take a miracle to help her, doncha think? I mean, caught with the murder weapon and all? Talk about bad timing."

I frowned. "Is there something I can help you with?"

"Not really." She waved her hand carelessly. "I was here a few days ago, and I thought I might have left something here I need . . . Oh, hello." Her eyes widened as she caught sight of Nick at my feet. "Wow. He's some big cat."

Nick regarded her with a cool stare, then minced over to the braided rug in front of Lacey's vanity and stretched out both forepaws, bottom in the air. He turned around twice and then plopped down, lifted his hind leg, and began grooming his privates.

Jenna burst out laughing. "He sure ain't shy." She dragged her gaze back to me. "Anyway, like I was sayin', it'll take a miracle to help your sister, or isn't it true she's been charged with first-degree murder?"

I nodded. "Yes, it's true. She was arraigned this morning."

"They didn't waste much time." Jenna pushed past me into the room, walked over to the dresser, and picked up the bottle of perfume. She sprayed it into the air, then leaned forward to catch the droplets on her skin as they fell. "I feel bad for her," Jenna said. She walked around the room, her eyes darting to and fro, taking in every detail. "Don't get me wrong—I don't condone murder—but if anyone had it coming, Pitt did." Her voice dropped to a conspiratorial whisper, even though we were quite alone. "He wasn't a very nice man."

"Really? All the accounts I've read paint him as a wonderful humanitarian."

Her brow arched. "You believe everything you read? That's all hype. Publicity." She waved her hand. "Just ask anyone who took his class. He was a class A creep."

"You sound as if you've had personal experience with him. Did you take any of his classes?"

"A few." She nodded. "But I dropped out to pursue my real interest, sculpture. I've got loads of friends who have taken his classes, though, and trust me, none of them had a good word to say. None ever actually threatened him, though, until your sister did. I happened to be waiting for a friend in the hall outside that classroom. The door was partially open, and I heard every word, along with about a dozen other people." I noted her gaze never met mine but rather focused on Lacey's open closet, almost as if she were taking a mental inventory. "I took a peek inside. Your sister was all red in the face, and she was screaming at the top of her lungs. I'm surprised they didn't hear her in China."

I moved closer, intrigued by the fact Jenna was apparently a witness to Lacey's impassioned declaration. "And Pitt? How did he react to all this? It sounds pretty shocking, to say the least."

Jenna shrugged. She'd moved over to the desk and stood, absently pulling drawers open, glancing inside, then shutting them. I was just about to point out the rudeness of her actions when she turned to me and said, "It's not like any student never had a meltdown in one of his classes before. He just stood there with a sour expression until she was done screaming, and then he picked up the rest of the portfolios and started handing 'em out, calm as you please. I don't know what happened after that. My friend showed up so I left." She picked up a snow globe from the desk, shook it absently, and then set it down, letting her fingers trail over the other items on the smooth surface. "I happened to be outside Pitt's office just last week—my professor's office is on the same floor—and his door was partially open. I don't know who he was talking to, but was he mad! I was sure glad I wasn't on the receiving end of that call."

"Wow," I said. "Was it another student?"

She shrugged. "Could have been. I really couldn't tell. I didn't want to be nosy."

"Of course," I murmured. "By the way, do you know Kurt Wilson?"

Her head snapped up. "Who?"

"Kurt Wilson. He's supposed to run a local gallery that showcases students' works."

The puzzled expression cleared somewhat, and she nodded. "Oh yeah, him. Let me think. I might have seen him once or twice at a distance. But I don't believe I ever actually *met* him. My sculptures were never considered for display. Although, come to think of it, I'm not sure he ever actually met any of those students, either."

"That seems a bit odd. Who did he make the deals through? Pitt?"

"Probably. Or maybe directly through the office. Like I

said, I was never selected, so to be honest, I've never even gone near the place." She shrugged and glanced at her watch, then plucked at the sleeve of her sweatsuit. "Sorry, but I've got to go. I have a sculpture class in an hour, and I can't be late. I've got Professor Grant; she's just as tough as Pitt used to be, and her pet peeve is tardiness."

She flounced out with a wave and a smile, and once her footsteps had disappeared down the hall I tapped my chin thoughtfully. "She was lying," I murmured. "About that argument. I don't think she overheard anyone else. I think it was her. She just didn't want to admit it. I think she came here to snoop around." I nudged Nick with the toe of my shoe. "What do you think?"

Nick blinked twice.

I nodded. "Yep, I feel the same way. Well, one good thing. Now we know for certain there were quite a few others who didn't have Pitt at the top of their hit parade. If I want to clear Lacey, I'm going to have to get into the nitty-gritty of PI work and get some answers on my own." I reached in my pocket, whipped out my cell, and punched in a number.

"Hey, Ollie," I said when the PI answered. "Remember when you said you'd be glad to help me? Well, I could sure use your advice. It's been a while since I've done this.

"I need to go undercover."

SIX

The naked guy climbed down from the rounded platform, plucked up a fluffy terrycloth robe, and headed for a table in the far corner of the large room on which a large coffee urn and a huge platter of donuts rested.

"Take ten, everyone," the tall, gray-haired woman standing in the front of the room said. Her gaze drifted to the doorway where I stood and then back to the ten students now milling around the refreshment table. She thrust her hands into the pocket of the blue smock she wore over her dress and walked over to me. "I am Professor Wilhelmina Pace. And you are—"

"Abigail St. Clair." I extended my hand to the woman. She stared at it, then removed hers from the smock and gripped mine tightly. I winced as I extracted my hand from her iron grip. "I'm a potential student. I've always liked to dabble with drawing and painting, and this school was very highly recommended."

"Dabble, eh?" Professor Pace raised one eyebrow. "Being a successful artist requires a bit more than dabbling. It requires concentration, dedication."

I swallowed. "Exactly. I'd like to learn, and, as my dear, departed grandmother used to say, 'Why not learn from the best?'"

She actually laughed. "Your grandmother sounds very wise. It's true, and you couldn't have chosen a finer school. The Pitt Institute is one of the premier art institutes in the state of California." Her gaze drifted back toward the refreshment table. The handsome model was chatting with several of the female students, a donut clutched in one hand. "Taft," she called out. "Watch the sweets." She rubbed at her stomach area with one hand. Taft's gaze narrowed and he deliberately turned his back.

Professor Pace turned to me and whispered, "A handsome boy but headstrong! We don't like our models to be sticks, but we don't like them too zaftig, either. We like them proportioned." She made an outline of an hourglass figure with her hands.

I shifted the brochures and folder the woman in the admissions office had thrust upon me and nodded toward the group. "He looks like a model. He's so handsome. Is he a student as well?"

She cast another wary glance his way, and I saw a muscle clench in her jaw. "He has a certain talent. I'm not certain I'd refer to it as art." Her cell phone rang just then, and she reached into her pocket for it, moving a few steps away from me. She flipped it open, listened for a few minutes, then called out, "Ten more minutes. Then we will begin again."

She moved out into the hall, speaking earnestly into her phone, and the students began to slowly drift back toward their easels. All, I noted, save Taft, who'd plucked another donut from the tray, this one a Boston crème, and lounged against the back wall, chewing and staring out into space. I shifted my gaze to the window just beyond the table and sucked in my breath. Nick was perched on the outside sill, and his paw moved impatiently back and forth against the glass, as if beckoning me to come closer to where Taft Michaels stood.

My brainstorm session with Ollie paid off big-time. Since visiting the school as myself was out of the question (I mean, they'd arrested my sister for the founder's murder. Who would tell me anything?), Ollie suggested I pose as a prospective—and wealthy—student interested in the pursuit of art. It was a plan I wasn't totally averse to. I'd played out lots of similar scenarios back in the day in Chicago, with not half-bad results, if I had to say so myself, and I'd mentally slapped myself more than once that I hadn't thought of doing this first. Ollie even went on the Internet and looked up the names of several wealthy heiresses in the California area who might be so inclined to pursue such a project. Abigail St. Clair was the closest to my age, and while upon a close inspection we probably wouldn't pass for twins, we both had the same build and coloring. I'd picked up a burner phone at Wal-Mart, and I gave that number as my contact information. With any degree of luck, they wouldn't do any in-depth checking and find out that the real Abigail St. Clair was incommunicado this week, having gone off to some retreat in Switzerland. I had my fingers crossed that they wouldn't start any sort of thorough background check until I actually agreed to sign up, and that I might actually learn something useful today.

I moved over to the table and selected a chocolate donut. Taft turned as I approached and gave me the benefit of a full grill smile that revealed a set of perfect white teeth with dimples at either corner of his lips. I decided his Facebook picture didn't do him justice. He was even more strikingly handsome in person, with or without clothes.

"Well, hello," he said, letting his sea blue eyes rove over me in a none-too-subtle once-over. "You're a new face."

I gave him my best rich heiress haughty smile. "Actually, this is the face I've always had."

He laughed. "Touché. What I meant was, you're a new face here. Let's see. You're a bit too well dressed to be a student, and Pace is falling all over herself with you, which means the front office told her to play nice, so that can mean only one thing . . . You've got money, am I right?" He wagged his finger in the air.

I extended my hand. "Abigail St. Clair. And yes, you could say I've got a bit of money. I'm thinking of spending some to study art here."

"Abigail St. Clair. Your name oozes wealth," he chuckled. "So you want to study art, huh? What's the matter, bored with the society set?"

I lifted my chin. "Not at all. It's just something I've always wanted to do, so I decided, why not?"

"Why not indeed?" He looked me up and down once more and then thrust his hand forward. "I'm Taft Michaels. Pleased to meet you."

"Likewise." I returned his smile, certain his renewed interest was more in Abigail's bank account than anything else. "So, what can you tell me about the school? Besides the obvious fact it's one of the best in the country."

"And one of the toughest. We've got an eighty percent dropout rate."

"Really?"

"Oh yeah. The professors are all good—top-of-the-line—but they're tough, just as tough as the founder of this school. Thaddeus Pitt was a notorious perfectionist."

"Was? Has he changed?"

He stared at me. "You haven't heard? Wow. You must be one of the few people on the planet who don't know." He leaned in closer and dropped his voice. "Pitt was murdered a couple of days ago. Killed right here in the school—in his own office." He made a jabbing motion with his hand to his chest. "Stabbed right through the heart by one of his own students, no less."

I put my hand up against my mouth, gasped, and widened my eyes, hoping I'd conveyed a proper amount of shock. "Really? How awful?"

"Yeah, well." He shrugged. "Pitt had a way of pushing people's buttons, driving them beyond their limits." He leaned in closer. "Trust me. There aren't too many shedding tears over his demise, teachers or students." He cast a furtive glance over his shoulder toward the doorway, then snagged another donut from the tray, this one a cinnamon glaze, and wolfed it down in three bites. He brushed crumbs from the edge of his lip and tossed me an apologetic glance. "Sorry. I skipped breakfast, and with my schedule today, lunch is a remote possibility at best."

I poured myself a cup of coffee. "Murder is so—so drastic, though. Are they absolutely certain this girl did it?"

"Let's put it this way. She threatened to kill him in class, and a few hours later, he turns up dead. Not only that, they caught her standing over the body with the murder weapon. Not too bright. If it had been me, I'd have chosen a much more subtle method." He scrunched up his lips in an expression of distaste. "Stabbing's so messy. I'd have used poison. You'd be surprised how many poisons there are that don't show up in an autopsy, you know, that make it seem like a heart attack. Take arsenic, for instance. It causes severe gastric distress, vomiting, and diarrhea with blood. If you give the victim a big enough dose, the autopsy will only find an inflamed stomach—maybe a trace of arsenic in the digestive tract, but that's not the norm. If it's given out over time you can only find it in the victim's hair, nails, or urine, if one would think to check. It's classic, really.

"Then there's succinylcholine. That's one not normally tested for in toxicology screens. It's a strong muscle relaxant that paralyzes the respiratory muscles. An autopsy would show the victim died of a heart attack.

"And let's not forget aconite, the 'Queen of Poisons.' It can be detected only by sophisticated toxicology analysis using equipment that's not always available to local forensic labs. The perfect poison for murder, according to experts."

I swallowed. "If you don't mind me saying so, you seem particularly well versed on the subject."

His eyes crinkled at the corners, and he gave me a slow, lazy smile. "What can I say? People talk about different things, and I listen. I'm like a sponge." He waved his hand dismissively. "Hey, enough of that doom and gloom, right?

After the next set I've got a pretty long break. If you'd like, I could take you down to the exhibition hall and show you around."

"That's very kind of you, but I'd hate to be a bother."

"No bother at all." He gave me a saucy wink. "It'd be my pleasure."

"I'll think about it," I said. "By the way, I understand there's a local gallery that sometimes showcases the works of the students."

He nodded. "Yep. The Wilson Galleries. Nice place."

"You've been there?"

He chuckled. "Once or twice."

"Ever meet the owner?"

Taft's eyes narrowed at my question, but he was spared from answering as Professor Pace reentered the studio, her sharp gaze focusing on Taft and me huddled together near the refreshment table. She clapped her hands together and boomed out, "Okay, break's over. Time to resume." She tossed a pointed look our way. "That includes you, Taft."

He reached out and his fingers closed over mine, gave them a quick squeeze. "The Dragon Lady speaketh. Listen, I'll be here another hour. Stop back, if you're interested, and I'll give you that tour."

He ambled back to the platform, doffed his robe, and leaned on the stool, posing in all his naked glory. He did have a ripping bod, but there was just something about him that seemed off, aside from his unnatural fascination with poison. I tamped down a shudder, set my coffee cup on the table, and hurried out of the studio. As far as I was concerned, Taft Michaels bore a further look, but right now I was more interested in seeing the inside of Pitt's office.

As Ollie so succinctly put it, "Nothing can give up a clue like the actual scene of the crime." I hurried down the corridor and paused, trying to get my bearings. The door to my left was half open, and the placard off to the left read in big, bold letters: PROFESSOR ARMAND FOXWORTHY—PORTRAITS AND SCULPTURE. I glanced casually inside. Six students were grouped around easels, listening to a man I assumed to be said professor speak in the front of the class. Foxworthy was a middle-aged man trying to appear about twenty years younger. He wore his graying hair long and clipped in a ponytail down his back, secured by an expensive-looking black onyx clip. He was bare chested beneath a brown jacket that looked as if it had seen far, far better days. His jeans were well worn and had holes at the knees. A pair of heavily tinted wire-rimmed glasses were pushed up on his beak-shaped nose, masking his eye area. I wondered how he could see, because the lighting in the room wasn't the best. I glanced over at the far wall, which consisted of two long shelves holding various pieces of sculpture and several paintings hanging next to the shelves: all of naked women, or rather, all of *the same* naked woman.

And then, suddenly, she was there, standing right in the room. She'd entered through a door in the back, wearing the same white robe as Taft Michaels had. She lazily ascended the platform to the right and shrugged off the robe. There she stood under the spotlight in nothing but her birthday suit, and there was no hint, no expression, no indication of self-consciousness whatsoever. Although if I'd had a body half as good as hers, I might not be averse to showing it off, either. Her body was firm, her muscles were taut, her breasts high and in proportion to her frame. She was tall—my height, maybe an inch taller—and she had long, coltish legs that seemed to go on forever.

I raised my eyes to her face and was struck by her classically beautiful features: wide, beautiful blue eyes; lips full and fleshy, arranged in a sexy pout; thick dark hair that cascaded across her slim shoulders and down her back like a waterfall. A niggling sense of familiarity struck me as I stared at her. I was certain I'd seen this girl before, but just where eluded me.

Possibly if she'd been clothed, I might have remembered.

I started to turn away when I saw a familiar figure enter the studio through a side door. Jenna Whitt. She marched right over to Foxworthy, whispered something in his ear. His lips tugged downward, as if he weren't pleased. Then he got up and followed her out the back door. But that wasn't the only interesting thing. The model onstage had turned her head slightly and was watching their every move. It was curious, but right now I had bigger fish to fry. I turned and started down the long hall. A young girl, portfolio tucked under one arm, passed me, and I reached out, touched her on the arm.

"Excuse me." I smiled and held out my hand, clutching all the pamphlets the secretary in the office had given me earlier. "I'm thinking of enrolling here, and I'm a bit lost. I was wondering if you could just tell me where all the offices are? I'm looking for—I'm looking for Professor Grant's office," I said, offering the first name that came to mind. "I—ah—want to discuss the possibility of studying sculpting under her. Someone said upstairs, but—I'm kinda lost. I know I saw an elevator somewhere, but—"

"Yeah? Old Grant's taking on new students? Wow, you

must either be really dedicated or a glutton for punishment. As for the elevator, heck, it's broken more than it works." She pointed a bloodred fingernail toward a door marked STAIRS. "That's the fastest way. Top floor. Her office is all the way at the end of the hall. I'd escort you up, but I'm late myself."

"Oh, no problem. I'm sure I can find it."

"Great. Well, then, good luck," she said, and breezed off.

"Good luck, thanks. I'll need all the luck I can get," I murmured, and made my way to the door.

Two steep flights later I found myself in a darkened, empty corridor. Apparently none of the professors were occupying their offices at the moment, which suited me just fine. I made my way down past the sea of closed doors. I passed the one marked PROFESSOR ADELINE GRANT, and the moment I turned the corner felt like shouting, "Bingo."

I hurried down the corridor and paused before the entrance. The door was tightly closed, covered top to bottom with yellow and black tape in a crisscross design. I sighed. How many times back in Chicago had I seen this? Ah, memories. The fact the tape was still up indicated to me that the police felt there was still something to be learned, possibly something they'd overlooked. That thought sent a surge of hope pulsing through me. I was relatively certain it was a misdemeanor, at the very least, to break CSI tape, but if it would help Lacey . . .

I hesitated, hand poised over the tape, and suddenly, my whole body stiffened, assailed by the sudden feeling I wasn't alone. The next minute a heavy hand clapped down on my shoulder.

"Before you do something stupid you'll probably regret, miss, would you like to tell me just what you think you're doing?"

I froze. I knew that voice. And it wasn't good. I turned and came face-to-face with my past.

SEVEN

*G*reat didn't even begin to describe how Leroy Samms looked, but the adjectives *yummy* and *mouthwatering* came instantly to mind. Even though it had been fifteen years at least since I'd last seen him, he hadn't changed a bit. If anything, he'd gotten better looking, and he'd been pretty perfect to start off with. He wore khaki pants and a cream knit sweater that hugged his chest and hinted at the muscular, rangy body beneath. His hair was still the odd shade I remembered, an inky blue-black that exactly matched the deep-set eyes; eyes that were trained right on me. When he said nothing, I thought with a modicum of relief that he hadn't recognized me, but then a glimmer of recognition lit up his eyes, and the corners of his full lips twitched slightly upward.

"Nora Charles," he murmured, touching two fingers to his forehead in a brief salute. "Oh my God, it is you, isn't it?"

"Last time I looked," I said, assuming a casual tone as if

I ran into ex-flames every day of the week. "How've you been, Samms?"

Those broad shoulders lifted in a careless shrug. "I can't complain." He took a step toward me. "I can't believe I ran into you, here of all places, after all these years."

"Yeah," I said. "Life's funny, huh?"

Those navy eyes raked me up and down. "You haven't changed a bit."

I forced a laugh. "You're being kind."

He shook his head. "No, truthful. So you still with that Chicago paper?"

I shook my head. "That's yesterday's news," I said lightly. "Now I'm Nora Charles, small business entrepreneur. I inherited my mother's sandwich shop."

The eyebrow lifted even higher. "You gave up reporting? That's hard to believe. Last time I saw you—" He stopped, ran a hand through his hair.

"Was our last night on the college paper," I said softly. "That was . . . quite a night." *And one I'd rather not rehash, thanks very much.*

His gaze was unfathomable. "Yes," he said softly. "It was."

We both stood there awkwardly for a minute, the silence so thick you could cut it with a knife. And then we both said, at exactly the same time: "What are you doing here?"

I answered first. "I—ah—I'm here trying to help my sister."

He frowned. "Your sister? Who's . . ." He slapped his palm against his forehead. "Oh, wait . . . Lacey Charles, the murder suspect? *She's* your sister?"

My chin jutted out. "She didn't do it, Samms. My sister's not a killer."

His left eyebrow twitched slightly. "Still calling me by my last name, I see."

I shrugged. "Old habits die hard. So I answered first; now it's your turn. What are you doing here?"

"Well, for starters, I heard an Abigail St. Clair was at the school, asking a lot of questions about the curriculum, the students, the teachers."

"Oh," I gave a careless wave, "can you keep a secret?" I leaned in a bit closer to him, so close I got a faint whiff of his aftershave—Brut? "That's me. This is my sister, after all. I'm just trying to help the police out."

"I see. What if the police don't need any help?"

I cocked my brow. "Trust me, the police always need help."

His lips thinned. "Thanks, but no, thanks. I'm—or should I say the police are—doing just fine."

I frowned. "What?"

He pulled back the side of his jacket, and I saw a shiny badge clipped to his belt. "Let me formally introduce myself. "I'm Detective Leroy Samms of the St. Leo Homicide Division. I'm in charge of this case."

OMG, if there was a hole nearby, I would have crawled inside and pulled it in after me. I felt my cheeks grow warm with embarrassment, and for at least a minute, I couldn't think of a thing to say. Finally, I managed to get out, "You're a homicide detective? More specifically, you're the good-looking detective who arrested Lacey? My aunt's friend's words," I added hastily. "Not mine."

He rubbed absently at his temple. "I should have made the connection when she mentioned an older sister in Cruz. Although I can't recall you ever mentioning anything at all about your family, or much else personal, during the time we—ah—worked together."

"I've always been a private person." I jammed my hands deep into the pockets of my jacket, determined to keep the conversation far, far away from college and auld lang syne. "You said you came here because you heard Abigail St. Clair was asking questions?"

His eyes sparkled, but his expression remained impassive. "I'm buddies with the head of the real Abigail St. Clair's home security. He asked me to check it out, since he knows the real Abigail St. Clair is out of the country."

Rats, just my luck. "I can explain," I said.

He held up his hand. "You already did. You came here to see if you could help your sister, maybe find a clue we might have missed in our initial sweep."

"Exactly." I pulled back my shoulders, a motion that made my breasts snap to attention, and my chin jutted forward. I noticed Samms's gaze linger on my chest for a brief moment before he raised his gaze to meet mine.

He looked at me and then let out a laugh, a deep, rich sound that sent a little tremor racing up and down my spine. It wasn't exactly an unpleasant feeling. I could equate it to having champagne bubbles stuck in your nose on New Year's Eve.

Huh? I gave myself a mental slap. Oh no. I wasn't going down *that* road again, no sir.

Samms's laughter subsided and he pursed his lips. "I read the accounts of what went down a few weeks ago with the Graingers. So, what, Red, you get lucky once and now you think you're Nancy Drew?"

My temper started to rise, more because of his use of his old nickname for me than being compared to America's favorite girl detective. "No, I do not think I'm Nancy Drew," I snapped. "I'm just trying to help out my sister. You and I both know once the DA settles on a suspect, further investigation goes out the window. And, believe it or not, I know my way around a crime scene. Just ask anyone at my former paper." I paused. "And don't call me Red, Samms."

"Still sensitive, I see. Do I get upset because you refuse to use my first name?" His brows drew together, making a deep V crease the center of his forehead. He brushed an inky bang out of his eyes and leaned in a bit closer. "How about if I call you Brenda?"

"Brenda?"

"After Brenda Starr." His voice grew soft. "I called you Brenda, that last night we worked together on the paper . . . or don't you remember?"

I was starting to remember things it had taken me years to forget. Fortunately, I was spared answering as two students rounded the corner, their arms overflowing with portfolios. Another figure walked, shoulders hunched, behind them, and I thought for a second I recognized the bare chest and ponytail of Professor Foxworthy, but I blinked, and when I looked again, Foxworthy (if indeed it had been him) was nowhere to be seen. I shook my head, wondering if I might be starting to hallucinate, as the students passed us, casting curious looks our way.

Samms eyed me. "I think this discussion is best had in quieter quarters." As soon as they'd gone, he reached out and grasped my elbow. I felt a surge of . . . something . . . shoot through me at his touch, and I abruptly pulled my arm away.

"I'm capable of walking on my own," I ground out. "I am an adult, after all."

He raised both hands in a gesture of surrender. "Fine. Please act like one." Without waiting for me to answer, his arm snaked out and in one motion ripped the yellow tape from the doorway. "Now we're gonna go inside, and you are not going to touch or disturb anything. Got it?"

I raised my chin another inch. "Like I told you, *Detective*, I'm familiar with the protocol."

His stern expression softened, but not by much. "Okay, okay. Just checking."

I followed him inside and stood for a moment to get my bearings. A cherrywood desk stood catty-corner, with two expensive file cabinets made of the same wood off to the right. The left wall was one massive bookcase, filled to over-flowing with books, save for the center shelf on which rested what appeared to be several expensive pieces of modern sculpture. One I actually liked. It depicted a hand holding a face, or a mask, supported on its left side by another hand. They were arranged so the mask seemed to be suspended in midair, making the piece just odd enough to be appealing, unlike some of the others in the case. The back wall held several expensive-looking oil paintings in equally expensive-looking frames. I noted a large faded rectangle on the far right, as if something had hung there but been removed. Light filtered in from a wide bay window just in back of the desk, highlighting the large, ugly red stain that marred the thick beige shag carpeting. Aside from the slight fading on the wall and the stained rug, the office was impeccably furnished and oozed wealth, position, comfort.

It was a shame Pitt had to die there.

I raised my eyes again to the other paintings. Two depicted

ballet scenes, one racehorses in a field. I moved a bit closer to study them.

"Nice, aren't they?" Samms said, almost at my elbow. He squinted at them. "Degas, I think. He liked to paint ballet and horses."

I ignored his comment and tapped the faded spot on the wall. "Looks as if he might have removed one of these. I wonder why?"

"Maybe he wanted to switch off. Pitt was a big collector," Samms went on. "These are only a few of his prized possessions. He's got some on display in one of the rooms downstairs, and the rest are in his private museum at his home." His gaze flicked to the bookcase. "Liked sculpture, too. Mostly modern stuff. Personally, I can't get into it, but to each his own." He took a step back and folded his arms across his chest. "So, you wanted to see the scene of the crime. Satisfied?"

My eyes traversed the length of rug and settled on the red blotch by the desk. A shudder ripped through me, and I dragged my gaze upward to meet his. "Hardly. I won't be satisfied until my sister's name is cleared." Against my will, my eyes strayed back to the blotch.

Samms walked over to the stain and nudged the edge of it with his toe. "There's about ten to twelve average pints of blood in a male human body, slightly less in a female. That stain looks bad, but actually it only accounts for one, maybe two pints."

"Thanks for that information." I swallowed. "Did the coroner pinpoint the time of death?"

"Sometime between nine thirty and ten. Probably closer to ten."

I suppressed a shudder. Lacey couldn't have missed the killer by much. "I imagine you've gotten the report back on the murder weapon by now?"

His stern expression sobered, and he sounded almost kindly. "As I informed Mr. Dobbs earlier, the only prints we found on that knife were his client's—your sister's."

I sucked in my breath. Damn!

He tapped his finger against his dimpled chin. "Seriously, though, even you have to admit she's a natural suspect. She had words earlier in the day with Pitt, threatened to end his life, no less, was quoted by several witnesses as saying 'I'd like to kill that bastard' and 'I'd like to put the professor on ice,' and then she's found standing over the body clutching a weapon that only her prints are on." He tossed me a pained look. "Tell the truth, now. If you were in charge of this investigation, you'd have arrested her, too."

"Maybe. But I'd try to keep an open mind and do a lot more digging into other possible suspects, too, of which there are plenty, by the way."

"Oh really?" His eyes sparked with defiance. "And what makes you think I haven't been doing just that?" The smile he tossed me bordered on indulgent. "I'd be remiss in my job if I didn't investigate other possibilities now, wouldn't I? It's the DA's office that's satisfied. They tend to get a mite overzealous when they get means, motive, and opportunity handed to them on a silver platter."

I recalled Irene's earlier comment and remarked, "I understand the DA's got a pretty good record with regard to murder convictions."

"Yep, she does, and getting better all the time." His eyes darkened as he added, "I just want you to know, Nora, I haven't stopped investigating this, not by a long shot. I consider myself a pretty good judge of character, too. Your sister doesn't seem like the murdering type. She's a bit of a prima donna, and spoiled, but a murderer?"

A tiny ray of hope blossomed anew. "So, you say you're still investigating. I realize most of what you find out has to be confidential, but is there anything else you feel comfortable sharing with me? I wouldn't ask, except . . . "

"Except it's your sister." He hesitated and then added, "I checked out the wife—the second one—first thing, because, as I'm sure you know, ninety percent of all murders are committed by the spouse. Giselle signed a pre-nup, so with a divorce she'd get zippo, but with a murder? Well, let's just say she stands to inherit a TON."

I remembered Chantal's tarot reading and nodded. "Sounds like a prime motive to me."

"Did to me, too, at first. But the alibi she gave us for the time in question checks out."

I bit down hard on my lip to conceal my disappointment. "Okay, then. What about Pitt's son? I heard they had a disagreement recently."

He pinned me with that navy gaze. "You certainly ask a lot of questions."

I shrugged. "Old habits die hard," I said lightly. "You can take the gal out of reporting, but . . . "

"Yeah, yeah, I get it," he said roughly. "Well, I quizzed him, too, and before you ask, his alibi for the TOD checked out."

The sigh that tumbled from my lips didn't even begin to express the frustration that welled inside me. "All right, but even if you eliminate them, there are others to investigate. Take Taft Michaels, for instance. Pitt is supposed to have picked on him a great deal, plus he has knowledge of poisons that seems to me to be way beyond what any art student slash model should possess. Then there's Kurt Wilson; it's possible they argued recently, too. And Julia Canton. She and Pitt were supposed to be having an affair. Maybe he broke it off, and she reacted as a woman scorned."

He started to say something, then stopped as his cell phone beeped impatiently in his pocket. He flashed me an apologetic look as he fished it out and flipped it open. "Samms here." He listened for a few minutes, then said, "Fine. I'm on my way." He snapped the phone shut and dropped it in his pocket. "Sorry, but I've got to go. An appointment that I completely forgot about." He made a sweeping gesture with his arm. "After you."

I stepped over the threshold and paused. Out of the corner of my eye I caught a flash of movement. I turned my head just in time to catch a glimpse of a gray-streaked ponytail disappearing through a door far down the hall. I glanced over my shoulder at Samms.

"It might be a good idea to seal the room up again. You know, to protect it from people curious about the scene of the crime."

His blank, unreadable face stared at me pointedly. "Of course I'm keeping it sealed for now. But you're right, some enterprising individual might take advantage of an opportunity to take a look around and help themselves to a little souvenir to sell on eBay. I think I'll speak to Ms. Dinwiddie, have her put one of the guards on this floor. Not that I don't trust anyone, but . . . aw, hell. I don't." He snagged my wrist and looked straight into my eyes. "Look, I know you're concerned about your sister, but you should leave this to the professionals. I'd certainly hate to see anything happen to you because you took it upon yourself to play Brenda Starr, or do you prefer I call you Nancy Drew?"

I jerked my hand free of his grip. "I prefer it if you don't call me either. And regardless of what you think, Samms, I know what I'm doing."

"I'm sure you think you do, but think about it. If your sister didn't kill Pitt, then the real killer is out there. And I'm sure he or she won't take kindly to someone trying to expose them." His lips twitched at the corners. "Our department is down manpower right now. One murder is about all I can handle at the moment."

"Agreed, but—"

"No buts. I'm sorry to bail on you right now, but please promise me that you'll leave the detecting to me and my team. I can see it's hard for you, but—" He shoved his hands into his pants pockets. "Things have a way of working out. So do I have your word you'll leave the detecting to the professionals?"

I promised, hoping he couldn't tell I had my fingers crossed behind my back. He turned and hurried back down the hall, and I leaned against the wall with a heartfelt sigh. Leroy Samms was the last person I'd ever expected to see again, and to top things off, he was the detective in charge of the case. Funny, wasn't it, how life worked out sometimes? Well, his warning had only served to strengthen my resolve to continue my investigation into Pitt's murder. I was just about to start walking back to the door marked STAIRS when it suddenly opened and a girl wearing jeans and a flannel shirt emerged. She toted a large sack in one hand, and the manner in which she held it suggested it might be heavy. As she started to cast a furtive look around, I ducked into a small alcove and flattened myself against the wall. Peering cautiously around the corner, I held my breath as I caught a better glimpse of her face. It was the nude model from downstairs, only now that she was clothed, recognition kicked in.

Julia Canton.

What the hell was she doing up here, and what on earth could she possibly have in that sack?

My cell phone chose that moment to start blaring out my new ringtone. Usually I sang along to Katy Perry's "I Kissed a Girl," but right now I scrabbled in my purse, desperate to shut it off. I wasn't fast enough. Julia's head jerked up; she gave a quick look around and hightailed it in the other direction. I sighed as my fingers closed over the phone, and I pulled it out and looked at the number. It was a local one, not familiar. Thinking it might be Peter, I flipped it open. "Hello?"

A lilting, feminine voice asked, "Is this Nora Charles?"

"Yes," I replied. "Who is this?"

"I've got to see you, Ms. Charles. As soon as possible."

I remembered the last time someone had said that to me. I'd ended up finding a dead body. "Who is this?"

"Mrs. Pitt. We need to meet. I have some information concerning my husband's murder."

A tingle inched its way up my spine. I gripped the phone and glanced around. Why would Giselle Pitt want to share anything with the sister of the woman who supposedly murdered her husband? "What sort of information, Mrs. Pitt?"

"I can't go into it over the phone, but let me say this. I do not think your sister killed him. In fact, I'm relatively certain she didn't."

That was surprising. "You are?"

"Let me just say this. There are others with far better motives than her. For example, I can tell you that the alibi that blond tart married to my husband cooked up needs to be looked at closely. Much more closely than the police did."

Wait a minute? Wasn't I speaking with the blond tart? "Excuse me, I'm sorry, you did say you were Mrs. Pitt?"

"Yes, and I'm the one who should be sorry. I should have been clearer. I'm Althea Pitt, Thaddeus's first wife. I live at 4576 Victoria Lane in Pacific Grove. Be here in an hour. Trust me, Ms. Charles, this is a meeting that will be well worth your while."

Then the line went dead.

EIGHT

Twenty minutes later I parked my SUV in front of the address Althea Pitt had given me, a small bungalow tucked back in a shady corner on a quiet street lined with huge elms and flowering shrubs. I locked the car and walked up the neatly trimmed walkway to a wide enclosed porch. I rang the front doorbell, and a few minutes later the door opened to reveal a demure woman with short medium-brown hair, snapping hazel eyes with flecks of gold in the center of their irises, and a wide, full-lipped mouth. Her dove gray suit looked lightweight and comfy, and a U-necked blouse in black was the perfect foil for the thick braided gold chain around her neck. I judged her age to be somewhere in her middle fifties at least—a very well-kept middle fifties. Our eyes met and her lips parted, revealing teeth so perfect they had to be caps, and she held out a perfectly manicured hand.

"You have to be Nora Charles. Do come in. I'm Althea Pitt. It's a pleasure to meet you."

I stepped over the threshold, and she wiggled her fingers, motioning for me to follow her down the narrow hallway. She led me into a dim room that I assumed was the parlor, and she turned on a table lamp with a fringed shade. An off-white damask upholstered sofa and love seat were positioned in front of a fireplace, and she motioned for me to take a seat. I settled down on the sofa and scooted to the edge of the seat.

Mrs. Pitt moved over toward an oak table on which an antique silver tea service rested. She picked up the pitcher and held it aloft. "Tea?"

I really didn't want any but didn't want to seem rude. "Yes, thank you."

"Do you take lemon?"

"No, thanks. Just a bit of cream and sugar."

She poured the tea into two fragile-looking china cups, which she placed on the long mission-style table in front of me, along with a sugar bowl and small pitcher of cream. As I prepared my tea I took a moment to study my surroundings. The room had a slightly musty odor to it, and the walls were painted a faded ivory color. I noticed several lighter rectangle shapes on the wall where pictures had obviously been removed. The Oriental carpet covering the hardwood floor was thick but threadbare and fading along the edges. A white grand piano bearing several framed photographs sat off to one side in front of a massive bookcase whose shelves were only partially full. My eyes focused on one photograph positioned off to the side, and a niggling sense of familiarity immediately swept over me. I didn't have much chance to dwell on it, though, because Althea leaned forward and spoke in her soft voice.

"I appreciate your coming, and I won't keep you too long."

I gave her a long, slow look. "I confess, I was surprised to hear from you."

She chuckled. "Well, your cell phone number isn't un-listed, my dear."

"That's not what I meant. Why call me at all?"

"Why not?" Althea returned my look with an equally long, slow one of her own. "Once the police informed us of who they had in custody, I did a thorough Google search on your sister, and on you. You have an impeccable reputation as a true crime reporter, not to mention the excellent job you did on the Lola Grainger case." She leaned forward. "You and I both know once they have who they feel is the perfect suspect in custody, the police have a tendency to stop look-ing elsewhere."

"And you're not sure my sister is guilty?"

Her lips twitched. "Let's just say I want the right person convicted of this crime." A slight pause and then, "No matter who it is."

I took a sip of the tea and balanced the cup on my knee. "You said on the phone you knew something. Is it about his murder?"

She let out a long sigh. "Thaddeus and I were happy, back in the day. We lived here when we were first married—oh, this was a grand house, full of life and love, and objects d'art. I love art in all its forms: paintings, sculptures, antique books, everything. It was one thing Thaddeus and I had in common. Unfortunately, over the years I've found it neces-sary to . . . part with some of my treasures."

Well, that explained the faded squares on the wall and the empty places on the bookshelf. "That's a shame," I murmured.

Her eyes took on a dreamy look. "Fame does things to people, my dear, especially to ones who are not prepared for it, and Thaddeus wasn't. He started believing his own press, and I didn't exactly support him back then. The fact my marriage ended was my own fault. Our son was grown, and the common bond of art we'd always shared was over-shadowed by his commercial fame. Thaddeus was ripe for the plucking, and Giselle saw a golden opportunity. My husband was smack-dab in the midst of a midlife crisis, and she saw a chance to grab the brass ring." Her hand fluttered carelessly. "I'm sorry. I don't mean to bore you with what is obviously not your problem. The current state of this house is in no way Thaddeus's fault. He gave me a generous settlement when we divorced—guilt will often be a benefactor—and gives a generous monthly allowance still." She shook her head. "I couldn't complain about him in that respect."

"Funny, Mother. I could."

I turned toward the doorway. The speaker was a tall, thin man in his late twenties, with close-cut red hair, deep green eyes, and a firm jaw. He wore a navy suit, which I judged to be an Armani, and a light pink and undeniably expensive shirt. He moved over to the bar and poured himself a brandy, downed it in one gulp, then poured himself another.

Althea's eyebrow rose. "A bit early isn't it, darling?"

He shrugged. "Not really. What is it they say? It's five o'clock—or happy hour—somewhere." He raised the glass. "Cheers," he said, and downed the second.

Althea's lips twisted into a half smile that in actuality resembled more of a grimace. "This is my son Philip. Philip, this is Nora Charles."

"Ah." He moved forward and extended his hand. I took it, noting as I did so the long, tapered fingers and the nails, which were impeccably manicured and shone with just a hint of clear polish. Somehow that didn't surprise me. "They arrested your sister for my father's murder," he said, and raised his empty glass. "Well, Mother and I believe in the old adage, innocent until proven guilty." He refilled the glass and settled himself in a high-backed Queen Anne chair. "Especially when there are so many other more likely candidates."

"Really? Who?" I couldn't resist asking.

He bit out a laugh. "The wicked stepmother, for one. Actually, the only one, in my book." He slid his mother a glance. "I still think Giselle is the reason Dad got cold feet about the painting."

I looked questioningly at Mrs. Pitt. Her finger toyed with the hem of her skirt. "Allow me to explain," she said. "As I started to tell you, the current state of my home is not Thaddeus's fault. Other expenses cropped up he didn't know about. No, let me amend that statement. To be quite honest, and I intend to be nothing less with you, dear, I didn't want Thaddeus to know about those other expenses."

Philip coughed lightly. "She means me, Ms. Charles."

Althea nodded. "My son has always been headstrong, impetuous, and outspoken." Her laugh tittered out. "His father's son, no doubt about it. A smart boy, but lazy." When Philip made no move to protest, she continued, "I can say that about my son, because he *is* my son. He has the mental capability to do something really great with his life, but he has no ambition, no direction."

Philip coughed again and shot me an apologetic look. "Do excuse the cough. I just can't seem to shake it."

"You've got to stop smoking," his mother admonished. "I told you, that only makes it worse."

"But Mother, I've got to have some vices, after all." He pulled a package of Newports from his pocket and tossed them on the table. "I even switched to menthol. Doesn't help. Anyway, getting back to my mother's assertion. It's rather harsh." He turned to Althea. "I have lots of ambition, Mother. You and Father just don't appreciate what the ambition is for."

"Yes, racing and blackjack." Althea spit the words out and then turned to me. "I blame Thaddeus and myself for the way he turned out. I couldn't have any other children after he was born, so I'm afraid we spoiled him rotten—"

Philip cut her an eye roll. "Not this again," he muttered.

Althea ignored him. "He knows it's true. He's never had a real job, never worked at any hard labor. He plays at things. Right now he's playing at investment banking." She leaned forward and dropped her voice to a whisper. "And he's terrible at it. It's only a matter of time until he gets fired, and then he'll move on to something else. The only constant in his life is gambling." She bit the last word out as if she'd spit out a hot pepper. "There were times when he'd be quite lucky at it, but more often than not he ended up owing extravagant amounts of money, amounts my monthly income can no longer cover."

Philip rose out of the chair and walked over to where I sat. "And before you ask," he said, "they thought about sending me to GA—Gamblers Anonymous—but my shrink told them it wouldn't do any good. One has to want to be cured, and quite frankly, I don't want to be. I enjoy it too much."

Althea slid me a look that said more plainly than words, *You see what I have to put up with?* "It's true," she gritted out. "My son refuses to admit he has a problem. I've sold whatever I could to help him out, but in recent months the well has, as they say, finally run its course."

"Yes, Mother insisted she couldn't support my habit anymore, so . . . last month I swallowed my pride and took the problem to the old man. After all, I'm the fruit of his loins, too." Philip spread his hands. "Imagine my shock when he agreed to help me."

Now I raised both eyebrows. "He did?"

Philip nodded. "Yep. He said he'd give me one of his paintings to sell. There was a condition attached, of course. I had to pay off my debt and then put any surplus in the bank and not touch it for a period of two years. He wanted me to leave it to grow, try and accumulate a nest egg." He paused. "He also wanted me to give up gambling entirely for the same length of time. Father thought if I could do that, well, there might be a chance I could give it up for good."

"And did you agree?" I asked.

He nodded. "Sure. What choice did I have? It was either agree to the old man's terms or get my kneecaps busted. The people I owed this money to aren't exactly the forgiving type. I was to meet with him last week, sign an agreement, and he was going to turn over the painting to me. Then I got a call, informing me the deal was off."

I swallowed. "You must have been furious."

"I was." He twirled his now empty glass in his hand. "But not enough to kill him, if that's what you're thinking.

Besides, I have an alibi for the time of death. I was at a fund-raiser the entire night."

That jibed with what Samms had told me. "But you did argue with your father."

"Yes. I couldn't understand why he so abruptly changed his mind. I wanted—needed—an explanation."

"And did you get one?"

He shrugged. "He seemed very evasive. Just told me he'd changed his mind and that was that. The entire call lasted about five minutes." He blew out a breath. "I was angry and disappointed, but in the long run it didn't matter."

"Why not?"

Althea answered, "Because the following day a check for the exact amount of Philip's debt arrived by special messenger. It was drawn on the school account. So I knew, right then and there, my husband's decision had nothing to do with Phil's situation, but rather with the painting itself. I'm positive of it."

I let out a low whistle. "That is interesting. Do you happen to know which painting?"

Both shook their heads in unison, and then Althea answered, "Thaddeus never said which painting it was to be, but I have an idea it might be one he recently acquired. There were two. A Cezanne and an Engeldrumm." Her lips twisted into a rueful smile. "Engeldrumm is a modern artist, a bit out of Thaddeus's comfort zone but very rare and hard to get. It would have been just like him to gift Philip with that one."

"And you think his current wife had something to do with his decision?"

"My father was besotted with that witch," Philip spat. "And she hates me and Mother. It would be just like her to insist Father not give me the painting. She'd love to see me squirm and suffer."

Althea nodded. "She would indeed, and as much as I'd like to lay the blame at her feet, I can't shake the feeling there's more to the story."

"I honestly don't know why Father stayed with her—oh, wait, sure I do. Giselle's great in the sack."

"Philip," Althea remonstrated. "Don't be crude."

He thrust his lower lip out. "It's true, though. That's why he married her but maybe not why he kept her around. I never could figure that out. I mean, it's not as if she could rake in the dough in a divorce. She signed an ironclad pre-nup. And she was cheating on him."

"Tit for tat." Althea sighed. "He was cheating on her, too."

I looked at her. "You know about his affair?"

She laughed. "Oh, of course. He told me. We always told each other everything, even after the divorce. We were married for so long, you know. We just never got out of the habit of confiding in each other."

"Do you think his current wife knew he was unfaithful?"

She smoothed the hem of her skirt with her long, tapered fingers. "Believe me, if she did, she wouldn't care a whit. Thaddeus knew she was cheating on him, too. He told me. He'd found it out a few days ago, but he didn't know with whom. He was determined to find out, though. And when he did—" Her shoulders lifted in an expressive shrug. "Let's just say Giselle wouldn't have been a happy camper." She rose, crossed to the piano, and plucked the photograph that nagged at me from its space. She returned to her seat and held the photo out, one long nail tapping at the female face. "This is her, in the Bahamas with Thaddeus. He gave this photo to Philip. I was going to destroy it at first, but Thaddeus looks so handsome I just didn't have the heart." Her hand moved across the frame in a caressing motion. "She called him Teddy. Can you imagine? The first time I heard her say it I damn near threw up. You could soak a load of pancakes in her tone, it was so . . . so dripping with phony affection. It was an Institute party—I still sit on the board, so I attend—and she sat there like a queen, dripping diamonds, more on display than anything else. 'Teddy, get me a glass of wine,' in that breathy voice of hers. I always called him Thaddeus, which is, after all, his given name. But he ate it up, didn't seem to mind a bit, so . . ." She let out a long sigh. "I guess that old adage is true: There's no fool like an old fool. And now he's a dead one."

I moved closer for a better look at the woman leaning on Pitt's arm. With her long, lustrous, perfectly coiffed mane of blond hair and her perfectly shaped, pouting, pillowlike lips, Mrs. Pitt the second made Angelina Jolie look like a scullery maid. Althea's voice broke into my thoughts. "She looks like a woman used to living the good life, right? Well, with the pre-nup she signed, if he'd divorced her, she'd have gotten nothing. As his widow, she'll get millions. Now if that isn't a splendid motive for murder, I don't know what is."

"I thought the same, but apparently the police seem satisfied with her alibi."

Althea Pitt picked up her teacup and took another sip. "They gave up a bit too easily. Her alibi can be broken, trust me. It will just take one tenacious person to do it."

"You sound very sure of that."

"She might be involved, or she might not. I can't say for sure, but one thing I do know. If you want to clear your sister, find out why he reneged on his promise. I'll bet more than likely it will lead you straight to his killer."

I set down my teacup. "That's a pretty tall order."

"Tall, but not impossible. I can even tell you who might be able to help," Althea offered. "Julia Canton."

My eyes widened. "His mistress?"

She glanced at her son, and then the two of them started to laugh. "Goodness no," she said at last. "Thaddeus wasn't sleeping with Julia. Far from it. Their relationship was focused strictly on objets d'art.

"Julia's not only a model, you see. She's also an art broker. She works part-time at the Wilson Galleries, in Pacific Grove. She's the one who got Thaddeus the Engeldrumm and Cezanne."

NINE

"**N**ow there's an interesting turn of events. Julia Canton works for Kurt Wilson at Wilson Galleries and recently acquired two valuable paintings for Pitt. Pitt offers one to the son, then reneges on the deal. It all means something. I just need to figure out what."

It was Sunday, and the Institute was closed for the day in honor of Pitt, with a brief service planned for late that afternoon. Since there wasn't too much I could do right now in the way of investigation, I had returned to Cruz late Saturday night, intending to use my free time to outline a plan of attack. Unfortunately, at the moment I just wasn't quite sure what I should be attacking. Chantal had come over early, and it was a good thing, since the Sunday breakfast crowd seemed a bit more hefty than usual. Now it was the lull between breakfast and lunch, and we sat grouped around the counter in the kitchen. I had the fixings for a brand-new sandwich in front of me, and Nick lay on the floor at my feet, hopeful of swiping a paw at any little bits that might inadvertently find their way to the floor.

"You will, *chérie*. But you must exercise caution. I am certain this person would not hesitate to kill again if they thought they were on the verge of being exposed."

"That's a given." I picked up the bowl with the mayo and Italian dressing mixture and started spreading it on a hoagie roll. "I must confess, though, that it's much easier for me to imagine Julia Canton in the role of scorned mistress than it is art broker. Maybe it's because I saw her naked." At Chantal's raised eyebrow, I gave a quick shake of my head. "Don't ask."

My friend's lips quirked, but she said in a bored tone, "Wasn't going to."

"Liar." I spread spicy mustard on the roll and then arranged a layer of turkey, speck (an Italian meat made from boned pork leg), and Colby-Jack cheese, topping it with fresh dill pickle slices. I closed the sandwich and brushed the bread liberally with olive oil. "It's good to be home and talking to you about all this. Every time I mention anything about Lacey or the murder around Aunt Prudence, she starts to get hysterical."

"Well, you really cannot blame the woman, *chérie*. After all, she is not as used to murders and criminals as you are."

"True." I set the sandwich brush down and wiped my hands on a nearby dishcloth. "Her friend Irene seemed much more interested in all the gory details. Now there's a character." I rolled my eyes. "It's hard for me to fathom just how those two became such fast friends."

"Opposites attract."

"Those two are polar opposites, all right. Irene seemed to actually enjoy speculating on whether or not they'd give Lacey the death penalty or just life imprisonment. I kind of got the feeling Irene's a closet shamus; you know, the sort who watches reruns of *Murder, She Wrote* and *CSI* and tries to figure out just who the killer is."

"Maybe you should have discussed the case with her, then," Chantal suggested. "Who knows? Perhaps she might actually have given you some good insight."

"I might have except I got the distinct impression she thinks Lacey's guilty. Getting back to the original topic, though, what would make a man like Pitt think twice about letting his son have a valuable piece of artwork, to virtually deny him a second chance at making something of his life other than a hot mess?"

"Um . . . finding out his son was involved with his current wife?" Chantal suggested.

I cut her an eye roll. "That's pretty good, but considering Philip Pitt thinks of his stepmother as the plague, not very likely."

"That could have been just talk, designed to throw people off the track."

I paused. "Maybe," I said after a second. "But I don't think so."

I walked over to the stove and slid the sandwich into the skillet I'd had heating there. I placed the press down on top of the sandwich and set the stove timer for a minute and a half. "Pitt and his son didn't get along too well, so his offer to help wasn't one made lightly. It had to be something really, really big that caused him to rescind. But what?"

I stepped away from the stove and let out a gasp as I felt something crunch underneath my shoe. Looking down, I saw four Scrabble tiles.

"Nick," I said, bending down and scooping up the tiles. "Damn that cat. He always seems to get his paws into these no matter where I put them, and I was certain they were in my nightstand drawer."

"Well, maybe he wants to play," Chantal suggested wickedly. "His former master was teaching him, right?"

I didn't answer. I was looking at the tiles in my hand. EKAF. Rearrange them and they spelled out—

"FAKE! That's it." My eyes popped wide just as the timer on the stove went off, and I pinned Chantal with a searing gaze. "A fake, a forgery." I whispered the word as if it carried a disease. "If I were going to give my child a valuable painting, and I suddenly discovered it were a forgery, why . . . I'd renege. I'd make up some excuse."

Chantal reached around me, shut off the stove, and then leaned one elbow on the counter. "But if he suspected a forgery, wouldn't he have notified the police or the FBI, *chérie*?"

"Maybe not," I said thoughtfully. "After all, he considered himself to be a consummate art connoisseur. He wouldn't want word to get out he'd been hoodwinked." I transferred the sandwich to a plate, cut it diagonally, and held it out to Chantal. "Taste. It's a variation on a Cuban."

"So he would have taken matters into his own hands? Not very smart." Chantal took a bite and made little mewling noises deep in her throat. "Ooh, this is good, *chérie*. I like the different cheese you used. And I like the taste of the speck."

"Yeah, it's slow smoked. I thought it would work." I

wiped my hands on a nearby dishrag. "Thus is born my new *Andy Garcia Cuban Special*. So with that out of the way . . . Like I said, Pitt considered himself an expert. Knowing his giant ego, he'd most likely get in touch with whoever sold him the painting and call them on it."

"Oh," Chantal's eyes widened. "That would be a prime motive for murder. He discovered the duplicity, called Julia on it, and she could not risk exposure. Plus, she saw an opportunity to frame your sister for the crime."

"Neat and tidy for sure, only . . . I'm not sure anything's been forged . . . yet. It's only an assumption, the same as Julia being the one behind the scam. It's possible she might be working for someone else, someone higher."

"Ah, the gallery owner?"

"Possible," I sighed. "I sure wish Daniel was around. The FBI investigates forgeries. He might be able to help."

The bell above my door tinkled, and I blinked at the tall, handsome man who crossed its threshold.

"Daniel!" I squealed. "I was just talking about you."

Daniel Corleone chuckled as he walked up to my counter. He nodded at Chantal and then turned twinkling eyes toward me. "Good things, I hope."

"Nothing but." I frowned. "I thought you were going away on a case?"

"I'm still on the case, but the lead we had turned out to be a dead end. Think I could get one of your famous tuna melts? I skipped breakfast and"—he glanced at the clock on the wall—"I'm due for an early lunch."

Chantal tossed me a knowing look over her shoulder and picked up her purse. "My cue to leave," she hissed in my ear. She said in a louder tone, "Well, I have to be getting over to the flower shop. I shall report back here for duty tomorrow morning bright and early, *chérie*."

I gave her a grateful smile and as she sailed out the front door turned to Daniel. "If your stomach isn't grumbling too badly, maybe I could toast you a bagel for now. If you can hang out for a bit, I'm trying out another new recipe, a variation on turkey meat loaf."

He licked his lips. "Sounds good, but unfortunately, I have to get back to work in about an hour. I'd be glad to take a rain check, though."

"Sure." I eyed him. "They've got you working on Sunday?"

"The FBI never rests," he said solemnly, "and neither do criminals. Crime occurs every day of the week; you know that."

I had to agree. "Okay, then, one *Thin Man Tuna Melt* coming right up."

I pulled the tuna salad and cheddar out of the case, then crossed over to the bread box for some rye. Danny eased his six-foot-plus frame on one of my hard-backed counter stools and watched me at work.

"How's your sister?" he asked. "Anything new there?"

I spread tuna liberally over the rye. "Her prints were the only ones on the murder weapon. The DA's satisfied she's their perp, but fortunately, the investigating detective has doubts."

"Leroy Samms, right? What'd you think of him? I've heard he's very thorough."

"He seems to be," I said noncommittally. I set the sandwich on the grill and then said over one shoulder, "Art forgery or theft is considered a major crime, right? Have you ever worked a forgery case?"

"There's a special task force assigned to such cases." His

eyes narrowed. "I imagine there's a reason behind that question, and do I want to hear it?"

"Probably not," I sighed. I hit the highlights for him, finishing up at the same time the tuna melt was done. I put it on a plate and set it in front of him. He dug in with gusto and wiped his lips from the gooey cheese before he answered me.

"I do hope you're not thinking of doing what I think you are."

I assumed an air of mock innocence. "And what would that be, exactly?"

He took another bite of his sandwich. "You know darn well. You aren't planning on doing a little independent investigating, are you?"

"Goodness no. I'm not *planning* on it," I answered, hoping he didn't notice the inflection I put on the word *planning*.

Fat chance. He set down his fork and crossed his arms over his chest. "That means, no doubt, you've already started. Please, Nora, if you want your sister to get out of this in one piece, leave the investigating to the pros. I know it's hard. She's your sister and you, well, you're you."

I bristled. "What does that mean?"

"It means investigative reporting runs through your blood, same as cooking. But cooking is safer." He grinned and then sobered. "Seriously, Nora, don't do anything stupid. Don't do anything that might endanger you, or hamper your sister's chances of being proven innocent."

"Trust me," I sniffed. "That's the last thing I want."

We heard a soft "*Meow.*" Daniel looked down and smiled. Nick was sprawled underneath the stool.

"Well, Nick looks fat, happy, and sassy." Daniel suddenly frowned. "He's got something in his paws."

My head shot up. "Not more Scrabble tiles?"

"Scrabble tiles? Likes to bat 'em around, does he? Well, it's not tiles." He bent down, straightened a moment later, and held two objects out to me. I groaned as I recognized the page from Atkins's journal, and the photograph, and reached for them.

"Where, indeed. He's been in a lot of places he shouldn't be lately." I gave Nick a dark look, and he got up and scurried out from under the stool and burrowed underneath the table in the back.

Daniel surrendered the photo but eyed the paper. "There are notes on here about a guy named Bronson A. Pichard," he said. "Where did he get this?"

I snatched the paper out of Daniel's outstretched hand. "It's from his former master's old journal. I thought I'd locked these up, but apparently getting his paws into locked places is one of Nick's many talents."

Daniel took another bite of his sandwich and laid his fork down. "Nick Atkins was investigating Bronson A. Pichard? Why?"

"Apparently he investigated him several years ago, for a divorce case. It seems the guy held a major grudge against Nick." I eyed Daniel. "Why do you ask? Is this guy familiar to you?"

"Only by reputation. You were talking about forgeries, and Pichard was supposed to have dealt heavily in them. Nothing was ever proven, though."

"Nick Atkins apparently thought Pichard's dealings were questionable. Ollie told me he was the one who tipped off the authorities."

Daniel frowned. "Is that why you think Pichard might know something about what happened to him?"

"Well, it seems a good possibility, and I really have no other lead right now."

"Do you need to have a lead?"

My eyes widened. "What do you mean?"

"Atkins was a good investigator, but from what I've heard, more than a bit eccentric." He paused and then added, "Do you really want to find Atkins? It could be asking for trouble."

I made a face. "You sound just like Ollie, so I'll tell you the same thing I told him. Not only do I find his disappearance puzzling, I'd also like to resolve the question of Nick's ownership." I sighed. "It's a moot point, though, because I've got no time to try and pin down Pichard; not with everything going on with Lacey."

Daniel leaned back, let his shoulders relax. He nodded. "Wise decision. Your sister's welfare is certainly more important than tracking down some lowlife, no question."

I raised an eyebrow. "Once this business with Lacey is settled, though, I plan to see what I can find out about Pichard."

I leaned over the counter, letting my hands rest lightly on top of Daniel's. "A thought just occurred to me. You have a ton of resources at your command. Maybe you could get a lead on him for me? Ollie said he was a master at disappearing, but, well, after all, you are the FBI. No one can hide from you guys for long, right?"

Daniel shifted on the stool. "You'd be surprised. And who was Ollie talking about? Atkins or Pichard?"

"Very funny." I swatted him lightly on his shoulder and leaned forward. I batted my eyelashes ever so slightly. "You know, if you could help, I'd be really, really, really, really grateful."

His lips twigged upward. "That's a lot of reallys."

I bounced my eyebrows. "And there's more where those came from. Seriously, I know you're on a case, but so am I, unofficially. I'm not in a rush for the info right now, because I can't follow up on it yet. But if you could turn up something, say, in the next few weeks . . ."

"I know," he laughed, "You'd be really, really, really, really grateful."

"At least think about it."

"That I can do." His fingers brushed against the photograph, which I'd laid on the counter. "Mind if I take this, then? It might come in handy."

I shrugged. "Help yourself."

Daniel pushed off the stool, flipped a ten on the counter, then leaned in and gave me a quick kiss on the lips. "I've really got to run. I'll be in touch, I promise."

"You'd better," I called after his retreating back. "You've got a rain check on that meat loaf, don't forget."

The door closed behind him, and I flopped down in the nearest chair. Nick's head popped out from under the back table.

"Meow."

I shook my finger at him. "And just what were you thinking, pawing around in those journals? If you don't stop ripping pages out, Nick, we'll have no clues to go on." I glanced around and frowned. "That's odd—where is that paper? I could have sworn I put it on the counter . . ." I looked sharply at Nick. "Did you take it again?"

He blinked. "Er-owl."

"Yeah, right. Well I imagine you'll drag it out again, when you're good and ready." I flopped back in the chair and closed my eyes. Right now I couldn't worry about Bronson A. Pichard or Nick's penchant for ripping up journals. Right now I needed to concentrate on my next move in the investigation I'd promised Daniel I'd stay out of. And logically, I knew exactly what it should be. I stood up and looked at Nick.

"Well, I'm in the market for an Engeldrumm of my own—or rather, Abigail St. Clair is. And guess who I'm going to ask to find one for me?"

TEN

A few minutes past seven thirty that evening I pulled up in front of the Wilson Galleries in downtown Pacific Grove. The building didn't look like much from the outside—plain white clapboard, with a small black sign hanging over the doorway. The broad picture window had a few oil paintings displayed on easels, and a few pieces of "molded clay" sculptures flanked either side of the window. It wasn't very impressive, to say the least. As I unclipped my seat belt, I went over the story Ollie and I had spent the better part of the afternoon perfecting. Rich heiress, very anxious to acquire this rare painting, and the money's burning a hole in my pocket. I was ninety-nine point nine percent sure the money part was why Julia Canton had agreed to meet me at the studio that evening.

Ollie's words rang in my ears as I hurried up the walkway. "If you come off like enough of a desperate sucker and she thinks she can get away with pawning off another forgery, she'll make a move." Hell, I was counting on it. I might have double majored in English and History, but one of my minors had been Theatre Arts. I hadn't exactly been good enough to send talent scouts flocking my way, but I didn't stink, either. Besides, I reminded myself, there were plenty of times tracking down stories in Chicago when I'd indulged in a bit of role-playing. Tonight was no different from one of those times.

The gallery door was locked (it figured, considering there was a large sign that said CLOSED ON SUNDAY right in the front window), but there was a buzzer on the side, and Julia had told me to ring it twice. I did so, and not a minute later the door was flung open and Julia stood in the doorway. Tonight she wore a short pink/purple/orange flowered dress that hugged all her curves in all the right places and a beautiful pair of eggplant purple Christian Louboutin strappy heels I would have personally killed for that added at least three inches to her already impressive height. Her long, dark hair was pulled off her face, twisted into a bun at the nape of her neck.

In a nutshell, she looked even more fabulous fully clothed than I could ever hope to, and I felt frumpy as hell in my tailored pantsuit and ruffled blouse. Something else niggled at me, too—a wisp of a thought—but I put it from my mind as she smiled at me, and I caught an assessing gleam in the depths of those brilliant blue eyes. "Ms. St. Clair?"

I channeled my inner snooty rich bitch self, which I found surprisingly easy. "Yes, Ms. Canton, I presume? Thank you for seeing me on such short notice. I do apologize for bothering you after hours, and on a Sunday, no less."

"Not a problem. I'm always happy to help out a friend of Gloria Christian's. She's one of our best customers."

"So I heard. I mean, I heard about how pleased she's been with her purchases here," I amended, as Julia's laser-sharp gaze raked over me. "She—ah—couldn't stop raving about the last one."

Julia nodded. "Ah yes. The David Patchen. An excellent example of a hot glass blown sculpture. I'd hoped she was pleased with it." Her full lips curved upward. "I sold it to her."

I gave Ollie another mental thank-you for doing such quick and thorough research on artsy acquaintances of Abigail St. Clair's, and on actually finding one that had done business with the Wilson Galleries. The fact it had been Julia who'd made the sale was a not unpleasant bonus. I followed her inside and over to a small table right in front of the wide picture window. As I settled myself into the velvet-upholstered chair she asked, "Can I get you anything? Some coffee, tea . . . champagne?"

My eyes widened. "You have champagne?"

Her laugh tinkled, like wind chimes. "Of course. Didn't Gloria mention that? We keep it for the preferred customers."

"Oh yes, yes, I forgot."

"Can I get you a flute?"

The offer was tempting, but I needed to keep a clear head. "I'll pass, thanks." I smiled at her as she eased herself into the seat across from me. "You look rather young to be such a connoisseur of art. Been doing this long?"

"Long enough," she answered shortly. "You said you were interested in acquiring some rare paintings?"

"Yes, I am. I have a rather extensive collection, and I'm interested in adding to it. Your gallery came highly recommended to me, not only by Gloria, but by some of my other friends as well." I crossed my fingers under the table that she wouldn't want a list.

Apparently the Gloria connection was satisfactory, because she smiled. "That's nice to hear." She flourished her pen. "Now were there any artists in particular you're interested in acquiring, or a particular era?"

"Well . . ." I giggled and leaned forward. "I've always had a passion for the unattainable, and I've heard this gallery specializes in acquiring pieces that are just that. Am I right?"

The smile stayed in place, but the friendly gleam vanished from the eyes. "I'm sorry. I don't understand."

My hand shot out, covered hers. "No need to play coy." I leaned over and, before she could make a move, pressed my lips to her ear. "What I want is a painting . . . an Engeldrumm."

She pulled away, a deep frown creasing her smooth forehead. She set the pen down on the table and leaned back in her chair. "An Engeldrumm? Well, you certainly don't fool around, do you?"

"Where art is concerned, I never kid."

Her breath came out in a gentle whoosh. "You do realize that Engeldrumms don't fall out of the sky. She's a legend in the fields of lyrical and geometrical abstract. Her work is damn hard to find."

I twisted my lips into a pout. "I can appreciate that, but . . . you managed to find one for Professor Pitt, did you not?"

Another slight widening of the eyes. "Yes, but—" She cleared her throat. "You didn't mention that Professor Pitt was one of your references."

"To be truthful, he wasn't. The details of how I learned

of the transaction aren't important," I added quickly, waving my hand in the air. "What is important is the fact you found him one, and if you found one, then you can find another, correct?"

Something flashed in her eyes, but it was gone in a second, her smile still perfectly in place. "I must tell you, in all honesty, that the acquisition we made for Professor Pitt was a rarity. The chances of finding another are slim, very slim indeed. Now, a van Eyck or a Turner would be much easier to get."

I laid my hand over hers. "Honey, if anyone can get me a gen-u-ine Engeldrumm, it's you. I told you, I've got a sixth sense about these things."

"I'm very flattered," she said slowly, "but I'm afraid who-ever told you this information is incorrect. I'm not the one who acquired the paintings for Professor Pitt."

I frowned. "Oh—it wasn't you?"

"No." She paused and then said, "That transaction was handled personally by the gallery owner."

"Ah, then maybe that's whom I should be speaking with. Kurt Wilson, is it? As I said, my heart is set on an authentic Engeldrumm, and I'm prepared to pay cash—and pay very, very well."

Her tongue darted out, slicked at her bottom lip. "Mr. Wilson is not—"

"Pardon me. Did I hear my name mentioned?"

Julia and I both turned at the same time. A tall, wiry man with a bald head and a neatly trimmed goatee was walking through a door at the far side of the room. His Brooks Brothers suit was immaculately pressed, and as he extended his hand I could tell the nails had been professionally manicured, but there was just something about him that made a shiver inch its way down my spine, especially when he raised my hand to his lips and planted a soft kiss in my palm.

"Forgive my boldness," he said in a well-modulated voice. "I am Kurt Wilson, the owner of this gallery. And you are—"

"No—Abigail St. Clair," I corrected myself quickly. "Well, this is an unexpected surprise."

Julia, in my opinion, looked far from pleased to see her boss. "I didn't expect you to be here, Kurt," she said. "I thought you were going to Los Angeles for a few days. That buying trip?"

He smiled a very oily smile. "Plans changed. I'll be in town until Thursday." He shifted his attention back to me. "I believe I overheard you inquiring about an Engeldrumm?"

"Yes. I'd heard the late Professor Pitt had acquired one from here, and Ms. Canton informed me that the owner arranged it." I batted my eyelashes. "That would be you, correct?"

He nodded. "Yes. Finding that painting was a real coup. I can have Julia make a few calls. Who knows, we might get lucky again." He stroked at his chin. "I must warn you, if we do manage to find one, it won't be cheap. Pitt paid two hundred fifty thousand for his. Considering their rarity, it's a good assumption this one will be higher priced. I'd say at least four hundred fifty thousand, and that's on the low side."

I gulped inwardly and waved my hand carelessly. "Is that all? I said money is no object. That's a mere drop in the bucket to a St. Clair." I snapped my fingers in the air for emphasis, and I could almost see the dollar signs light up in Wilson's eyes.

"Excellent." Wilson turned to Julia. "You know what to

do." He bowed to me, and I breathed a silent sigh of relief when he made no move to take my hand again. "I must go now, but I trust we'll meet again—under very satisfactory circumstances."

He turned on his heel and walked back through the rear door. We watched him go, and then Julia scraped her chair back and rose to her feet in one fluid movement. "It's a tall order, Ms. St. Clair, but let me see what I can do. Can you give me a few days?"

"Honey, I'll be in the area for the week. Let me give you my cell. You can call it day or night."

I scribbled down the burner cell's number on the back of a card and handed it to her. She glanced at it and then shoved it into the pocket of her dress before glancing pointedly at her watch. "I'm sorry, I completely forgot about another meeting I have in ten minutes. I'll be in touch." She walked me to the door and all but pushed me over the threshold, slamming the door soundly behind me once I was outside. I walked down the cobblestone path, right past my SUV, and paused before a sleek Jaguar parked there. I fiddled with my purse until I saw the curtain in the front window fall back, waited a few minutes more for good measure to be certain neither Julia nor Kurt were still watching, and then cut across the lawn around to the back of the gallery. There was a small, dirty window there, and if I secreted myself behind the azalea bush and stood on tiptoe, I could just barely see inside. Fortunately, I'd been in similar situations in Chicago before, so I'd come prepared. I'd just pulled the opera glasses out of my purse when the light flicked on, illuminating a small, seedy-looking room that boasted a rolltop desk, a table with four chairs, and a phone that looked as if it had come out of the Stone Age. Julia entered. She walked over to a closet, opened it, and rummaged around inside, emerging at last with a thick, rolled piece of paper clutched in one hand. She sat down at the desk, which was right beside the window, picked up the phone, punched in a number. Her head turned slightly in my direction, and I ducked, not wanting to take any chances. I waited a few minutes, but when I raised my head, I let out a disappointed cry.

The room was dark. Julia was gone.

No matter, I thought, squaring my shoulders. Thanks to my trusty opera glasses, I'd managed to see the number she dialed. I hurried back to my SUV and climbed in. I turned the key and the motor sprang to life. I drove up and down the narrow streets until I came to a dead end, where I pulled over, cut the ignition, and took out my cell. Holding my breath, I punched in the number I'd seen Julia dial. A minute later my heart skipped a beat as an all-too-familiar voice boomed in my ear.

"St. Leo Homicide. Detective Leroy Samms."

ELEVEN

I skidded to a stop in front of the police station. Thankfully, there was an empty spot right in front. I shut off the car, pocketed the keys, and stomped toward the station, where I took the short flight of stone steps two at a time. I burst right through the plate glass doors and into the small lobby, where a large counter protected by what I assumed was bulletproof glass loomed in front of me. I walked straight up to it and saw a desk with a few filing cabinets in the room beyond. A stern-faced, gray-haired woman wearing a crisp blue uniform sat behind the desk, her attention focused on her computer monitor. I looked over to the side and saw a sign: RING FOR ASSISTANCE. I pressed the buzzer and heard a loud *bzzt* on the other side of the glass. The woman glanced up, frowned, then slowly rose and lumbered over to the window.

"Yes?" she asked through the microphone. "Can I help you?"

"I'd like to see Detective Samms. It's urgent."

Her gaze was so chilly, I was surprised I didn't get frostbite. "I'm not sure if he's even in."

I glanced toward the small waiting area, which boasted a hardwood bench. "Then I'll wait, if I may. If he should be back there, could you tell him Nora Charles needs to see him? It's urgent."

Her lip curled at one end. "It always is, sweetie."

"Thanks." I returned her frosty gaze with one of my own. "You might also tell him I plan on waiting here for him *all night* if necessary."

I no sooner settled myself on the uncomfortable bench than Samms himself swung through the plate glass door. He glanced my way, started to walk toward the door, paused, did a double take, then retraced his steps back to where I sat. He folded his arms across his chest and scowled down at me.

"Well, well, to what do I owe this honor? Did your secret decoder ring break? Or maybe you've found you've missed me, after all these years?"

"In your dreams." I jumped up and poked my finger against his broad chest. "I have to talk to you. Right now. It's important."

He stared at me for a minute, then nodded toward the door. "Follow me." He motioned to the woman at the desk, and she hit a buzzer. A few moments later I trailed behind him down a narrow hallway to a frosted plate glass door at the end. HOMICIDE—DETECTIVE LEROY SAMMS was etched on it in black letters. He opened the door and ushered me inside. Smack in the center of the room was a large metal desk, its top covered with papers and files. In front of the desk were two worn-looking leather chairs, and behind the desk, a leather captain's chair, equally worn. Off to one side were two file cabinets. The drawer of one stood partially open, and I could see it jam-packed with manila file folders. A Bunn coffeemaker with a half-full pot sat on a small table underneath a large window. He waved me into one of the worn chairs, then slid into the one behind the desk, leaned back, and steepled his fingers underneath his chin.

"So, tell me. To what do I owe the pleasure of your charming company tonight? What do you have to tell me that's so important?"

Never one to beat around the bush, I met his stare straight on and said, "You spoke with Julia Canton tonight, didn't you? Don't deny it—" I held up my hand as he started to speak. "I know you did. I know she called you."

He leaned back in his chair, propped one foot up against the desk's edge. "Well, sure she did. Why would I deny it?"

His admission took me by surprise, and my jaw dropped. "You—you're admitting it?"

He actually had the temerity to look amused. "Why shouldn't I? Has a new law been passed I'm not aware of? Is it now a crime to receive phone calls from concerned citizens?" He shot me a look I felt sure he usually reserved for crazy people. "Or are you going to deny you were at the Wilson Galleries earlier, asking her and Wilson to find you a very rare Engeldrumm, *Ms. Abigail St. Clair*?"

I swallowed over the giant lump rising very fast in my throat. "Oh."

"Yeah. Oh." He took his foot down and leaned across the desk, hands folded in front of him. "So what have you got to say for yourself?"

I shifted from side to side in the chair, curled my fingers around its arms. "I can explain."

"Like you can explain calling here about fifteen minutes ago and hanging up when I answered?"

I gave myself a mental slap upside the head. Of course he'd have known it was me—every police station was equipped with caller ID. "I can explain that, too."

"Okay. I'm waiting, Nora, and I warn you, it had better be good."

I flashed him a dark look as I answered, "Fine, I'll tell you. On Friday I received a phone call from Mrs. Pitt."

"Why would Giselle Pitt call you?"

"Giselle didn't. This was the original Mrs. Pitt, Althea. She thinks the police should do some further checking on Giselle's alibi for the night of Pitt's death."

"She does, does she? And what, she thinks you have some pull here? That you can arrange it?"

"She knows I'm concerned about Lacey, and, unlike some people, she doesn't want to see an innocent person go to prison," I shot back.

He fixed me with a level stare, and we sat in silence for a few minutes; the only sound was Samms, drumming his fingers on his desktop. At length he stopped and steepled his hands in front of him. "So she called you over to discuss the ineptitude of the police department . . . and then what? Why did you go to the gallery and pose as Abigail St. Clair? Don't tell me it's because you've suddenly become a patron of the arts."

"No, of course not. Pitt promised his son a valuable painting to help alleviate his financial troubles, then reneged on the deal at the last minute. I went to the gallery because Althea thought Julia was the one who sold Pitt the painting he was going to give their son." I let out a breath. "I wanted to find out if it were possible the gallery somehow sold him a forgery."

Samms leaned back, picked up a pencil from a tin cup on the desk, and scissored it between his fingers. He did this for a short time, and just when I thought I couldn't take it any longer, he said, "Is this what you did as an investigative reporter? Take a button and sew a vest around it?" He swiped at his mouth with the back of his hand. "You've got no proof the gallery sold Pitt a forgery, let alone Julia knowing anything about it. All you've got is conjecture. You're assuming a situation that may or may not be true."

"I think there's a good chance it is true," I burst out. "You know, you were a lot more on the ball when you were on the college paper than you are now. Granted, there's no concrete proof—yet—but if one of those paintings was forged, and if Pitt discovered it somehow, he'd have been very upset. He might have taken steps to confront whoever he thought responsible, and that person might have wanted to silence him . . . permanently."

Samms's eyes narrowed into slits. "And you think this person is Julia Canton?"

"I don't know if it is or isn't, but if one doesn't let oneself be blinded by her stunning good looks, it makes sense. She works at the gallery. She argued with the deceased a few days before his death. I'm certain she was involved somehow in the sale of the paintings." I paused for a breath. "Do I have to go on?"

"No." He shook his head. "You don't. Like I said, all

you've got is a theory and no proof." He got up, walked around the desk, and eased one hip against its edge as he looked down at me. "Look, I appreciate the fact you'd like to see your sister cleared of a murder charge, but fingering another innocent person—"

I jumped up with such vehemence I felt my breasts jiggle underneath the thin fabric of my shirt. "I may not have proof she's guilty, but there's nothing that proves she's innocent, either."

Both his bushy eyebrows bounced at either my jiggling breasts or my comment—I wasn't sure which. "So you're a lawyer now, too? Okay, then. I appreciate where you're coming from, but poking your nose into matters that don't concern you isn't going to help. You've got nothing that'll stand up in court." He blew out an exasperated sigh. "God, if this isn't just like old times, you so stubborn—"

"Why did you become a detective?" I asked sharply, cutting him and his dissertation of my virtues off.

He stared at me. "What?"

"Why did you become a detective? You had a lot of promise as a reporter. What changed your mind?"

"The usual reason people change direction in life." His lips thinned. "I had a lot of pressure from my family—my father, in particular—to follow in his footsteps."

"Ah." I did remember Samms talking about his father, a former San Francisco homicide detective. "That's too bad," I said. "You were good at your job."

"Yeah, well . . . sometimes life throws us a curve ball." His gaze met mine and held it. "Ever wonder about what your life might have been like if you'd made a different choice?"

Now that was a loaded question. I shook my head. "No. I've found it does no good to rehash the past. It's much safer to live in the present."

"Maybe so." He ran his hand through his thick mass of hair. "And speaking of the present, I told you I didn't think your sister was guilty of the crime," he continued. "But if you don't rein it in, you're going to do her more harm than good."

I raised a hand to rub at my own throbbing temples. "There's something you're not telling me, isn't there? There's more here than meets the eye, and for some reason you don't want to share it."

"I have nothing else to say to you, Nora. You're just going to have to put your faith in me for a bit longer." His tone softened as he leaned toward me. "Please. Don't do anything stupid, anything you'll regret."

His nearness was disconcerting; even though he didn't touch me, I started to tingle, like I'd touched electricity. It took me back, for an instant, to a night, long, long ago, a night when . . . Abruptly I pushed back my chair, stood up, and smoothed down my skirt. "The only thing I regret at the moment is thinking you'd be of some help. I thought you were someone who cared about justice, who wouldn't want to see someone put in prison for a crime they didn't commit. I guess I was wrong about you. Good evening, Detective Samms."

I walked out of his office, my head held high, feeling the heat of his steely gaze sear my back as I went. I hurried down the corridor, past the reception desk, and I'd just stuck out my hand to push through the plate glass door when I realized my gold bangle was missing. I nibbled at my lower lip. I'd been fiddling with the catch while Samms and I sparred. I must have loosened it enough for it to fall off my wrist when

I got up. I hesitated. As much as I didn't want to look at Samms again, that bracelet was the last thing my mother had given me, and I wasn't about to leave here without it. I turned and walked back into the reception area. There was a different woman minding the desk now, and she didn't bat an eye when I explained what I wanted, just buzzed me through with a sympathetic smile. As I approached Samms's office, I noticed the door was closed. I'd just raised my hand to knock when I heard his voice from behind the door.

"Julia? It's Lee."

Feeling like I'd just been doused with a bucket of ice water, I rubbed my suddenly clammy hands down the sides of my slacks. Lee, huh? So much for impartiality. I pressed my ear closer to the door, eager to catch every word I could.

"Yes, she was here. I think I managed to put her off the scent, though—what's that? You found the *terma*? Are you certain?" There was a moment of silence and then, "Billings Warehouse at ten. Got it. I'll meet you there."

I heard the sound of a chair scraping back, and I turned and walked swiftly in the direction I'd come from. Fortunately, the receptionist was busy on the phone and hardly acknowledged my halfhearted wave. I hurried over to my SUV, climbed in, and leaned my head against the seat rest, struggling to process recent events.

It was pretty obvious now why Samms was reluctant to follow my lead. There was some connection between him and Julia, but what? Of course there was the obvious assumption that they were lovers, but was that all there was to it? Or could there be something more? I'd seen a lot of dirty cops when I was in Chicago. Heck, I'd even been on stakeouts with some of them. But I had difficulty picturing

Samms as a cop, let alone a dirty one. Of course, it had been a long time since we'd seen each other, but . . . a person didn't change *that* much. There was also the possibility Samms was onto her, that he'd been onto her all along, and perhaps meeting her at this warehouse tonight was a trap. That might explain his insistence I keep my distance. He could want to keep me out of any possible cross fire.

There was only one way for me to find out the truth, and that was for me to go to the Billings Warehouse and see for myself just what was happening. Worst case scenario, I could always contact Daniel and get the feds involved.

I glanced at my watch. There was still an hour and a half before the proposed meeting. Enough time for me to pay a little call on Mrs. Pitt the second and find out just how airtight that alibi of hers really was.

TWELVE

I ran a Google search on Giselle Pitt on my iPhone and got an address in the more exclusive section of Carmel. About twenty minutes later I pulled into a gated drive on a quiet, tree-lined street. I rolled my window down as the intercom just beyond it started to squawk. I announced myself saying, "Nora Charles. I'm associated with the SFPD," and a minute later the gates parted, revealing a winding circular driveway lined with overhanging elms and dogwood trees. At the very end was an exquisite English Tudor residence, flanked on one side by a spacious side-by-side garage. One of the doors was open, and I caught a glimpse of a candy apple red Mercedes Benz, black convertible top down, before the door shuddered and began its descent. I couldn't help but notice the license plate: TRPHYWF. I wondered if it had been Pitt's idea. I parked over to the side, got out, and stood for a moment admiring the house.

It was well built, featuring a high-peaked slate roof with a façade of half timbers and cross-hatching, symmetrically paned picture windows, and leaded glass sidelights. Handsome herringbone brickwork on the elegantly landscaped walkway led up to the entryway, where a pair of tall hammered columns rose to a balcony/flower box high overhead. The setting reminded me of formal English gardens I'd seen in magazines, the front garden boasting colorful blooms, lush greenery, and sculpted boxwoods. All in all, it was a feast for the eyes. I was halfway up the cobblestone walkway when the front door suddenly swung open.

The woman who stood framed there looked anything but grief stricken. Giselle Pitt was even more striking in person than in her photographs. Long straight hair cascaded around her slim shoulders like a golden waterfall. Her skin, tanned to a golden honey brown, looked to be unlined, smooth and creamy as a baby's bottom. I judged her height to be about five-six or five-seven, even without the benefit of the spiky-heeled black Manolo Blahniks gracing her tiny feet. She couldn't have weighed more than a hundred pounds soaking wet, but it was a curvaceous hundred, shown off to perfection in her formfitting Isaac Mizrahi sheath—in black, of course. Eyes the color of a Tahitian sky fixed on me, the stare steady and unblinking. She extended a perfectly manicured hand. "Nora Charles? I'm Giselle Pitt. Do come in."

I followed her into a vestibule fairly reeking of elegance and money, with a cross barrel vault ceiling and arched leaded glass sidelight. She caught me gaping and smiled. "Beautiful, isn't it? My husband lived for art in any form, Ms. Charles. He knew what he was doing when he purchased this," she said with a nod. "This house was designed by a popular interior design group in collaboration with the previous owner, who was also an artist. It's been published in architectural periodicals."

I took in the deep crown molding, polished hardwood floors, and expansive picture windows and nodded. "I'm sure. It's . . ." I struggled to find an appropriate word. "Magnificent."

"There's custom lighting throughout every room of this place. It was designed specifically to focus on art and objects d'art for its owners, who were not only artists, but well-known collectors, much like my husband. There are five bedrooms, four deluxe baths and two half baths, a living room with a fireplace and den alcove, a formal dining room, a library, a custom kitchen, a media room . . ." She waved her hand in the air. "Before I married Teddy I came from a rather modest circumstance. I worked in a restaurant, and I lived in a two-room apartment. To go from that to this, well, it was quite a change. Quite."

"I can imagine. It certainly takes one's breath away."

"Yes." Her lips twisted into a wistful expression. "Quite a lot for a simple girl from Kansas City to take in, but you get used to it. If I wanted to stay married to Teddy, I had to." Her arm swept out in an encompassing gesture. "Please, let's talk in the living room. It's cozier in there. Sometimes the rest of the house—well, without Teddy around, it just feels like an empty museum." She sucked in a breath. "I do miss him—more than I ever thought I would, actually."

She led me into a room that did indeed seem both warm and inviting. A classic white marble fireplace graced one end of the room, set against walls that appeared to be beautifully hand painted in a soft rose color. The furniture consisted of a sofa and love seat combo upholstered in an expensive-looking beige velvet and a cherrywood mission-style coffee table positioned between them. A high-backed Queen Anne chair in a rich brown of the same material was just off to the left. A lighted display case near the large bar area held several pieces of modern sculpture, similar to the ones I'd seen in Pitt's office.

"Sit anywhere," Giselle said with a brisk wave. "Can I get you anything? Tea, coffee, a soft drink?"

I shook my head as I eased myself onto the sofa. "No, I'm fine."

She sat down on the love seat opposite me and picked up a gold cigarette case from the coffee table, shook out a cigarette, put it between her lips, then fumbled in the pocket of her dress and withdrew a gold lighter. She lit the cigarette, took a deep drag, and then leaned back, eyes slitted, studying me for a moment. "You said you were with the police?"

"Yes. I'm—ah—I'm helping them with the investigation into your husband's murder."

"That's still going on?" She took another drag on the cigarette. "I was under the impression the murder had been solved and the culprit apprehended, and at the scene of the crime no less. One of Teddy's students."

I had to agree with Althea—the nickname sounded way too syrupy. "We just want to be certain all the possibilities have been explored. The accused is pleading not guilty, you know."

Her eyes rolled. "She was caught holding the knife. Goodness, why bother pleading not guilty. Unless she plans to add by reason of temporary insanity." She flicked an ash into an expensive marble ashtray on the coffee table. "Now *that* I could understand. Teddy didn't exactly endear himself to his students. I'm sure more than one harbored thoughts of murder at one point or another. And he certainly knew how to push people's buttons. I could easily see someone flying off the handle, perhaps stabbing him in a fit of rage . . ." Her voice trailed off and she glanced over at me. "I can understand it, but it doesn't mean they should go unpunished. She took a human life. There's a price to pay."

I reached into my shoulder bag and removed my notebook and pen. I opened it and balanced it on my knee. "If you don't mind, I have just a few questions."

Her sigh was audible. "Go ahead. Of course, I want to cooperate in any way I can to ensure Teddy's killer is brought to justice."

God, stop calling the deceased Teddy or I might kill you myself. I smiled and asked, "So, would you mind telling me where you were the night of the fifth between nine and eleven p.m.?"

Her eyes narrowed. "Don't you have this information already? I told all this to the detective who came around the next day—Samms, I think his name is. Can't you get this from him?"

"Detective Samms is working another matter right now," I said, thinking fast, "and the DA wants to bring this to trial as quickly as possible, so we need to make sure our facts are accurate. So, if you don't mind . . ."

"No, of course not. It just seems like a lot of wasted energy, but if you think it's important." She waved a heavily jeweled hand. "I was at a party in Sea Cliff. The Van-Blandts'. It was a post-fund-raiser celebration. I helped them raise some money for a children's charity, and we exceeded our goal by ten thousand dollars. Lina VanBlandt sits on the charity board, and this was their way of showing appreciation for all our hard work. Lina and her husband footed the bill, of course. And added another ten thousand to what we'd already raised."

"I see." I scribbled in my notebook. "And of course, you have witnesses who can testify you were there at the time of the murder?"

"Of course. I was there the entire evening. Wait." She rose, crossed to a rolltop desk in the far corner of the room, and returned a few moments later, a small photo album in hand. She handed it to me. "I showed this to Detective Samms. A friend of mine took photos, gave each of the board members that book as a souvenir. There are date and time stamps on them."

I set my notebook aside and opened the album. The very first photo was of Giselle, wearing a skintight red cocktail dress, hair done in a French twist, holding a flute of champagne and standing between two other women in what appeared to be a very elegant foyer with a winding staircase as the backdrop.

She tapped the picture with a bright red nail. "That's me, flanked by Dorothy McCambridge and Mercedes LeBon. They co-chaired the fund-raiser with me." Her nail skimmed the edge of the photo. "Note the date and time."

I looked in the bottom right-hand corner. The photo was dated the fifth of this month, and the time was 9 p.m.

I raised my head and stared into those brilliant blue eyes. "Your husband was murdered sometime between nine thirty and ten p.m."

She sighed. "Look at the other photographs."

I flipped through the album. Giselle was in practically every photograph, some candid, some posed. The times of the photographs were varied, but all were between 9:30 and 11 p.m. I flipped to the last page, and suddenly my heart did a double flip-flop.

This photo depicted Giselle seated on a leather sofa in what appeared to be a den, with dark wood walls and soft lighting. She was seated facing a man wearing a shirt open at the collar. His dark hair was mussed, and he clutched a flute of champagne in one hand, the look of adoration on his face unmistakable as he gazed into her eyes. A portrait of a setting sun hung just over their slightly lowered heads.

With a jolt, I realized where I'd seen a setting very similar to this before. Taft Michaels's Facebook page. And no wonder, since Giselle's companion was none other than Taft Michaels. And just like that, I realized what it was that had bothered me ever since I'd seen that photograph of Giselle at Althea's.

Giselle was the blonde Taft Michaels was kissing in his Facebook photo. Which to my mind, could mean only one thing. Taft was, in all probability, Giselle's lover. I looked at the date stamp in the corner of the photo. It had been taken on the fifth, at 9:30 p.m.

My head jerked up sharply. "Who is in this photo?"

She leaned over and shrugged. "A friend."

I tapped at the photo with my own nail. "This is Taft Michaels. He's a model at your husband's school. Apparently you're friendly enough with him to ask him to accompany you to a fund-raiser in your husband's place?"

She jerked her fingers down on the necklace, so hard I thought it might break and pearls scatter over the hardwood floor. "He didn't accompany me. Taft also worked on the fund-raiser. I happened to meet him there. I went alone, because Teddy said he had to work late that night, but you already know all this. It should all be in the statement I gave Detective Samms."

"To be honest, I haven't read your statement, so if you don't mind going over it once more?"

"Oh, for pity's sake." Eyes flashing, she jumped up from the couch. "Why are you treating me as if I'm a suspect in my husband's murder?" She reached down and tapped at the photographs. "I never left the party. You can ask anyone who was there." She paused. "You can ask Taft, if you must. We were together the entire time between nine and eleven."

"I see. He'll swear to that?" At her nod I said, "That's rather . . . convenient. You give each other a perfect alibi."

The look she shot me was blacker than a thundercloud. "I'm not certain I like your line of questioning, Ms. Charles. It almost sounds as if you're trying to pin my husband's murder on me."

"I'm just trying to make sure justice prevails, Mrs. Pitt. Do you want to see an innocent woman convicted?"

Her lips pursed in a pout. "Heavens no—*if* she is innocent. However, the DA has assured me all the evidence points to the fact the right person is in custody."

"Evidence can be interpreted many ways."

"It's hard to misinterpret catching one standing over the body with the murder weapon." She took another drag of the cigarette, exhaled, and looked me up and down. "You *did* say you were working with the police, didn't you? Because you act as if you're on the defense team."

I blew out a breath. "Was your husband aware you and Taft Michaels were lovers?"

Her gaze flickered but didn't waver. "I didn't say we were lovers."

"You don't have to. If one can't tell from the way he's ogling you in this picture, then they can check out his Facebook page. He's practically got his tongue shoved down your throat in quite a few pictures."

"Damn fool." She swore softly under her breath before turning back to me. "Teddy was hardly in a position to throw stones."

"So you don't deny it?"

"Why should I? Apparently it's out on Facebook for the whole world to see." She choked out a tight laugh. "Yes, Taft and I were—are—lovers, but it's not as if my husband was as pure as the driven snow. He's had his share over the years. Oh yes, I've had him watched, as I'm sure he's had me watched as well. I wanted to get a bit of ammunition of my own, you know—just in case. I've even seen a blonde leaving his office, late at night. The suspect in custody is a blonde, correct?" Her arm swept out, a gesture that encompassed the large, airy room. "I mean, do you think I'd want to give up all this? He made me sign a pre-nup. If either of us filed for divorce, I walked away with just what I came into the marriage with, and that amounted to virtually nothing." She flicked a stray hair out of her eyes in a casual motion. "I didn't kill him."

"And Taft, your lover, can swear you were at this party, and vice versa."

Her eyes glittered like stones. "If you're insinuating we'd lie to protect each other, you're wrong. There's no need to lie. Whatever differences my husband and I had," she said, her finger tapping the edge of the album after enunciating each word, "I was very fond of Teddy. I still am. Just because we had lovers doesn't mean we stopped loving each other." She rose, plucking the photo album from my lap as she did so. "I think we're through here, don't you?"

I walked with her to the door, spun around as I reached the threshold. "One last question, Mrs. Pitt. Did your husband ever mention anything about any of his artworks possibly being forgeries?"

Her eyebrow shot up. "Teddy had an obsession with art and went to great lengths to ensure the pieces he collected were authentic. I guess it's logical, when you consider the amount of money he spent on his little hobby."

"So to the best of your knowledge, all his pieces are authentic?"

"I sincerely hope so, since once all this is settled I'll probably be selling the bulk of his collection." She let out a short laugh. "I wouldn't know a genuine Renoir from a fake, to tell you the truth. Teddy did, though. If something was amiss with any of his treasures, he'd have caught it, sooner or later. Unless, of course, the forgery was near perfect. Then maybe not—who knows." She paused, eyes heavy lidded. "Come to think of it, he was upset over something the morning he died. I'm not quite sure what." Her brow creased and she closed her eyes, only to open them a second later. "Oh yes. He called the gallery. I'm sure of it because the number was written on the pad by the phone. I seem to recall he did speak with someone—rather heatedly, too."

I leaned forward eagerly. "Julia Canton?"

"Maybe. I couldn't say for sure. I never paid much attention to Teddy when he was talking about artwork. I think he did say something about a flaw he'd found, but . . ." She shrugged. "I'm afraid that's all I can remember."

I took an oblong piece of paper out of my purse and scribbled my name and cell number on it. "If you do remember, please get in touch with me."

She glanced at it, then tapped it thoughtfully against her chin. "Charles, Charles. Now why does this name sound so familiar—wait a second." Her eyes narrowed. "The suspect in custody—isn't her name Charles as well?"

I didn't answer, just moved swiftly across the threshold. "Good night."

I hurried down the steps and over to my SUV and climbed in, feeling the stabbing heat of Giselle's stare boring into my back. I strapped on my seat belt and peeled out of the driveway at a speed Mario Andretti would have approved of. Once I was a few blocks away, I slowed down and reviewed what had transpired.

For my money, Giselle Pitt was still an excellent suspect. I was willing to bet Hot Bread's receipts for the weekend that the trip from that house to Pitt's school and back could be accomplished in less than an hour, which could leave her enough time to commit the deed. I was willing to bet another weekend's worth of receipts that her "airtight alibi" was none other than her boyfriend, Taft Michaels. As for the blonde she claimed to have seen leaving her husband's studio, well, I was darn sure that wasn't Lacey, and it probably wasn't Julia, either.

Who, then?

I had the feeling if I could find that out, I'd be one step closer to proving who really killed Thaddeus Pitt.

"*Meow*."

I jumped at the sound, and the next moment a ball of black-and-white fur had leapt from underneath the backseat into the passenger side. Nick blinked twice, made a quick circle, then plopped himself down and began washing his front paws.

"Good God," I grumbled. " How did I not see you? Have you been in the car all this time?"

Nick's nose twitched, then he rested his head on his forepaws.

"I guess I may as well give up trying to figure out just how you do what you do. Are you certain you were Nick Atkins's cat? You didn't belong to a magician, like maybe David Copperfield, perhaps? Or did you borrow the cloak of invisibility from Harry Potter?"

Nick rolled over on his side, stretched out his forepaws.

"Fine, be that way. You have your secrets, and I have mine. But right now, we're going to see if we can learn one of Detective Samms's secrets. What do you say to that?"

His mouth snapped open in a wide, unlovely cat yawn.

So much for small talk.

I pulled up in front of the Billings Warehouse at five to ten. I got out, went over to the passenger side, and opened the door. Nick hopped out, did his kitty stretch while I locked the car. We stood for a moment, surveying the dark, oblong-shaped building. The warehouse was sandwiched in between a meatpacking warehouse and what looked to be an abandoned bar. Not exactly the glitzy neighborhood I'd been used to hanging around in the last few hours. We entered through the cargo door, and I stood for a moment, letting my eyes adjust. Even though there was lighting from half-dead fluorescent tubes in the ceiling, it could only be considered minimal at best. Fortunately, my key chain boasted a tiny flashlight I could use just in case the bulbs gave out. The area appeared as deserted as a cemetery on Halloween, and twice as eerie. Nick trotted along beside me as we made our way deeper into the warehouse. Suddenly, he froze, tail upright, the hairs puffed and fluffed out like a giant fan.

"What's wrong?" I whispered, even though I knew he couldn't answer. We stood in silence for a moment, and suddenly, I did hear something. A very faint sound, from far away . . . like a door closing.

"Come on," I hissed. I lifted my head, sniffed at the air. It smelled pretty stale, but there was another scent, cigarette smoke. I racked my brain, trying to remember if I'd seen either Julia or Samms smoking.

Nick's tail swished, and he pawed at arrows painted on the ground. He trotted ahead of me at a brisk pace, and I fell into step. We followed the painted arrows along a white-tiled hallway down to a door with a shade pulled all the way down. A sign placed haphazardly in the window proclaimed it CLOSED.

I tried the door, which seemed to be stuck. I looked at the doorframe, which appeared to be less than sturdy, and checked it for alarm wires. Seeing none, I raised my leg and gave the door a swift, hard kick. It clicked open an inch, and I pushed it all the way open. We walked into a tiny office not much bigger than a postage stamp. A large metal desk and battered file cabinet took up the majority of the space. Another door at the far end stood partway open. Nick suddenly tensed, and I saw the hairs on his back rise. His tail fluffed out, and he started to growl, deep in his throat.

I frowned. "What's wrong? What do you sense?"

Nick reared up on his hind legs and then shot through the partially open door. I had no choice but to follow. The room I now found myself in appeared to be a slightly larger version of the previous office. Nick crouched in front of a large metal desk, and as I entered, he shifted his body slightly. I caught a glimpse of two feet, very still, shod in the pair of eggplant Louboutins I'd admired earlier in the evening.

"Oh crap," I cried. "Please tell me that's not what I think it is." I walked around Nick and peeped around the edge of the desk. I saw a twisted figure in a white raincoat bunched up around shapely legs, a tumble of dark hair covering its face, the neck bent at an unnatural angle.

"Shit," I said.

"*MA-ROW!*" Nick yowled.

I heard a sound behind me as Nick dived under a nearby chair. My heart started to beat wildly in my chest. The last time he'd pulled something like that I'd been caught next to a dead body and hauled off to the police station. His fat rear had barely wiggled out of sight before the door slammed back and I found myself looking first down the barrel of a .45 and then, as I raised my gaze, at the grim, unsmiling face of Detective Leroy Samms. He looked at me, then at the feet, then back to me again. He lowered his arm, slipped his gun back into his shoulder holster. "Well, well. Look what the cat dragged in."

I responded almost automatically. "He didn't drag me. I walked in on my own."

One eyebrow quirked. "Pardon? It's an expression, Nora."

"Oh, sure. I knew that." The queasy sensation in my stomach was getting stronger, and I really felt like gagging. I started to push past Samms, but his strong fingers reached out and encircled my elbow in a grip of steel.

"No need to run off."

I pressed my palm against my cheek. "I—I'm not. I just felt a little . . . squeamish."

"Of course you do," he said, still not cracking a smile. "I've got some Pepto back at the station. Fix you right up. Then we're going to have a chat, you and I." His grip on my elbow tightened. "Ms. Charles, you've got some explaining to do."

THIRTEEN

An hour later I found myself once again in Samms's office. He'd called in the coroner and the CSI team, and then ushered me out of there faster than the speed of light. Back at the police station and true to his word, he'd produced some Pepto-Bismol tablets and a tall glass of water; I downed it all in one huge gulp. He left me alone for some twenty minutes while he conferred with another officer, and when he came back into the room he pulled out his chair and eased himself into it, staring at me with hooded eyes, his face expressionless.

"Okay, Nora. Care to tell me just what you were doing down at that warehouse?"

"Isn't it obvious? I was looking for a dead body and, lo and behold, I found one."

"Ha-ha. I don't find that funny at all, Nora," he said, his tone humorless. "As a matter of fact, I'm beginning to think finding dead bodies runs in your family."

I rubbed at my forehead with the tips of my fingers. "Leave Lacey out of this," I growled.

"Okay, then, *Nora*. Or is it still *Abigail St. Clair*? Care to tell me what you were doing at the warehouse?"

I folded my arms across my chest and hugged myself, a typical defensive stance. "If you must know, I was waiting for you to show up."

His face remained expressionless, a perfect blank. The only visible sign my words had gotten to him was the muscle twitching at double time under his left eye. "Did I hear you right? You were there waiting for *me*?"

"Yes, I was. You aren't going to deny you had an appointment at that warehouse at ten o'clock with the deceased, are you, Detective?"

If looks could kill I would indeed have been at least six feet under. Both his eyes and face were darker than the proverbial thundercloud. "How did you know that?"

The temple above my right eye began to throb, but I fought the impulse to rub at it and to ask if he also had any Excedrin lying around. Instead I forced myself to lean back in the chair and stare straight at him, unblinking. "I have my ways."

"I don't doubt it."

He bent down, looked underneath the desk. Then he ran his arm beneath it, tapping at the wood every so often. He got up, felt underneath his chair, then he walked around to where I sat, knelt down, felt underneath my chair. He stood up, gave me another black look, and returned to his seat. When he picked up his phone and started to unscrew the receiver, I couldn't take it another minute. I jumped to my feet. "Good God, there's no listening device in here. What do you think I am, the CIA or something?" The words came out in a torrent. "If you want to have a private conversation, I'd advise speaking in a lower tone."

"Don't be ridiculous. I know you're not CIA." His stare didn't waver. "And I don't talk that loud. You've either got incredible hearing or your ear was pressed to my door."

"How I heard what I did is irrelevant," I snapped as I sat back down. "What is relevant is the fact you've been lying to me—covering something up. I came to you in good faith with my suspicions regarding the Wilson Galleries and Julia Canton, and you brushed me off like I was some sort of deranged lunatic."

His smile was indulgent, the type I felt sure he reserved for his more psychotic suspects. "Not a lunatic. That's a bit strong. A little nuts, overzealous, maybe."

I resisted the urge to stick my tongue out at him. "Maybe you could tell me now why you were having this secret rendezvous with Julia Canton?"

"It wasn't a rendezvous."

I raised my eyebrow. "A late-night meeting in a deserted warehouse? Sounds like one to me. So, come on. What was it all about?"

"You were the one I found standing in the room with the dead body, remember? Therefore I get to ask the questions, not you."

I leaned back, laced my hands behind my neck, and tried to sound bored. "Go ahead. Ask away. I've nothing to hide."

"Great," he muttered. "So, you went inside the warehouse looking for me. Is that how you came across the body?"

"Yes." A sudden thought occurred to me, and I asked, "It was Julia Canton's body, right?" At his look I added, "I never saw the victim's face, but I thought I recognized the shoes."

The frown deepened, cut a sharp V in the middle of his forehead. "Shoes?"

"Yeah. Eggplant Louboutins, really nice. I noticed them when I was at the gallery. I mean, what are the chances another woman had that same exact pair? I'm pretty sure they're limited editions. Must have cost a small fortune."

"Shoes," he repeated, shaking his head. "Figures that's what a woman would notice."

It was on the tip of my tongue to call him out on his sexist remark, but instead I counted to ten and then asked, "How was she killed? A gunshot wound to the head, a knife through the heart? I didn't see blood but then again . . . I didn't look that close."

"Sorry to disappoint; it was nothing that exciting. She was strangled. We found a scarf near the body. We'll test it for prints, but I don't expect we'll find any." He leaned across the desk. "Just what did you think going to this warehouse would accomplish, Nora?"

"I was hoping to get some of the answers you seem reluctant to give me," I burst out. "I'm willing to resort to any means I have to in order to prove my sister's innocence. I firmly believe Julia Canton might have known something. Maybe she wasn't the one who offed Pitt, but she knew . . . something. And now we'll never find out just what that something was."

He plucked a pencil out of a tin cup on his desk and scissored it between his long fingers. "I agree completely. Julia Canton is dead because of something she knew."

"Something about Pitt's forged painting, I'll bet."

"You forget we haven't yet established whether or not the painting was forged. That's just a vague assumption. So far the evidence indicates your sister killed him over a bad grade."

147

I flopped back in the chair. "You are impossible. I thought you told me you didn't think my sister was a murderer."

"I don't."

"Then why, dammit? Tell me why." I pushed my hand through my hair, pulled at a stray curl. "Why do you refuse to investigate any other leads?"

He stood up, walked around the desk, placed both his hands on my shoulders, and gently pushed me down into the chair. Then he edged one hip onto the desk and stared down at me, arms folded across his broad chest. "I believe I did tell you I was investigating other avenues. Right around the same time I told you to ease up and leave the detective work to the professionals."

"Why should I?" I shot back. "The professionals don't seem to be doing too good a job. One of the prime suspects just bit the big one."

"No, one of *your* prime suspects just bit the big one. Julia Canton was never a suspect in my book."

"And why is that, exactly?" I sneered. "Because you *just know* she had nothing to do with selling Pitt the painting? Or because the two of you shared a much closer relationship?" The corners of his lips twitched, a gesture that only served to inflame me more. "And just why do you find that so amusing?"

His voice shook with repressed laughter as he answered me. "Thanks for the compliment, but Julia wasn't my type, and you should know that."

I ignored both his remark and the rush of heat I'd felt at hearing it. Instead I snorted. "Are you kidding? She was every man's type. She was—well, from what I could see, she looked pretty perfect."

"Now, see, that's it right there. I find perfection . . . boring." His stare raked me up and down. "Now you . . . Trust me, Nora, you're far from boring."

"And what is that remark supposed to mean?"

He eased himself off the desk and walked back to sit in his chair. He spread his arms wide. "It means some people aren't too fond of my bedside manner."

I tossed him a rueful smile. "You could use a bit of work in that area. I'm willing to overlook your deficiency, though, if you'll tell me why Julia Canton *really* called you."

He hesitated slightly then said, "I told you—she wanted to check up on you. Make sure you were legit—*Ms. St. Clair.*"

"Uh-huh. And you had to arrange a meeting to reassure her of that? Or did your rendezvous have another purpose?"

He gave me a stare so blank I wondered if he'd spent time practicing it in front of a mirror. "Our rendezvous, as you put it, was police business. Speaking of which, I understand you were involved in a little police business yourself after you left the station."

The hairs on the back of my neck pricked to attention, and I could feel little beads of sweat start to pop on my forehead. "I'm sorry?"

He quirked one eyebrow, giving him a sort of devilish look. A sexy devil. "Don't play coy. I'm sure you wouldn't dream of lying to a police officer, now would you? Or are you going to deny *you* paid Giselle Pitt a little visit? Very cooperative of you to use your real name, this time."

Uh-oh. So she'd checked up on me. She was smarter than I'd given her credit for. "Someone had to do something. Both Althea Pitt and her son think her alibi is crap, and—"

"Stop right there."

Samms's hand came down hard on the desk, effectively cutting me off. He leaned over, stopping when his nose was only about an inch away from mine, and pinned me with his hawkish gaze. "Do you know what the penalty for impersonating an officer of the law is, Nora?" he asked, softly.

I swallowed. "Not offhand."

"Then let me spell it out for you." He reared up, and the rough, tough officer tone was back in his voice as he said, "California Penal Code 146a—Impersonating an Officer and Punishment. In a nutshell, that code states that anyone who falsely represents himself or herself to be a public officer and tries to intimidate an individual is subject to imprisonment in a county jail, a two thousand five hundred dollar fine, or both." He splayed both palms across the top of the desk and said more gently, "Now, you don't really want to be next to your sister in the slammer, do you?"

My finger shot up. "Giselle Pitt got it all wrong. I never said I was a police officer. I said I *was associated* with the police. And I am, in a sense."

"Yeah. Associated as in messing things up." He shook his head and made a clicking sound. "Mrs. Pitt was quite upset, you know. She figured out you were related to the defendant, and she was almost ready to call her lawyer. I had to do some fancy talking to convince her that you were just an over-zealous nutcase and wouldn't bother her again." He picked up a pencil, tapped it against the desk. "If I were you, I'd stick to sandwich making. It's safer and less complicated."

I slumped lower in my chair. "Gee, thanks," I mumbled.

"You should thank me. However, now, thanks to you, she's under the impression we're suspicious of her alibi."

My head jerked up. "Are you?"

He shrugged. "We questioned everyone. No one can say with absolute conviction that they saw her between the hours of nine and eleven—except, surprise, surprise, Taft Michaels."

"Yes, apparently they were there together. She showed me the photo album. And assured me there was no need for them to lie for each other." I cleared my throat. "What about the person who took the photos?"

"Ah. He's conveniently away somewhere in Greece on a photo shoot and unavailable for comment at the moment. We're checking into whether or not he and Giselle have a closer relationship than appears."

I looked at him. "Geez! If you suspected she had some-thing to do with her husband's death, why didn't you just tell me when I asked?"

"Oh, for the love of—" He sighed and ran his hand through his hair. "There's a lot going on with this investigation, Nora. Things you're best off not knowing. Trust me. It's better for you—and safer—if you just restrain yourself, sit tight, and let the pros handle it."

"Okay." I half rose from the chair. "You've had your say, and now I'll have mine, Detective. The DA is pushing for a quick trial, and there's a good chance my sister is going to get convicted on this circumstantial evidence unless the real killer is found. I realize you don't know me, and you have no reason to believe it, but I'm actually pretty good at investigating. I recently as-sisted the FBI on a very sensitive case. The agent in charge of that doubted me in the beginning, too, but I proved him wrong."

One eyebrow quirked. "Did you now?"

"Yes, I did. Whatever's going on here, I can handle it. I can help you."

He sat down heavily in his chair, fingers drumming on the desk. "You're like a pit bull with a bone," he said at last. "I suppose in order to get you to lay off I'm going to have to reveal certain things to you. I want you to promise me that when I do, you'll be satisfied and stop poking into this."

I thrust out my jaw. "I can't make that promise until I hear what you have to say."

He swore softly and let out a breath. "Okay. Fine. Julia Canton couldn't have been involved in whatever's going down at the gallery because . . . she was working with us."

FOURTEEN

For a minute you could have heard a pin drop in the room. Finally, I managed to squeak out, "What do you mean, Julia was working with you? You mean like a CI—confidential informant?"

He rose. "I think this is where our conversation ends. I said I'd reveal certain things to you and I did. I've explained why Julia Canton was never a suspect, and I've told you why. Now I expect you to keep your promise and back off."

"Hell no!" I shook my head. "I said I'd hear what you had to say before I promised, and I'm far from satisfied with your answer."

"I'm sure you're not, not with that endless curiosity of yours. However, any more information I could possibly share is strictly on a need-to-know basis, and you don't."

"I don't what?"

"Have a need to know."

"Oh-ho, that's where you're wrong. My sister's in jail awaiting trial for a murder she did not commit. This business with the forgeries is somehow connected to it. Exposing the person behind them could also expose Pitt's real murderer, so I'd say that qualifies as a very big need to know." I held up my hand as he opened his mouth. "And please don't say there's no proof the forgeries are connected to Pitt's death. You know damn well they are."

"I know no such thing, yet," he barked. "What I do know right now is I've lost my inside track. I'm going to have to figure out another way to get the answers I need."

"Hello?" I turned my hand inward and pointed at myself.

He shook his head. "Thanks, but no, thanks."

"Why?"

"For one thing, you're too close to the situation. It's bound to color your work. For another you're not a trained investigator."

"That's true, I'm not. But neither was Julia, or was she?" I paused as the expression on his face changed from annoyance to consternation. "Wait a minute. She was more than a CI—Julia was a member of the force, wasn't she? An undercover cop?"

"Like I said," he ground out. "Information's on a need-to-know basis. You don't need to know that. As a matter of fact, it would be great if this entire conversation could be forgotten, but it won't be, will it?"

"Heck no."

He sighed. "I didn't think so. Let me just give you some friendly advice. Stop sticking your nose in where it doesn't belong. I realize that in your prior career that was a way of life for you, but, as you said, you're on a different path now. I'd hate to see you get hurt, for old times' sake."

I glanced up swiftly at him, but his face was impassive. Stony, even. He had, as we used to say in Chicago, his "cop face" on. I slumped back in my chair, sniffed, and said, "You don't have to treat me like I'm some greenhorn, Samms. I've worked undercover with the police in Chicago, actually many times. I'm familiar with the protocol and procedure."

He rubbed at his temple. "You aren't going to drop this, are you?"

"No. So why don't you save us both a lot of trouble and just tell me what Julia found out about the forgeries." I paused. "She did find out something, right?"

He sat for a minute, his eyes hooded, his expression guarded. Finally, he said, "Fine. In light of our . . . long association, I'll tell you, but on the condition you promise to let up and not interfere?"

Oh hell. No way was I making that promise. "Let me put it this way, you've got a better shot at me doing that if you share what you know. For instance, what made her the most qualified operative?"

He exhaled a deep breath. "She has—had—a background in art history. Once she got into the gallery, she started to notice things. Odd things. Paintings would come in, and the customer would not immediately be called. Sometimes it would be a week, maybe more, before Julia was instructed to get in touch with the customer. She'd go into the store-room and at times could not find a particular painting that had come in, and then magically it would reappear a few days later. She'd ask Wilson about it, and there always seemed to be a good reason, but she just had a bad feeling about it. About a month ago a Van Eyck came in. Julia thought she recognized it from photos she'd seen as a painting that had been lifted from the Bleekers Gallery a year ago. She was trying to ascertain if it was the same painting when it mysteriously disappeared from the back room. A few days later the painting reappeared, but she could swear there was something different about it."

"Different? In what respect?"

"I'm no expert, mind you, but buying a piece of artwork is an investment. Of course, the purchaser wants to ensure the artwork they purchase is an original creation, but unfortunately, more sold pieces than you would think are forgeries, and they make their way into auction houses and galleries even with highly trained scholars on the lookout. It's even worse when the gallery owner is in on it. Someone trained in art appreciation—like Julia and Pitt—is more attuned to the little nuances that can distinguish the genuine article from a knockoff; but some forgers are so damn good, it's hard.

"For example, Julia told me that the Van Eyck the Bleekers owned originated in the eighteenth century. Yet when the painting reappeared in the gallery, it was held in the frame by staples."

"Staples weren't around in the eighteenth century," I said. "So—wow! Does that mean Wilson engineered the theft and when he got a demand for that particular painting, had someone copy it and sell it as an original?"

"That's the way we were thinking," Samms nodded. "She wanted to make a more thorough appraisal, but the painting didn't hang around long enough."

"Giselle said Pitt called the gallery the day he died, and

she thought he mentioned something about a flaw. Could he have been talking about one of his paintings?"

"Maybe, but he spoke to Julia about it a few days before he died. Pitt was positive that the painting he'd originally seen had been switched. He hadn't put it on display yet, and when he went to unwrap it to give it to his son, there were some things about it that gave him cause for concern."

I scooted to the edge of my seat, interested. "Things like what?"

"He claimed the brushstrokes in the background were off. Also the lighting in several places where it had not been before. Most important, it had a faint oily smell."

"Why was that important?"

"Oil paintings have an oily smell for many years until the oil fully dries. The Engeldrumm that Pitt purchased was more than a few years old, and it shouldn't have smelled at all.

"Needless to say, he told Julia he trusted her. He wanted her to get an authentication, and then he'd make contact with the person he believed responsible, and they had damn well better make restitution or else."

"And did she get the authentication?"

Samms hesitated, then nodded. "It was a forgery, all right. She never got a chance to confirm it with Pitt, though."

"Pitt probably went ahead with his demand for restitution without her." A mental picture of Wilson reared itself in my mind's eye, and I suppressed a shudder. "Only met Wilson once, but he didn't seem like the type that liked to be crossed or asked for refunds."

"It might not have been Wilson."

My eyebrows went up. "What? I thought Wilson owned . . ."

"He does, along with someone else."

"Who?"

He brushed a hand through his hair. "We don't know. All we know is he's got a silent partner." He dropped his hand and looked at me. "Now Nora, I've told you all I can. Honest. If I were to say any more—well, to be perfectly blunt, I can't. Not without permission."

"Permission? From who? Your captain?"

He held up his hand. "Sorry. That's all I can tell you. Will you drop it now, and leave the rest to us?" His other hand shot across the desk and captured mine. His thumb rubbed against my knuckles. "I promise you," he said softly, "I will do all I can to ensure your sister does not go to prison for Pitt's murder."

It was hard to think as his finger caressed my skin, and I forced myself to focus. It wasn't easy. "How can you possibly make a promise like that?"

"I can. I just did." He leaned even closer, so now his face—and his well-shaped lips—were just scant inches from mine. "Once upon a time we worked together pretty well. Do you trust me, Nora?"

I breathed in his scent—soap and water, his clean male smell—and my head nodded of its own volition. "I guess so," I said finally. "As much as I trust anyone."

He folded my hand into his and squeezed. "I guess that's as close to a yes as I'm gonna get out of you," he said. He released my hand and leaned back. "And who knows . . . once all this is said and done, and you see I'm right, maybe you'll decide to start calling me Lee."

That remark made my lips twig upward in a half smile. "Never happen," I said. "I'm afraid I'll always think of you as Samms, the guy who made my last year reporting on the university paper hell."

His gaze met mine with an intensity that sent heat searing my cheeks once again. "Not all of that year was hell," he said softly. "Was it?"

I rose quickly, nearly toppling the chair over. "I don't think we need to revisit memory lane," I said roughly. "And while I can appreciate what you're saying, I'm just not sure I can look the other way when so much is at stake."

He swore softly. "You are still the most stubborn female God ever created. Well, you're forcing my hand. I didn't want to play this card, but I guess I have to." He chuckled for the first time since our conversation started. "There is, as I mentioned before, a little matter of you breaking the law."

I stared at him. "You can't be serious."

He tossed me a look he probably meant to resemble innocence but that actually ended up looking smug. "Hey, trust me. I did what I could, but Giselle Pitt doesn't need much provocation to press charges. And for the record, even just saying you're associated with the police, specifically when you aren't, could still be construed as impersonating an officer."

"Fine." I let my lips part in a wide, obviously phony smile. "I guess I have no choice. If I don't want to spend quality time behind bars, I'll leave the investigating up to you."

His eyes narrowed. "Do you mean it, or are you just trying to humor me?"

I raised both hands in a gesture of surrender. "No, no. I know when I'm beaten."

"Uh-huh."

"No, seriously. I can't take the chance of you making good on your threat. It won't do Lacey any good for me to be behind bars, too."

He considered this a moment, then nodded. "Okay, good.

I'm glad that's settled. So, will you be going back to Cruz tonight?"

I inclined my head pointedly at the clock on the wall. "It's late, and I'm tired. I'll crash overnight at my aunt's and then head back in the morning for a day or two." I offered him a thin smile. "In spite of Lacey's problems, I still have a business to run, you know. I have a friend looking after it for me, but I can't impose on her forever."

He gave me a long, searching look, then shrugged. "Good. Come on, I'll take you to get your car."

Whether Samms would admit it to me or not, I was convinced Pitt's murder and Julia's were both related to whatever was going down at that gallery. And, in spite of what he thought, I knew damn well it was up to me to prove it.

FIFTEEN

An urgent phone call claimed Samms's attention just as we were headed out the door—a call he couldn't ignore, according to him—so instead one of the other officers (a baby-faced cop who looked like a dead ringer for Richie Cunningham, right down to the close-cropped red hair and freckles) ended up driving me back to the warehouse to pick up my SUV. The CSI truck was still parked there and I could see about half a dozen yellow jacketed team members still milling about. I glanced furtively toward the building, wondering if Nick were still inside. The question was answered as I saw a long black shadow stretch up, up, up and lengthen itself against one of the warehouse's dirty second-floor windows. It was gone before I could blink, and I hoped none of the CSI team had happened to glance that way. I walked purposefully over to my SUV, unlocked the door, hopped in, and started the engine. I gave young Richie a casual wave as

I sailed past him onto the deserted street. I made a sharp left at the corner, went down a block, then made a sharp right and then another sharp left into a cobblestone driveway. The drive was long and wide, and I drove all the way to the end and then pulled as close to a giant wall of shrubbery as I could and killed my lights. I sat in the darkness for a few minutes, then reached over and snapped open the glove compartment. I pulled out my mini flashlight and fished the latest issue of *Mystery Scene* magazine out of the side panel of the driver's door. I leaned back against the headrest and read the magazine from cover to cover—twice—before checking my watch. Well over an hour had elapsed. I started the engine up again, hopeful the CSI team had completed their job and departed. When I turned back onto the block I breathed a sigh of relief—the truck was gone. I parked my SUV, pocketed the keys, and walked swiftly toward the warehouse.

There was no long black shadow to be seen in the windows as I hurried down the walkway, my heels clicking against the concrete. I let myself in once again through the cargo door, peered into the semidarkness, and hissed, "Nick. Nick, where are you?"

"*Meower.*"

Moonlight slanted in through the slatted windows, reflecting off a diamond of pointy sharklike teeth. Furred sides scrubbed against my calves. I reached down and hefted Nick into my arms.

"You rascal," I whispered into his fur. "Sorry, Nick. I had to make sure no one would follow me back here. We can go now."

Nick squirmed in my arms. I set him down, and he immediately trotted off in the direction of the offices where Julia's body had been found.

"Hey!" I called after the black shadow. "Nick, come on. That's a crime scene. Nothing more to be learned there."

He turned and paused to grace me with a look of catly disdain before disappearing around a corner. I sighed and followed, retracing the route we'd taken earlier. When I got to the offices I stopped and regarded the myriad of yellow crime scene tape that seemed to be everywhere. I placed my hands on my hips and looked at Nick, waiting expectantly by the door. As I watched him, he rose on his hind legs and pawed at the wood.

"What, you want me to go back in there? Sorry, pal. No can doosey." I pointed to the yellow tape. "That place is an official crime scene now, and all I have to do is get caught by my old pal Samms defacing it. He's just looking for an excuse to slap me in a cell and throw away the key."

In answer, Nick wiggled under the yellow tape and disappeared inside. "Okay, fine," I called after his retreating form. "I guess Samms can't arrest you, although I wouldn't put it past him to try." Nick reappeared a few minutes later, a ratty-looking burlap sack clenched in his sharp teeth.

I leaned over to relieve him of his burden. "What have you got there, buddy? Where did you find this?"

He cocked his head at me and blinked.

I eyed Nick's find dubiously. It did resemble the one I'd seen Julia with at the Institute. Then again, most burlap sacks did look alike, and there were no distinguishing marks of ownership, at least none I could see. Common sense dictated that if it were evidence, it shouldn't be removed from the scene of the crime. Of course, I hadn't removed it. Nick had. And since I didn't know just where he'd gotten it, well, how could I know if it were evidence? I shook it, and something fell out, making a clinking sound on the linoleum floor. Looking down, I saw three pieces of plaster. I bent over and picked up the largest piece. There were four medium-sized grooves in it, almost as if someone had stuck the balls of their fingers, or knuckles, in it while wet. I frowned. "This is weird. If this is Julia's sack, I wonder if this is what she wanted to show Samms? But if it is, why? She was supposedly investigating the forgery of paintings. What connection could there be among that, a bag of plaster, and two murders?"

Nick began to purr, and I saw he had something else clenched between his paws. I bent over to inspect it. "Hm," I said, extricating the cigarette butt from his talons. "Looks like a menthol brand. Yep, Newport. Of course, it doesn't mean it belonged to the murderer. Anyone could have dropped this."

Anyone indeed, except for the fact I'd definitely smelled cigarette smoke when I'd entered the warehouse the first time. I turned the butt over in my palm. "Althea Pitt's son smokes Newports. Giselle Pitt smokes, too, but I'm not sure of the brand."

I sighed. As much as I'd have loved to finger Giselle—that squealer—she'd never have made it to the warehouse before my arrival to kill Julia. Philip Pitt seemed a better bet, save for the fact I could picture him murdering Giselle, not Julia. Kurt Wilson? Maybe. If he figured out Julia were informing on him, it would make perfect sense, but I'd learned the hard way not all murders made perfect sense. In fact, most murders were pretty senseless, if you asked me. Chalk it up to the human condition.

I tossed the cigarette butt into the sack with the bits of plaster and motioned to Nick. "Come on, Nick. It's pretty evident I won't be getting much sleep tonight, so we may as well put what remains of the night to good use."

Nick yawned, revealing rows of sharp white teeth.

"Yeah, I'm tired, too, but there's work to be done. I heard Samms ask Julia if she'd found the *terma*. That's definitely a code for something, and it might be a valuable clue, if I knew what it meant, so . . . get your geek on, buddy. It's Google time."

As it turned out, looking up *terma* wasn't as simple as I'd hoped. The most popular site was a company called TERMA, which specialized in aerospace, security, and defense. I perused that site, but after a few minutes it became evident it wasn't what I was looking for. I also checked out some charitable foundations, even a resort and spa, and was just about to click on the one for an episode of *The X-Files*, when I heard a knock on my door. Thinking it must be Aunt Prudence, I called out, "Come on in," and almost fell off the chair when Irene entered, bearing a tray on which rested a small pitcher and a mug of steaming hot chocolate.

"Your aunt made this fresh. She thought maybe you'd like some." She set the tray down on the edge of the table and peered over the rim of her glasses at my laptop screen. "You like *The X-Files*?" she asked, nose wrinkling. "That show was a bit too 'far-out' for my tastes, although I've always liked David Duchovny."

"Actually, I was trying to track down the meaning of a word, and it happened to be the title of this episode."

Her eyebrow quirked skyward. "A word? Must be a pretty odd one."

"*Terma*. Ever hear of it?" I said, not expecting an affirmative answer, so when Irene nodded and said, "Sure I have," I almost fell off my chair *again*.

"You're kidding," I said. "Where?"

"It was a word in one of my crossword puzzles. Don't ask me which one, 'cause I do a ton of 'em, but I do remember that one because it's so unusual, and it was a bitch to look up. I finally found it, though. It's a Tibetan word, and if I'm not mistaken, I think it means 'hidden treasure' or something like that."

I typed *terma Tibetan* into the search engine and, sure enough, a few sites came up. I clicked on Wikipedia and quickly scanned the page. Irene was right. *Terma*, in a nutshell, was a term used to refer to a "hidden treasure" or an object that's been concealed or hidden.

"Well." I reached for the mug on the tray. "Thanks for the tip, Irene. This is certainly a help."

"No problem." She set the pitcher on the table and picked up the tray. "Is this something that will help your sister?"

"It might."

"Well then I'm glad I remembered it." In the doorway she paused and snapped her fingers.

"The *New York Times*," she cried. "That was the one. They always have the hardest, most obscure words. Damn."

Once she was gone, I glanced over at Nick, sprawled comfortably beside the laptop. "Looks like Julia used the term as a code for hidden treasure. Maybe she found something hidden inside the plaster, and that's what she wanted to show Samms, but if she did, where is it? There was nothing else in the bag."

I switched off the laptop, crossed over to the bed, and lay down. I closed my eyes, but I knew damn well I wouldn't get a wink of sleep. My thoughts were far, far too jumbled. Suddenly, I sat bolt upright, startling Nick, who'd just arranged himself comfortably across my ankles. He fell to the floor with a resounding thump as I dragged my hand through my hair.

"Althea was positive Giselle's alibi was bogus. Why? Does she have some sort of proof, or is it merely her own desire to see the woman who stole her husband get what she deserves?" I rubbed my hand across my forehead. "You know, it's possible there are two murderers. Maybe Giselle did murder her husband, and maybe Wilson and/or his mystery partner discovered Julia was informing on them. Having your forgery scheme unmasked is an excellent motive for murder." I gave my pillow a good punch. "I'll tell you the person I can't figure out in all this. Jenna Whitt. I'm ninety-nine percent sure she was at Lacey's room because she wanted to look for something, but what?" I frowned as a sudden thought occurred to me. Giselle Pitt said she'd seen a pretty blonde leaving Pitt's office late at night. She'd thought it was Lacey, but what if it were Jenna? Could my sister have something in her possession that might prove a connection between the two?

Nick jumped onto my lap. I caught a glimpse of something shiny clamped between his jaws, and I reached out, sunk my fingers into his ruff.

"What have you got now?" I asked as I extricated the object from his mouth. I groaned. "My Mickey Mouse watch! I paid over a hundred at Disneyland for this, Nick. I'll say this for you—you know quality when you see it." I jumped up and walked over to my dresser, replaced the watch in the top drawer. I shook my finger at Nick, who lay innocently sprawled on the bed. "I can't be worried about your Houdini-like habits now. I've got other matters, like this case that's got more twists and turns than a roller coaster." I shut the drawer, grabbed my purse, and fished out my cell phone. I punched in a number, and the minute it went to voice mail, as I knew it would at this ungodly hour, I said, "Hi, Peter, it's Nora. Sorry to call so late, but I've been thinking. There are some things I need to ask Lacey, so I was wondering if you could get me in to see her early tomorrow morning? Call me when you get this message."

I rang off and looked at Nick. "I hope my hunch pans out. Because as things stand right now, jogging my sister's memory could make the difference between a prison sentence or freedom. And you stay out of my drawers. Please."

He just blessed me with his unblinking stare.

I stretched out on the bed and closed my eyes. Might as well try to get some shut-eye. I felt Nick curl up next to my arm in a tight little ball. The last thing I remembered as I surrendered to the velvety arms of sleep was the comforting feel of his rough tongue against my palm.

I awoke to bright sunlight streaming in my window. A quick glance at my bedside clock assured me I'd managed to get a few hours of snooze time in—it was almost eight thirty. Nick had shifted his position to my feet, and I gave him a quick nudge as I rolled over and out of bed. My cell phone revealed Peter had called sometime around 7 a.m., so he was an early riser, too. His message said to meet him at the jail at ten o'clock. I arrived only five minutes late to find him sitting on a long bench, head bent over his briefcase, going over some notes. He tried to be cheerful, and I felt like telling him he didn't have to put up a brave front for me; in spite of Samms's assurances, I knew unless we could cut a break quickly, Lacey's wardrobe would soon consist of a bright orange jumpsuit. We went downstairs and through the same procedure we had the previous time. This time the guard was a dour-faced woman, whose starched uniform seemed a bit snug, particularly around her wide girth. She gave me an exceptionally sharp look as I passed through the metal detector and handed her my purse for inspection.

"You're part of the law team?" she asked. Her beady eyes pierced right through me, like a lion considering its prey. Not a good feeling. I nodded, and she gave me the evil eye as she handed me back my purse and waved me through. I could have sworn she mumbled, "You don't look much like a lawyer," as I passed.

We were shown into a room even drabber than the last time, with only two benches and a long table, no windows. A few minutes later a guard appeared with Lacey. She wore the same navy pants and shirt, and her hair appeared just as unkempt as the prior time. I wondered if they'd ever let her shampoo it at all. I noticed an angry pimple popping up on the middle of her forehead as she sat down. Her expression, oddly enough, appeared hopeful.

Once the guard had moved across the room, she leaned forward slightly. "Have you got good news? Are you close to finding out who really killed Pitt?"

I gave a little shake of my head, and my stomach plummeted as her face fell. "That's why we're here, Lace. The investigation seems to have stonewalled. Unless we can come up with something, things don't look good."

She slumped back on the bench, the corners of her lips drooping farther down. "Oh."

I cast a cautious look across the room at the guard and then leaned forward a bit. "Lace, I just know deep in your subconscious there's some sort of clue. I know it. We need you to think, and think hard. Is there anything you can remember about that night—even that day—that was odd, out of the ordinary?"

My sister let out a deep breath. "I've been doing a lot of thinking about it. I was just so upset, you know. At that low grade, at what he said . . . I think I blocked everything else but my anger out of my mind."

"And now?" I prompted as she grew silent.

"Now I'm trying to remember just what else happened. Details, anything, you know. But it's hard; it really is."

"Sometimes when one feels pressured, or under great stress, it can have an adverse effect on their memory," Peter interjected.

"Well, sitting in a jail cell sure is stressful." Lacey shot Peter a grateful look. "I'm sure I have you to thank, though, for the fact I'm in a solitary cell."

He smiled. "I may have had a bit to do with that. Can't promise anything, though, if you get sent to Chowchilla."

"We won't let it get that far," I cut in, and reached a hand out to Lacey. The guard saw me and turned. I pulled my hand back, twisting it with the other in my lap. "I know it's hard, but you've got to try and think. I know you. Something's buried in your subconscious, I can tell. You've got to try and dig it up."

"I've been trying, honest." Her hand fluttered up, pulled at a strand of hair. "Don't you think I'd like to take a decent bath, start looking halfway human again?"

"You look fine," Peter assured her.

She managed a smile. "Aren't you kind. But I know the truth. I want nothing more than to get out of here."

I looked at my sister simpering at Peter. I looked at Peter almost beaming at Lacey. Wow, I hadn't seen this coming. They were attracted to each other, not that it was necessarily a bad thing. Rather, I thought Peter might actually exert a calming influence on my sister, provided she didn't have to spend the rest of her life in an orange jumpsuit making license plates.

"We both want you out," I said. "So think! Help us get you free, please."

She coughed lightly. "I think Julia was standing there when Pitt told me to come by his office later. As a matter of fact, the more I think of it, the more positive I am. Julia had to overhear."

I shook my head. "That's not a viable lead anymore."

Lacey frowned. "Why not?"

"Because—" I glanced over at the guard and then leaned over as far as I dared. "Because Julia is dead," I whispered.

"Dead!" Lacey and Peter both cried out together. The guard's neck snapped around, and we all got a scathing look. "Dead?" Lacey repeated in a softer tone. "Good Lord, how?"

"Strangled, apparently. She was found in the Billings Warehouse last night."

"Are you certain?" Peter asked. "It hasn't been on the news yet."

"I'm positive. I'm the one who found the body."

"You?" they chorused again. This time the guard took a giant step forward.

"You're going to have to contain yourselves," he said stiffly, "or we're going to have to conclude this interview early."

Peter made the appropriate apologies, and that seemed to mollify him. When he was once again safely on the other side of the room I continued, "Julia was my prime suspect. As it turned out, she was working with the police. Did you know they suspect Kurt Wilson is dealing in forged paintings?" I'd addressed the question to Peter, but it was Lacey who answered.

"Really? Wow, that might explain it then."

I pinned her with a sharp gaze. "Explain what?"

"I saw Taft one day in town, at the public library. He was engrossed in a book. I thought it was odd, because Taft isn't exactly the type to frequent the library. He got up to go back down one of the aisles, and I walked over and took a quick peek at the cover." She wrinkled her nose. "It appeared to be a book about art. The title was odd, *Provenance*."

I shook my head. "Never heard of it."

"I have," Peter said excitedly. "It chronicles an investigation of art fraud. Specifically, paintings. *Provenance* refers to the paper trail that establishes a work of art's authenticity."

I frowned. "You're right. That is an odd choice of reading material. I wonder why he would be interested in that."

Lacey shrugged. "I don't know. I thought it might be because he worked at the gallery."

I stared at her. "What? He works there, too?"

"Oh yeah. You didn't know? Taft is the one who got Julia her job there."

Well, that was an interesting development indeed. "Are you sure?"

"He bragged about it often enough. How much money he made on the side, how this could open up new opportunities for him, yada yada. Julia said she was struggling, so he got her in. He offered to get me in, too, but I turned him down."

"Which was probably a good thing." I tapped my finger on the table, thoughts racing. Why would Taft be so interested in a book on art forgery, unless . . . Was he also working undercover? Or could he have something to do with the actual forgeries? Either seemed a good bet.

I switched to the reason I'd come to the jail. "I happened to be in your room the other day, Lace, and you had a visitor. Jenna Whitt."

Lacey's eyes widened slightly. "Jenna? What'd she want?"

"She said she thought she might have left something in your room, but I got the impression she was just there to snoop around."

"Oh geez," my sister grumbled. "I told her I didn't have her damn leather pouch. I guess she didn't believe me."

"A leather pouch?"

"Yeah. She cornered me right before Pitt's class, the day of the murder. She wanted to know if I'd maybe picked it up by accident when we'd left the Modern Art History class. I told her no, and if I had, I would have reported it to lost and found. I guess she didn't believe me."

I drummed my fingers on the table. "You're certain this

pouch was leather? It couldn't have been made of something else, say burlap, perhaps?"

Lacey gave her head an emphatic shake. "Nope. It was leather. I know because I saw her with it a few times." She held up her palm. "About so big, and really old and grubby looking. You know how leather can get. All faded and scuffed." She let out a huge sigh. "She said she needed to find it but it wasn't even hers."

"It wasn't?"

"No. Said it belonged to a friend of hers, and it had his medicine in it. He'd be real upset if she lost it."

"Medicine?"

"Yeah, tranqs, I think. She said her friend had panic attacks."

"That doesn't make any sense. If her friend needed the tranqs for his attacks, why would he give her the pouch?"

"Supposedly he'd misplaced it a few times, and she was hanging on to it for safekeeping. It sounded pretty fishy to me, but . . ." Her eyes rolled skyward. "I told her I didn't have it, and she should go ask Julia. I'd seen her with a similar pouch earlier that day. It might have been Jenna's or it might have been hers. Who knows? I really didn't care." She paused. "And now that Julia's dead, I guess we'll never know, will we?"

SIXTEEN

I let myself in the back door of Hot Bread a little after two. The store itself looked deserted, and Chantal was nowhere to be seen. Nick trotted off to his favorite spot in front of the refrigerator, and I set my overnight bag down in a corner and slipped out of my light coat. I was just making my way over to the register when the side door opened and Chantal walked in. "*Chérie*, you are home!" She hurried forward to envelop me in a bear hug to end all bear hugs. "I was not expecting you until later."

I extricated myself from her grasp and gave her a smile. "Thanks for watching the store for me. I thought I'd get home in time for the lunch crowd, but it took a bit longer at the jail than I expected."

"Ah. Well it is good to see you. Both of you." She turned to Nick, beaming. "Guess what! I have finished half a dozen new collars, Nicky. Just for you! What do you say to that?"

His rotund bottom gave a brisk wiggle, and then he dive-bombed underneath a table.

I laid my hand on Chantal's arm. "He'll get over it."

She waved her hand carelessly. "Oh, of course he will. Once he sees what I have whipped up, he will be anxious to wear them. At least I hope he is. Remy is planning to take some photos of Nicky to use in a brochure he designed. He plans on sending it to all the top retailers in the county."

Out of the corner of my eye, I saw the tablecloth move ever so slightly, and the tip of one black ear emerge. Modesty is definitely not one of my feline's virtues.

"I'm sure if you offer Nick some catnip he might be persuaded."

Satisfied purring sounds rumbled beneath the table. I chuckled. "He can be bought so easily," I whispered.

Chantal took my arm, and we walked to the table farthest in the back. Once we were seated, she looked me straight in the eye. "How is Lacey holding up?"

"Not bad, considering. Peter and I visited her this morning, and then we found out the DA's pushing for the trial to start this week."

Chantal's eyes widened and one hand went to her throat, rubbed lightly. "*Mon Dieu!* That fast?"

I nodded grimly. "The circumstantial case against her is airtight, according to the DA. The fact she was found standing over the body and then fled the scene carries a lot of weight. Peter was going to file a motion to delay, but he didn't think it would do much good. As of now, the trial is scheduled to start Thursday."

"Eeks. That's only three days from now."

"Yep. Which gives me even less time to figure out who

really murdered Pitt and Julia Canton. I've got a very strong feeling the two are connected." I sighed. "What have you been up to? How was business?"

"Quite brisk, actually. Thanks to the hoard of food you prepared before you left, I didn't have to make too many sandwiches. Believe it or not, that *Jennifer Aniston Garden Salad* has become quite popular, surprisingly with the male customers."

I chuckled. "Lots of people watching their weight lately, I guess." I studied her for a moment. "Is there something on your mind?" My friend has a horrible poker face. It's very easy for me to tell when she is preoccupied, and I wasn't wrong.

She shifted in the chair. "I did another reading." Her hand shot out, covered mine. "Do promise me you will be careful!"

The hairs on the back of my neck pricked up. Chantal had the gift, and lately it seemed her readings were more spot-on than ever. She'd certainly been right when she'd predicted Nick would walk into my life (although she claimed it was Daniel—six of one, I say), and her last prediction about me was the reason she'd sent Daniel down to my rescue only a few weeks ago. When she was upset over a tarot reading, it was darn near impossible for me to not take her seriously.

I swallowed. "That might be easier to promise once you tell me what you saw in the reading."

"I did a Fourfold Vision spread and asked if you would be able to clear your sister. The Seven of Swords appeared, reversed. That card is indicative of a hopeless situation, one that is too much for you to handle. The reading indicated you would find yourself caught in the middle of a desperate act of cunning or deception."

I ran a hand through my tumble of curls. "You're right, that does sound ominous."

"The rest is no better," she said grimly. "The Wheel of Fortune also appeared but reversed. It signifies an unexpected turn of bad luck, an inescapable descent due to Fate or Karma: Great changes, the result of earlier actions, that cannot be taken back. There is a bright spot, though."

I groaned. "I could use a bright spot. What is it?"

"It was crossed by the King of Wands. He represents a powerful influence. The King of Wands has the ability to reverse the misfortune, but it is all tenuous. There are evil forces at work, all around you. You will have to use great skill and cunning to defeat them."

"Well, I'm trying." Now was definitely not the time to tell her I'd found another dead body, too. Chantal got a bit squeamish at that sort of thing, and besides, she'd probably go back and be reading those damn cards all day, trying to find another bright spot.

"Just be careful, *chérie*. Someone does not want you to find out the truth, and they will go to great lengths to prevent it. Just be on your guard." She paused and then added, "If you get in trouble, you must call upon the King of Wands."

"Daniel? That might be a bit hard. Daniel's off on a case, MIA for all intents and purposes."

Her head shook to and fro. "How fast we forget, *chérie*. Daniel's court card is the King of Swords. This card is King of Wands."

"There's a difference?"

"Oy!" I could hear the frustration seeping into her tone. "The King of Swords is a high-energy person, a symbol of intellectual power and authority, one who has the courage and intellect to accomplish all that he desires. The King of Wands is a bit different. Whereas the other Wands court cards deal with actual creation and implementation, this King is more apt to take an idea and change the world to match his vision. He's a natural-born leader, a visionary who sets a goal and sticks to it, makes it happen. It's indicative of another type of person entirely." She touched my arm. "I get the impression it's someone you know, or have known in the past?"

A mental picture of Leroy Samms reared itself in my mind's eye, but as quickly as he appeared, I brushed the image away and forced a smile to my lips. "Sorry," I said lightly. "I can't think of anyone unless I count Nick."

"Sorry, the King is human, not feline." Her gaze swept me up and down. Unfortunately, my friend can also read me like a book. "Are you certain you have no idea who it could be?"

"Positive," I said shortly.

She hesitated, as if she wanted to ask something else, then apparently thought better of it. She shrugged and said, "Ollie called. He wanted to know the latest on Lacey, and how you were doing. And Lance has been asking about her, too."

I glanced at the clock and rose. "Well, since it's time to close up for the day, maybe I'll take a quick run over to the Poker Face and give Lance the lowdown in person. Maybe get a drink, too. I sure could use one."

Chantal laid her hand on my arm. "Whenever you need to go back, just say the word. Remy understands I'm on call here until this whole mess with Lacey is straightened out."

I gave her a quick hug. "Thanks. You're the best. I'll probably head back there tomorrow after closing. I need to put together a plan of attack first." I looked around for my purse and saw Nick, lying in front of the refrigerator, purse under his fat belly. I sighed and walked over to reclaim it. As I bent down, I saw Nick's paw snake inside the side pocket.

I narrowed my eyes. "What are you doing? Looking for food?"

I shook the purse and bit my lip as the object of Nick's desire came clear. I snatched up my Mickey Mouse watch from the floor and slipped it in my jacket pocket.

"What am I going to do with you?" I said to the cat. "I'm not even going to try and figure out how you got this out of my drawer . . . again. But what is this fascination with Mickey?"

"*Er-OW!*" Nick jumped up and pawed the air. I caught a glimpse of a crumpled bit of paper near his rear and bent down to retrieve it. I smoothed it out, recognized an advertisement that had come in the mail a few days before.

"What did you want with this advertisement for Finn Crisp crispbread?" I said, glancing sharply at the cat. "Oh, how I wish you could talk. You are trying to tell me something, aren't you?"

He blinked twice, then sat back, raised one leg, and began to groom.

"Good God! Mickey Mouse watches, bread advertisements, what next?"

I started to place the advertisement on the counter, then stopped mid-motion as a sudden thought occurred to me. I remembered back in Chicago tracking down a story where the victim had been drugged—or slipped a Mickey Finn— slang for tranquilizer. Pitt had been a big man, and strong. He'd also been stabbed right through the heart.

What man would stand there and let someone stab him right through the heart? Someone who didn't expect it or someone who'd been drugged.

I knelt down and rubbed the white streak behind Nick's left ear. He responded with a guttural purr. I snatched my cell out of my purse and punched in Samms's number. When it went to his voice mail, I left a message suggesting he check the decanter in Pitt's office for traces of drugs, particularly tranquilizers—a suggestion I was pretty certain would go over like a lead balloon—and then hurried off to the Poker Face.

"Hey, Nora. We were just talking about you. How's Lacey?"

It was a little after three when I stepped through the door of the Poker Face. I paused in the doorway, letting my eyes adjust to the dim lighting from the harsh glare of the afternoon sun, and saw Lance behind the bar. I caught a bit of motion out of the corner of my eye, and the next minute Louis Blondell stood in front of me, an anxious expression on his pinched face.

"Hey, Nora," he said. "How are things going? Any luck finding out who really iced old Pitt?"

I slid onto a barstool, propped my elbows on the counter, and shook my head. "Lots of possible suspects, all with far better motives than my sister, but no evidence to tie any of them to the crime. At least not yet."

"Ah, well, I'm sure something will turn up," Louis said. He fiddled with his tiny moustache with the tips of his fingers.

"Damn straight," Lance said with feeling. "Lacey's no killer, right, Nora?"

"If she were I'd have been dead long ago," I said ruefully. "We used to have some catfights, back in the day."

"You can say that again." Lance chuckled. "I remember

a few doozies myself." He eyed me. "Get you a drink? It's on the house."

"Yes, a good stiff one, please. I don't usually imbibe so early in the day but, heck, after the last few days I can use one."

"Hey, it's after five o'clock somewhere in the world, right? And I've got just the thing." A few minutes later he placed a cool-looking drink in a frosted glass in front of me. "White gin and tonic," he said in response to my questioning look. "Packs a good punch, and it seems to me that's what you need, right about now."

I took a sip and set the glass back down. "Strong, but it's good."

"It's a London dry, the most common of the seven types, but the best, for my money."

I took another sip and slid a glance at Louis. "How's the magazine doing this month?"

"Good." His hands fiddled with the bottle of Samuel Adams on the counter in front of him. "I got a lot of inquiries as to why there was no offering from you this month. It appears you've become quite popular."

"Why wouldn't she?" Lance said. He pulled a rag from underneath the counter and proceeded to wipe down the bar. "You're lucky to have Nora, Louis."

Louis's hand shot up. "I'm not disputing that at all. Her recount of the Grainger case made quite a splash, one I'd like to continue." He eyed me. "There is the column we talked about, you know."

I wrapped my hand around the stem of my glass. "The PI tips? Kind of hard to do that when I'm not a PI."

Louis lifted the bottle to his lips and took a swig. "Hey,

you could go for a license. I've got every confidence you'd get one with no problem."

"I'm certainly getting enough practice. Lacey's case alone is a PI's dream, or should I say nightmare."

Louis pushed his empty bottle off to the side, and Lance reached under the counter, put a fresh one in front of him. He looked at me. "You said there were plenty of other suspects, right?"

"Plenty from my POV, but apparently not from the DA's. Since Lacey was caught standing over the body and then saw fit to flee the scene, they think they have their perp."

"Knowing Lacey, she probably panicked. Her first inclination would be to run." Lance shook his head. "What about the wife? Don't they normally look at the spouse in a murder case?"

"They do, and they did. She has an ironclad alibi."

He set down his rag and cupped his chin with his hand. "I'm usually suspicious of people who have ironclad alibis. Why, nine times out of ten they can be broken. Just watch *Law & Order*."

"This is real life, not a TV show," I said, finishing my drink and pushing my glass toward Lance for a refill. "But in this case I have to agree with you. It just seemed a bit too pat, too perfect to me."

"What was her alibi, if I might ask?" Louis leaned forward.

"She was at a fund-raiser party. People did see her there, and pictures were taken, but there were none for the exact time of the murder. I searched Google for the distance from the party locale she mentioned to Pitt's office. It came in at just under three miles. She could easily have made it up and back and no one probably would have noticed she was gone." I sighed. "Unfortunately, it doesn't prove she actually left. And without proof . . ." I stopped speaking as a sudden thought occurred to me.

Lance glanced over at Louis and jerked his thumb at me. "See that face. That's the face she usually gets on when a lightbulb has gone off in that pretty little head of hers." He held the refreshed white gin and tonic aloft. "None for you until you spill. What idea popped into that brain of yours?"

I reached for the glass, but Lance held it out of my grasp. I made a face at him and then said, "Just this: Events like that fund-raiser party are always a nightmare. There are too many people and, oftentimes, too little parking. Giselle's got a fancy-schmancy car. No way would she trust parking it to a valet. She'd park it herself, and if she planned to make an early exit, she'd park it where there was easy access." I reached for the glass again, failed, then said, "You wouldn't have a laptop here by any chance?"

Louis was already reaching underneath his stool. "I do." He opened it, powered it up. "What am I looking for?"

"She was at a party in Sea Cliff the night of the murder. The VanBlandts', I'm pretty sure."

Louis pulled up the white pages, plugged in VanBlandt. "Six of 'em, but only one in Sea Cliff. Percy VanBlandt the Third. Chauncy Court." Louis's fingers flew over the keyboard. "If we pull up the town site it should be able to tell us what streets have parking restrictions. Ah, there it is!"

A swift perusal confirmed the fact Sea Cliff—and Chauncy Court in particular—had no parking restrictions. I nodded.

"So. She could have parked the car there and taken it out, undetected, at any time." I paused, my eyes slitted in thought. "Althea Pitt—that's Pitt's first wife—was particularly insistent that the police check her alibi. It makes me wonder why. At first I thought it was just bitterness and a desire to see Giselle convicted of the crime, but maybe not. Maybe Althea knows something."

"What could she know?" Lance asked.

"Damned if I know." I closed my eyes. "It could be possible Althea saw something that placed Giselle at the school at the time of the murder."

"If that's the case, she would have told the police," Louis said practically. "After all, if she wants to see the woman convicted of murder, you'd think she'd be shouting it from the rooftops."

"Maybe what she saw would place her at the murder scene," suggested Lance. "Although out of everyone, she's got the least motive, right?"

"Right. But what if she wasn't the one who saw . . . whatever?"

Lance's brow puckered in thought, then he brightened. "The son, right? She could be protecting the son?"

"But what might he have seen that could be so incriminating?" asked Louis. He was hunched forward, elbows splayed on the counter, a look of keen interest on his face.

"Maybe one of them was out that night and happened to drive by the school. Maybe they saw Giselle's car parked there, or something," I said.

"Possible," Lance agreed. "But how could one prove that?"

I lurched forward, almost toppling over the stool, and

gestured impatiently toward the laptop. "Look up the Pitt Institute in St. Leo. It's on Northumber Court. See if there are any parking restrictions by the school."

Louis grabbed the laptop, started typing. A few minutes later he let out a little mew of triumph. "There sure are. Three places, and one is in the very front of the school. No parking allowed on Wednesday nights. The murder occurred on a Wednesday, correct?"

I clapped my hands. "The only way I could prove Giselle was at the school would be if she parked illegally, and if said car received a parking ticket."

"It would be easy enough for Samms to check out, right?" Lance asked.

"It would be if the DA weren't so positive he had the right perp in custody. The red tape to get this info could take weeks." I sighed. "Why, oh why, did I never learn computer hacking when I worked in Chicago?"

Louis flexed his fingers. "Well, lucky for you I used to be a pretty good system hacker, back in the day."

Lance grinned. "Me, too. And old habits die hard. Hacking's like riding a bike—you never forget."

I looked from one to the other. "Do the two of you honestly think you can hack into the St. Leo police database?"

Louis puffed out his chest. "Darlin', I can hack into the New York City police database. As a matter of fact, I did, once." He flexed his fingers. "Haven't done it in a while, but Lance is right. I might be a bit rusty, but . . . one never forgets."

Lance glanced at the clock on the wall. "It's a good hour and a half till my happy hour crowd comes in. I'll get us all fresh drinks, and let's see what we come up with." He gave me a huge grin and rubbed his hands. "Boy, talk about memories . . . This is gonna be *fun*!"

To Louis's credit, it only took him forty-five minutes to come up with the information that a parking ticket was issued to a vehicle with the license plate TRPHYWF at 10:37 p.m. on the night of the murder.

"She's one careless doll," Louis remarked, taking a swig from his fresh bottle of Sam Adams. "She parked in the NO PARKING zone right in front of the school. Didn't even bother to hide the car."

I let out a low whistle. "Well, that's a break. It definitely sheds a whole new light on things. The ticket itself places her at the scene of the crime at the time of the murder, and while it isn't in itself enough to convict her of murder, it would go a long way in raising reasonable doubt in the minds of a jury."

"And get an acquittal for Lacey," Lance added excitedly. "So, now what happens? Who do you give this information to?"

I fished my cell out of my purse and punched in Peter's number. When he answered I said quickly, "Peter, it's Nora. Get in touch with Samms and have him go through the parking ticket records for the night of the murder, particularly for a vehicle with the license plate TRPHYWF. Tell him it's urgent and he should forgo the paperwork . . . No, I can't tell you any more than that, but trust me. Have him do it ASAP. And don't mention my name unless you absolutely have to. Even then, tell him he's not on a *need to know* basis."

I rang off and Lance cocked his brow. "That should go over big."

"Yeah, just as big as my earlier tip, I'm sure." I slid off the stool. "Well, thanks for all your help, guys. You'll visit me when Samms hauls me off to the slammer for interfering in a police investigation, right?"

"Heck, Nora, if anyone should go to the slammer it should be Louis and me. We're the ones who hacked the system," Lance said, scratching his head.

I blew them a kiss from the doorway. "Probably, but a good reporter never reveals her source, or squeals on her hackers. Wish me luck."

"Good luck," Louis said. "And stay out of jail. You've got a column to write."

"And delicious sandwiches to feed the hungry public," Lance added. "Keep me posted."

Back on the street, I squared my shoulders. It was pretty obvious Samms was going to know right where that lead had originated, and a good bet he'd be damn mad. It was even more obvious what my next move had to be.

I had to find Mr. Taft Michaels and grill him about lying to provide Giselle Taft with an alibi. Hopefully I'd be able to find out something that would make Samms forget all about pressing charges on me and focus his concentration in other areas.

SEVENTEEN

"I can't thank you enough for helping me with this, Ollie. Keep an eye out for Pine Street, won't you?"

It was the next afternoon. Chantal had agreed to take the last half of the lunch shift, and I'd picked Ollie up at his office at twelve thirty. When I'd outlined my plan to him the afternoon before, he was more than willing to go along. As a matter of fact, he had some very good suggestions. I slid a glance at him as I made the turn onto Clover Road that would take us to the Pitt Institute, and he smiled, his teeth sparkling against his coffee-colored skin.

"No need to thank me, Nora. I told you, I consider furthering your PI education an investment."

"An investment? How do you figure that?"

He chuckled. "The way I figure it, detective work is in your blood, same as reporting and sandwich making."

I slid him a glance. "You've been talking to Louis Blondell,"

I accused. "He thinks I should get a PI license, although he wants me to get it so I can write a magazine article on it."

"You should get it," Ollie said. "One of these days you'll realize this is what you really want to do, and I, most likely, will need a new partner."

I chuckled. "Giving up on Nick Atkins already? There's no proof he's dead, you know. No body's turned up, that we know of, anyway. For all we know, he could be wandering around California, an amnesia victim."

Ollie let out a loud snort. "A more likely scenario is one of his many secrets finally caught up with him, and if it didn't kill him first, he probably thought it prudent to just . . . disappear."

"Well, maybe we'll get lucky and finally find out the truth. I asked Daniel if he could look into it—into Pichard's connection to Nick, specifically. I know you disagree, but I still think he might know something."

"It's possible, I suppose. Pichard hung with a pretty shady crowd. For that matter, so did Nick. I always told him his daredevil ways would do him in—oh, damn, Pine was back there, sorry."

"No problem." I turned onto the first side street and made a quick U-turn. I found Pine, made the appropriate turn, and a few minutes later pulled up in front of the Pitt Institute. As I cut the engine I remarked, "Call me crazy, but I just can't shake the feeling that Little Nick chewed that page out of his master's journal for some reason."

"You think he's trying to send you some sort of message? Well, it wouldn't be the first time."

"No," I said, my lips twitching as I remembered Nick's "Mickey Finn" message. I had yet to hear back from Samms.

I'd have to give him another call. "That cat's blessed with a—a sixth sense. It's uncanny, the things he does. He's no ordinary cat."

"I believe I told you that the first time we met." Ollie reached over to pat my hand. "But we've got something far more important than Nick Atkins to worry about now, my dear. Clearing your sister must come first."

I nodded as I pushed my door open. Ollie was right. The mystery of Nick Atkins's disappearance would have to remain just that, at least for now.

A few discreet inquiries led us to the admissions office. The woman behind the reception desk appeared none too friendly when I told her we needed to get in touch with Taft Michaels on a matter of the utmost importance. She snorted and peered at me over the rims of the Joan Rivers readers perched on her beak-shaped nose, and she tucked a stray strand of iron gray hair into the bun at the nape of her neck.

"He quit," she said bluntly. "Yesterday."

"Quit?" I didn't have to pretend to be surprised. I looked at the bronze nameplate prominently displayed on the desk—Agatha Bowman—and thought the name suited her. "Are you certain, Ms. Bowman? That's rather sudden, isn't it? I mean, I saw him here just the other day. He seemed quite happy with working here."

"Well, appearances can be deceiving," she said with a sniff. "He said a golden opportunity had presented itself, and he couldn't look a gift horse in the mouth. Taft is a selfish man. He didn't even have the courtesy to give us two weeks' notice to find another model." She plucked a pencil from the tin holder on her desk and tapped it against her blotter. "It doesn't surprise me, though. In addition to being selfish, that boy was also vain. You could see it in his appearance, the way he carried himself. Thought he was a god, too good to be stuck here with the rest of us mere mortals. I always said it was only a matter of time before he went on his merry way."

"Yes, he did strike me as arrogant, and I certainly don't agree with his handling of the situation," I agreed. "Unfortunately, we really need to speak with him. I don't suppose you have a home address for him, or a phone number?"

"I do," she said, eyes flashing, "but I'm really not permitted to give out that information."

"Excuse me."

I jumped at the voice so close to my ear and whirled around. Armand Foxworthy, his arms filled with papers, stood so close to me you couldn't wedge a paper clip between us. I took a step forward, the edge of my hip coming in contact with the desk.

"Sorry," he said. He brushed past me and set the pile of papers down in front of Agatha. "These are my students' final graded exams. They have to be entered into the computer before Thursday."

Agatha's expression softened, and her voice took on a gentler tone. "Certainly, Professor Foxworthy. I'll get right to it, just as soon as I've finished with these people."

Foxworthy straightened and flashed Ollie and me a tight smile before he left the office. Agatha sighed audibly as we turned back to her desk.

"Such a nice man. He hasn't been on staff long, but he's a real gentleman. Too bad about his allergy, though."

"Allergy?"

She nodded. "To fluorescent lighting. It's pretty rare, and if he's not careful he could also become allergic to sunlight. That's why he wears the glasses. A pity, though—he's such a nice-looking man." She let out a long, drawn-out sigh. "I'll bet he's got really beautiful eyes."

"I'm sure he does." I leaned forward, my palms flat on the edge of her desk. "We don't want to take up much more of your time, Agatha—may I call you Agatha?" At her nod I continued, "We can see you've got a lot of work to do here." I indicated the pile of papers with a flick of my wrist. "I can tell you're a person with a good work ethic. I bet you've got a good sense of justice, too, am I right?"

A ghost of a smile played across the older woman's lips. "I believe very strongly in fair play, and the justice system."

"Ah, I knew it." I gave her a big smile. "That's just what we're after, Agatha. Justice. We can trust your discretion, I know. It's very important we track down Taft Michaels. We need to ask him some questions in regard to a recent murder."

Agatha pushed her glasses down lower on her nose, and her beady gaze skittered between me and Ollie. "Oh my Lord! Not Professor Pitt's?"

Ollie nodded solemnly. "Yes. The very same."

I didn't say anything, just raised one eyebrow.

She gave us another once-over. "You're with the police?"

I hesitated. Oh well, what the heck. I was already in deep doo-doo with Samms for telling a white lie to Giselle Pitt. What was one more at this point, especially if it helped crack this case? I held out my hand. "Abigail St. Clair. This is my partner, Mr. Oliver. We're associated with the investigation into Professor Pitt's murder."

Her brow puckered. "I don't recall ever hearing your names, Detective."

"Probably because we've just arrived from out of town," Ollie said smoothly. "Special consults. It's quite a baffling case."

More brow puckering. She shook her head. "I was under the impression the murderer had been apprehended . . ."

"There is a suspect in custody, yes. But our investigation is ongoing. Loose ends, you see," Ollie supplied.

I inclined my head toward the phone. "Call Homicide if you're unsure. Ask for Detective Leroy Samms. He's in charge of the investigation, and believe me, he's quite familiar with the name Abigail St. Clair."

Agatha Bowman's lips scrunched up as she thought. Meanwhile, I took a page from Chantal's book and sent out a mental message of positive programming: *oh please don't call oh please don't call oh please don't call.*

"Ah, Detective Samms," she said at last. "Yes, I remember him. Very nice man. And so good-looking." She gave me another cursory look and shrugged. "Oh well, in that case . . ."

I said a silent prayer of thanks my mantra worked as her head swiveled to her computer. She tapped out a few swift strokes on the keyboard, and a minute later I heard the soft hum of her printer. She plucked a sheet of paper from the tray and handed it to me. "Here you go. And do give Detective Samms my regards."

"I surely will."

Her voice dropped to a whisper. "I never liked that boy, not at all. And if he had something to do with the professor's death . . . well, I'd just like to know."

I gave her a wide smile as I tucked the paper into my

purse. "Agatha, we appreciate your cooperation more than I can tell you. I promise you, when we find out who killed the professor, you'll be one of the first to know. You have no idea how much help this is."

"My pleasure." Her lips tugged downward. "And if you find out Taft had anything to do with it—well, I hope he gets what he deserves."

"Believe me, we'll try our best to make that happen," I said.

Fifteen minutes later we pulled up in front of the Archstone Grove Apartments. "Well," Ollie said as he surveyed the complex. "Looks pretty ritzy for an art student slash part-time broker slash former model. I bet the rent's almost two thousand a month. You can't tell me he earned that much modeling for Pitt's school. After all, it's not like he posed for *GQ*."

"According to this printout he's only lived here a few months. Before this there's an address near Chinatown."

"Ah. A more modest district but a long drive."

"Something paid him enough to afford this. His gallery job, perhaps? Think about it; if he's involved in fencing forged masters . . . maybe this golden opportunity he can't pass up has something to do with that. Maybe he's going into it full-time."

We exited the SUV and strolled into the complex. The grounds were large and beautifully maintained. We passed a large kidney-shaped pool, and I paused to dip my hand into the shallow end.

"Nice. Maybe I should look for a place with a pool one day."

"Not a bad idea. Fill it with fish. Little Nick would love it," Ollie said.

We continued our perusal of the grounds. There was also a spa with a state-of-the-art fitness center, a large clubhouse, and, behind the two modern-looking buildings, a picnic area with gas barbeque grills. There was also a path that led, according to the brightly painted wooden sign, to a hiking and a biking trail. The buildings themselves were three stories of modern design that appeared to be rather new, and there were about two dozen of them, all without any visible numbers.

"Grand," I muttered. "Now how in hell do we find 1675?"

"Can I help you?"

I whirled around to face a woman who reminded me vaguely of Joan Collins in the old television series Dynasty. Her artfully coiffed black upsweep didn't have a hair out of place in spite of the fact the humidity was high. She wore a tailored suit—Dior, unless I missed my guess—in a shade of blue that matched her eyes exactly. The four-inch black Manolos on her feet added enough height so that she came up to just below my shoulder. She extended her hand, her French tips lightly brushing my wrist.

"I'm Marlene McKay. I'm the Realtor in charge of these apartments. Are you interested in renting one? I've got a few vacancies." She looked me over like an eagle about to pounce on a helpless mouse. I could practically see the dollar signs in the irises of her eyes.

"We are interested, but not—" Ollie began, but she cut him off with a brisk wave and a smile.

"Then you've come to the right place, all right. We're one

of the best complexes in Pacific Grove. We're near everything—shopping malls, transportation, major highways. Good schools nearby. Got kids?"

"No, just a tuxedo cat," I said, and Marlene let out a little squeal.

"Ooh, I love tuxedos! My favorite kind! They always look so well-groomed, like they're ready for a night on the town." She leaned forward and said in a conspiratorial tone, "I've got an apartment I think the two of you will just love. The guy next door has a Chihuahua—Pepe, he's a scrappy little thing—but don't worry, his owner never lets him out on his own. What's your cat's name?"

"Nick, but . . ."

She cut me off again with a brisk wave. "Nick's a cute name for a cat. I like it when the pets have human names. Personally I hate it when someone has a sheepdog named Fluffy or a cat named Percy—*Purr*cy, get it?" She laughed at her own very bad joke. "Now, a few things you should know." She started walking down the graveled path toward one of the buildings, leaving Ollie and me no choice but to follow her. "All the apartments have high ceilings and oversized windows. Ceiling fans in every bedroom; some living rooms have 'em, too. We've got spacious closets, a big walk-in one in the bedroom. There's high-speed Internet and cable TV. First-floor apartments have patios; second and third, balconies. Sorry, right now I have nothing on the first floor, but you probably wouldn't want that anyway. I might even have a furnished apartment, if that's what you're interested in . . ."

I cut her off before she could segue into another extended description. "It sounds lovely, really, but I'm not interested in renting an apartment. And we're not a couple."

"You're not together?"

"We—ah—work together."

"Oh." It was hard to tell if she was relieved or surprised. Her finger came up, jabbed the air scant inches from Ollie's nose. "She said she's not interested, but what about you? You in the market for an apartment?"

"Not really, no. Actually, we're looking for someone who lives in this complex."

Her hands fisted at her hips. "Well, goodness. Why didn't you say so in the first place? Who'd you want to see?"

I wanted to scream out, *Because you didn't give me a chance*, but instead I bit down hard on my lower lip and held out the piece of paper. "Taft Michaels? Building number 1675?"

"Oh." She gave me a cursory once-over. Apparently my deep coral prairie skirt, low-heeled sandals, and black gauze top passed muster, because she gave a little nod of approval. "Hm, you don't look like one of his usual models. They wear the skimpiest outfits."

"One of his usual models? I'm sorry, I was under the impression Taft is a model himself."

Both her perfectly arched brows rose. "He is indeed, but he's also a struggling *artiste*! And a rather brilliant one, if you ask me." She waved her hand dramatically. "He studies at the school and he also paints. Lots of different things— portraits, still life—you name it, he does it. He's not bad, either. Kinda cagey about his work, though. I brought a potential renter into his apartment one day—I knew he wasn't home, and I wanted to show off how he'd done his balcony—and my God, I thought he was going to take my head off. I practically had to swear on a stack of Bibles that

I hadn't brought the girl anywhere else but to the balcony and out." She leaned forward. "He had a painting up on the easel in the living room, though, and it was impossible not to look at it. It was excellent—a half-clothed woman—and so real you thought she'd doff the robe and walk straight off the canvas. Honest, his work is on a par with many I've seen hanging in museums."

Ollie raised a brow. "He's that good?"

She leaned in to us and said in a confidential tone, "That boy's got serious talent. He's going to make something of himself someday, mark my words."

I looked significantly at Ollie. "That's very interesting. I didn't realize he had that much talent. He mentioned to me he'd dropped out of his art class."

"Yes, it was too expensive. A real shame, if you ask me. Talent like that should be nurtured, not discouraged." She leaned in close to me, as if she were afraid someone might overhear. "He was particularly talented when it came to painting people, portraits, nudes. They looked like they could all jump off the canvas. I found it fascinating, since Taft is such an antisocial type of guy. He didn't seem to have any male friends. I saw one guy come over once—a real arty type, long hair, dark glasses—but he delivered a package, so I assumed he was some sort of business acquaintance. Now the ladies—well, there's another story entirely. He had two girls who used to come over regularly. One I know he met at the art school."

"Ah, I think I know the one you mean. Black hair, blue eyes, about my height, perfect figure?"

Marlene shook her head. "Oh heck no. Just the opposite. Real pale colored hair—almost white—and hazel eyes. Tiny frame, but well built, you know, kind of like Marilyn Monroe. She's only been here a few times. Goodness, the last time she was lugging a box bigger than her. But the other one, another blonde, more on the golden side, real sexy, that chickie was practically living here for a while." She leaned in and said in a low tone, "Personally, I think he's in for trouble with that one. I saw a wedding ring on her finger. But"—she raised both hands—"it's none of my business, really. I just notice things. Why, I've seen things around this complex that would set your hair on end. I really should write a book one day. Do you know there's a man in number 2025—"

I cut her off before she could recount any more escapades. "To tell you the truth, we came here to pick up a still life from Taft. It's, ah, a gift for my sister's anniversary party tomorrow, and he said it would be ready today. So if you can just tell me which building he lives in—"

"Oh, isn't that nice. What a thoughtful gift. She'll love it, I'm sure. But he's not home right now."

Disappointment arrowed through me. "He's not? But he's not at the school today, so I just assumed—"

Her finger wagged to and fro under my nose. "See, that's the problem when you assume. I know he's not at the school today. This is his day at Sip 'n Slip. He usually bartends most nights, but Tuesdays he works the morning and early afternoon shift—helps out with the cooking and waitstaff." She glanced at her watch. "It's not far from here. If you leave now, you might be able to speak to him before his shift ends." She shrugged her shoulders apologetically. "If he wasn't such a stickler about it I'd let you into his place so you could get your painting, but I don't need another scene, no sir." She clasped her hands dramatically in front of her. "If I did that, why, he'd be *very* upset. Very."

"No problem." I whipped a card out of my purse and scribbled my phone number on it. "If I should miss him, though, could you give him this and ask him to call me?"

She glanced at the card before shoving it into her pocket. "Sure enough, Ms. St. Clair. Gee, that name sure does sound familiar. Any relation to the Pacific Grove St. Clairs?"

"Distant," I answered. "Very, very distant."

Once we were out of Marlene's earshot, I let out the giant breath I'd been holding. "It seems as if our boy Tate might be involved more than we think. I wonder if he could be the one producing the forged paintings."

"Well, I greatly doubt bartending is the 'golden opportunity' he couldn't pass up. I've known quite a few bartenders in my day. They couldn't have covered their rent if it weren't for the tips, most of which went unreported to Uncle Sam, unless I miss my guess. It's what they call 'under the table' income. Even still, I doubt it would be enough to afford the rent on that place."

I nodded. "I wonder if the man she described could have been that Professor Foxworthy. He's an 'arty type' with long hair and dark glasses."

Ollie shrugged. "To be honest, guys that fit that description are a dime a dozen."

"True, and, as far as I know, he's got no ties to the gallery. I admit I'm far more interested in her descriptions of Taft's lady friends. One is Giselle, no doubt, and the other . . . it sounded like Jenna Whitt, to a tee."

"The girl you think wanted to snoop around your sister's

room. Hm." Ollie mused. "Wonder what that connection could be?"

I tapped my chin thoughtfully. "I'd sure like to know what was in the box she said Jenna brought over. I'll bet anything it didn't contain art supplies."

"Well, maybe now is the right time to get some answers."

We climbed in the SUV and I programmed the GPS for directions to the pub, which fortunately wasn't far away. We arrived at our destination in a little less than fifteen minutes, and I parked across the street from a low-slung black and red clapboard building in the business district of Pacific Grove. The gold lettering on the Sip 'n Slip sign was eye-catching set against the stark black background, but I thought there was an unnecessary amount of clutter and posters in the wide picture window that detracted from its overall appearance.

We got out and I locked the car, and we walked across the street. It took a minute for my eyes to make the adjustment from bright sunlight to dim interior, and once they did, I took a quick look around. The bar was a wide affair that took up the entire right side of the room, extending from far back to right next to the wide window. If the shelves overflowing with bottles behind it were any indication, it was well stocked. Two men in battered jeans and wrinkled T-shirts sat hunched over the bar near the window, deep in conversation, half-full mugs of beer in front of them. They looked up as I entered, gave me a once-over, and then resumed talking as if I weren't there. I wasn't sure if I'd just been insulted or not.

The floor was clean and seemed to be divided between timber and tiles. There were brown leatherette stools flanking the bar, and to its left, a green and brown bench seating area that appeared to be in good condition. In the midst of the bench seating was a fireplace encased in nice yellow brick. A solid fuel stove added more charm. The walls were painted green and white, and I could hear Irish music playing softly in the background. A flat-screen TV turned on to a game show played right above the bar area, and near a door that I assumed led to restrooms were a gaming machine, a dart board, and a cigarette machine. A jukebox was at the rear of the room near another door, which I assumed led to the kitchen area. That was confirmed a moment later when it opened and Taft himself, carrying a tray on which rested two orders of French fries, emerged. He walked over to the two men, set the fries in front of them. While he did that I slid onto a stool at the other end of the bar, and Ollie settled himself near the other two men. Taft finished with them, and Ollie ordered a Sam Adams. Taft set a frosty mug in front of him, then turned in my direction. His eyes widened a bit as he saw me, but I caught no flicker of recognition in them as he approached, a wide smile on his face.

"Good afternoon," he said. "What's your pleasure, miss? We've got some nice Guinness on tap today, and Michelob Light as well."

"Good afternoon, Taft," I answered. "I think I'll just have coffee for now."

"Coming right up." He moved over to a large pot on the back counter, filled a mug, and set it in front of me with a small pitcher of milk and a few sugar packets.

I poured some milk in, took a sip. "Mmm . . . good and hot. Thank you, Taft."

He leaned across the bar, elbows up, cupping his chin. "Have we met somewhere? You seem to know me . . . and you do seem so familiar." He stood back a bit and squinted at me. Then his expression cleared and he gave me one of his dazzling smiles. "Of course—now I remember. You were at the school. Abigail St. Clair, am I right? I never forget a pretty face."

Or a thick checkbook, I thought. "We did meet at the school, but I'm afraid my name isn't Abigail St. Clair."

His eyes clouded, and one corner of his lips tugged downward. "No? But I could swear—"

"It's the name I gave, but it's not my real name. I felt it best at the time not to divulge my real identity."

He barked out a laugh, but the look he shot me was a wary one. "Your real identity? I'm sorry, I don't understand."

"My name's Nora Charles. I'm Lacey's sister. With everything going on, I'm sure you can understand why I chose not to disclose my identity."

He reached underneath the counter, pulled out a rag, and started wiping down the bar. "Of course. It's not pleasant, having a sibling accused of murder—particularly when the chances are excellent that she's guilty."

I leaned forward to rest my elbows on the bar's smooth surface. "I think we both know that's not true."

His head jerked up, and his eyes narrowed into slits. "Now how would I know that?"

"You don't have to play dumb with me, Taft. I know you lied about the night of the murder."

"I beg your pardon? If anyone's lying here, it's you. I'm not the one hiding behind an assumed name."

I ignored his remark and continued, "You know, I've got a sort of sixth sense—I can tell when someone's not being honest."

"Can you now?" His lips clamped into a thin line. "Well, you've got it wrong this time. I've got nothing to say."

"Don't you?" I slammed my fist down on the bar with enough force that the two guys at the other end paused in their conversation to look up. "You said that you were with Giselle Pitt at that fund-raiser the evening Pitt was killed, but that's not true. Giselle left for a short time and went to the school."

His brows shot skyward, and he shot a quick glance toward the other patrons, who were regarding us curiously. "Not so loud," he hissed. "No one needs to know what we're discussing, do they? Besides, where'd you get an idea like that?"

I leaned closer to him and dropped my voice a bit. "A parking ticket was issued at ten thirty-seven to a red Mercedes with the license plate TRPHYWF. We both know who that plate belongs to, so why don't you drop the pretense and just admit you lied for her."

He stared at me, then let out a mirthless chuckle. "Lady, you've got it all wrong."

"Impossible," I bristled. "I've got the facts to back this up. You're trapped, Taft. All you can do now is blow her alibi right out of the water. She wasn't at that party; she was at her husband's office. Tell me—did she kill Julia, too?"

His face blanched, and his eyes got round as saucers. He gripped the edge of the bar so hard his knuckles bled white. "What?" he whispered. "Julia's dead?"

I nodded. "She was strangled the night before last, sometime before ten. At the Billings Warehouse."

"Oh God." He leaned against the counter, passed a hand across his eyes. "Julia . . . dead. I—I heard the account of that murder on the radio earlier, but they didn't give out the victim's name. I—I had no idea." He swallowed. "This could change everything," he murmured, so low I had to strain to catch the words.

"What does it change? Was Julia involved with this golden opportunity of yours? The reason you quit your job at the school?"

A flush climbed his neck. "My reasons for leaving are none of your business," he barked. His hand raked through his hair, and he took a step backward. "I—I'm sorry. I've got to go."

"Not so fast." My hand shot out and grabbed his wrist. "Where were you Sunday night, Taft?"

"Sunday night?" He stared at me blankly, and then his gaze hardened. "Oh no, no way. I see what you want to do. You're not pinning Julia's murder on me. I was here that night, working till almost midnight."

"Why should I believe you? You lied about what happened the night Pitt died."

He tossed his rag over to one side of the counter and splayed both palms on the counter. "You can ask Dave—he's the owner; he'll be in soon. He'll vouch for me, plus there are about fifteen other people I waited on who can, too. I'd be glad to get you a list of names, if that'll satisfy you."

"And what about Giselle Pitt? Could they vouch for her, too? Or are you planning to fabricate another lie to cover her?"

He let out another mirthless chuckle. "Giselle doesn't need me to provide her with an alibi for that night. It's her yoga night. Between nine and eleven, she was doing Rocking Boats and Dog Stretches in front of about twenty other people. Besides, she had no reason to kill Julia."

"Maybe not—but she had about a million good ones to kill her husband."

"She didn't leave the party. She couldn't have."

I balled my hand into a fist. "You don't have to lie anymore, Taft. The ticket proves otherwise."

"No, all the ticket proves is that the *car* was at the scene of the murder."

"The car? Sure, but someone still had to drive it there."

He let out a breath. "Giselle didn't drive to the school and park illegally. I did. Giselle was covering up for me."

I stared at him, hardly daring to believe what I'd just heard. Why had he confessed so easily? "It was you? You went back to kill Pitt?"

"No, no." He waved his hands back and forth. "I didn't kill Pitt. I argued with the old boy a few days ago but I honestly didn't understand what he was talking about. He just yelled at me one day, called me stupid, told me if I couldn't tell left from right I'd be hard-pressed to make it in this world."

"That is odd. What do you suppose he meant?"

"With Pitt—heck, who knows? He was eccentric to the point of being anal. It wasn't the first time he screamed and shouted at me over something that made no sense at all. Anyway, Giselle let me borrow her car, and she thought it best if we agreed to say we were together. It never occurred to me anyone would check on the parking ticket."

"Why did you go back to the school?"

He shifted his weight. "I—I had an appointment. I was meeting someone."

"Who?"

His eyes darted nervously around the room. "I'd rather not say."

"Well, you'd better say." I leaned forward. "Samms knows about the parking ticket. He's going to reach the same conclusion I did—that it was Giselle that went to the school. And if he puts pressure on her, do you think she'll keep your cover—or crack to save her own skin? The time for lies is past—the only way to stay out of trouble is to be honest. Now, shall we try this again?"

He bit down hard on his lower lip. "Fine. If you must know, I was meeting another girl."

Before I could challenge him on whether the other woman was Jenna, the door to the pub opened, and a tall girl with hair the color of corn silk entered. She glanced our way, shot Taft a shy smile, and wiggled two fingers in greeting before she disappeared through a rear door. I slid Taft a glance, and there was no mistaking the light in his eyes as he looked at her.

I jerked my thumb in the blonde's direction. "Her? Seriously? You arranged a secret meeting with her at the school?"

He nodded. "We've been seeing each other for a few weeks. Tammie's a student at U of C. She's majoring in art. We got to talking and . . . she thought she'd like to enroll at Pitt Institute after she graduates, so I was—ah—showing her around."

My eyebrows lifted. "At ten o'clock at night? Try again."

"Okay, fine. Giselle's great, but sometimes I get a yen for companionship nearer my own age. There's a nice big storeroom adjacent to Foxworthy's classroom."

I started. "Foxworthy?"

"Yeah. I did a few errands for him, and in return, he let me use the storeroom. And, if you're still not satisfied . . . we got, ah, a little vocal. Jake Rawlings, the night janitor, came to investigate. I paid him pretty good to keep his mouth shut, but if you get your friend Detective Samms to flash his badge, I'm sure he'd freely admit what he saw." He paused, a wicked gleam in his eye. "Then there are the nude photos on my iPhone—if one puts stock in photos, that is."

I set my jaw. At this moment I had to agree with the secretary in Admissions—I didn't like Taft too much, either. "So you cheated on Giselle with this waitress. Did you also cheat on her with Jenna?"

"Jenna?" He had the nerve to look insulted. "Heck no. Is that what you thought? Jenna and I don't have a romantic relationship."

"What sort of relationship do you have? The realtor said she saw her at your apartment a few times. Was she modeling for you?"

"Hell no. Jenna couldn't stay still long enough to model for a painting if her life depended on it."

"Well, then, why was she visiting you?"

He made an impatient gesture with his hand. "Fine. You want to know? Jenna's the one who got me into the gallery."

That startled me. I stopped toying with the handle of my cup and jerked my eyes upward. "*Jenna* got you in?" I remembered something Marlene McKay had said and leaned forward. "Does it have something to do with the big boxes the real estate lady saw her with? Was she delivering something to you? Maybe paintings to copy?"

I saw a muscle twitch in his lower jaw, and his eyes took on a steely glint. "For the record, Ms. Charles, let's get something straight. I had nothing to do with Pitt's murder, or Julia's, either, and I have witnesses—real witnesses—who can back me up. So now, if you'll excuse me . . ."

He started to turn away, but I wasn't finished. "Wait. Why did you quit your job at the school? Ms. Bowman in Admissions said you told her you had a golden opportunity. Did it have anything to do with Julia? Is that what you meant when you said it could change everything?"

He slanted me a glance over one shoulder. "Things might have been different, if Julia were still alive, but since she's dead, it's business as usual. I guess now I'm gonna have to grovel and do many mea culpas to get my modeling job back."

He reclaimed the rag and started to wipe down the counter, but I was far from finished with him. "What can you tell me about the forged paintings, Taft? You have something to do with them, don't you?" I paused as another thought occurred to me. "What did you do for Foxworthy in return for his letting you in to that storeroom? I'm sure he didn't do it out of the goodness of his heart. So, was it anything to do with the gallery?"

His lip curled. "You know, what I do or did do for people is none of your concern."

"There's been two murders. That's cause enough to be concerned about anything out of the ordinary, wouldn't you say?"

He let out an exasperated sigh, threw the cloth to the side, and whirled on me. "Let me give you some advice, Ms. Charles. You really want to avoid making accusations you can't prove."

"Julia was working with the police, Taft. How long do you think it'll be before this all blows up? If I were you, I'd think long and hard about what you want to do—about your future."

I'd gotten to him at least a little—I could tell from the way his face paled—but I had to hand it to him; he didn't flinch one bit, just picked the rag back up and continued wiping. "I think we're done here," he muttered and then moved down to the far end of the bar, putting the kibosh on our conversation. I pushed back the half-empty mug, slapped a bill down on the bar, and slid off the stool, giving Ollie a brief nod as I sailed past. I walked outside and over to the SUV, where I paced back and forth for a few minutes before I saw the tavern door open and Ollie emerge. He hurried across the street, and we both got into the SUV.

"Nice work," he complimented me when we were both seated. "I think you really rattled him."

"He's a cheater, and he's got an alibi for the time of Julia's murder, but he did seem pretty shaken up over her death—far more than if she were merely a casual acquaintance."

Ollie raised an eyebrow. "You think maybe they were involved sexually?"

I frowned. "It's hard to say, but somehow I doubt it. One interesting thing I did learn, though—even though he denied having a close involvement with Jenna Whitt, it seems she's the one who got him the job at the gallery."

"Really?" Ollie's eyes became slits in his mocha-colored face. "Now that is interesting. It would appear Jenna has closer ties to the gallery than anyone might suspect. What might they be, I wonder."

"Beats the heck out of me." I ran my hand through my hair and tugged on an errant curl. "She lied to me, Jenna did. The first time I met her, she said she'd never gone to the gallery, because they'd never displayed any of her work. She also said she'd never met Kurt Wilson, but if she got Taft that job . . ."

"Logically, it would follow that she'd know him—now what's wrong?" Ollie demanded, leaning in to peer at my face. "You've got one of those cat that ate the canary expressions. What gives? What idea's popped into that brain of yours?"

"I'm just thinking logically. It would seem dear Jenna has a vested interest in the gallery, what with hiring people and making deliveries, so . . ." I twisted in my seat, grasped my purse, and hauled it onto my lap. I rummaged around, found my cell, and quickly dialed Peter's number. He answered on the first ring.

"You must be psychic," he said. "I was just about to call you. They've moved up Lacey's trial date from Thursday to Wednesday."

"Wednesday? That's tomorrow!" I wailed. "Why so fast?"

"As I've said, the DA really believes it's open and shut. I'm confident I can get a postponement until Thursday, but I'm afraid that'll be it. It's an election year," he added, as if that should explain it all.

"Great. Listen, do you think you'll have time to look up something for me? It could help Lacey."

"I'll do my best. What do you need?"

"Can you get me the names on the deed for the Wilson Galleries?"

Brief hesitation, and then, "I should be able to. I know a girl in the property records office. But how will knowing that help Lacey?"

"I've got a hunch." I raked my hand through my hair. "It's complicated, but I promise to explain just as soon as I get confirmation."

I rang off, started up the SUV, and guided it into the stream of traffic.

"Care to share your epiphany with me?" asked Ollie.

"No. It's a long shot, and I could be wrong."

"You could be right, too."

I chuckled. "We've got less than twenty-four hours before Lacey goes to trial. I think Julia found conclusive proof of the goings-on at the gallery. Her call to Samms confirms that. I think one of the people involved silenced her for good; maybe the same one who killed Pitt, maybe a different one. There's proof lying around somewhere. I just know it. And I need to find it." I expelled a breath. "We've got one more stop to make, Ollie. I need to find Julia Canton's address."

He whipped a piece of paper from his jacket pocket and dangled it in front of me. "I had a feeling you'd want it. While Agatha was busy with the oh-so-charming Professor Foxworthy, I sneaked it out of her Rolodex."

I beamed at him as I made a quick left. "Ollie, you are a wonder. I do believe you are almost as perceptive as Nick— the feline one."

He laughed. "That is a compliment indeed. Now, might I ask just how you intend to get into Julia Canton's apartment?"

I grinned back. "You sure can. How are you at breaking and entering?"

EIGHTEEN

As it turned out, Julia's apartment building was only about a mile away from Taft's complex. I parked on the quiet street and surveyed the five-story brownstone building. I glanced up and down the street as I exited the car but saw no sign of any police cruisers, although there could just as well have been an unmarked car hanging around. After all, Samms's vehicle was an unmarked Ford Focus. And not even black. His was more of a silvery beige.

Ollie and I went up the stairs and into the vestibule. We looked at the names above the bells. Of course Julia's apartment would be on the top floor. We found the door marked STAIRS and about ten minutes later emerged on the top floor. Julia's apartment was catty-cornered, all the way at the end of the long hall.

I tried the door. Locked. I made a sweeping gesture with my arm at Ollie. "All yours."

He knelt in front of the door. "Got a credit card?"

My eyebrows rocketed upward. "A credit card? Really?"

"What, you thought I carried burglar tools around in my pocket? It's either that or ring the super's bell, say she's got something in her apartment of yours you need pronto. It would be somewhat less of a misdemeanor but much more attention calling."

"Which is what I want to avoid. Fine."

I fumbled in my purse and drew out my credit card holder. "Any card in particular?"

Ollie shrugged. "They all work pretty much the same."

I selected my American Express card and handed it to Ollie. He slid the card into the vertical crack between the door and the frame and wiggled it up and down. Nothing.

I expelled a breath. "Great. Did you happen to notice where the fire escapes are positioned? You know, just in case we need to make a quick getaway?"

He shot me an indulgent look over one shoulder. "Now, now, little bird. Patience. It's evident housebreaking was never on your resume."

I watched as Ollie repeated the first steps and then bent the card the opposite way. I thought I heard a slight pop, but when I tried the knob, nothing. Zippo, zingo, zilcho.

"Well, at least we know we'll never make it as petty thieves. Our victims would all have to leave their doors unlocked."

Ollie ignored me and slid the card in again, wiggled it some more, and then stopped as we both heard a very distinct click. Ollie straightened, handed me back my card, and gave an exaggerated bow.

"After you."

"One second." I reached into my tote and pulled out two

pair of plastic gloves. I handed one set to Ollie. "So we don't leave prints."

He gave me an approving nod as he slipped the gloves on. "You're learning, Nora. Trust me, you'll make a great PI someday."

I twisted the knob, and the door slowly swung inward. I stepped inside and took a quick glance around. The apartment was furnished in modern style—glass and thin chrome end tables and coffee table, a long black sofa flanked by two black chairs. There was a large black chrome and steel entertainment center with a forty-two-inch flat-screen TV along one wall, and near the window a recessed bar. There were no personal items visible, no bric-a-brac, no souvenirs, collectables, photos, nothing. The entire room seemed devoid of personality.

"It feels off," I said, scratching my head. "Like no one really lives here. It has a hotel room feel to it, doesn't it?"

"Like maybe this isn't her permanent residence?" Ollie walked around the room, his eyes darting to and fro. "Perhaps she wasn't a local gal. Perhaps she just stayed here while she was undercover."

"If she was a member of the local police force, why would she do that?" I mused.

"It also appears, from the antiseptic state, that the police might not have done their search yet. I wonder why?"

"Good question."

I moved through the living room and into the small kitchenette. The modern appliances here gleamed, still reeking of newness. The stove looked as if it had never been touched. I opened the refrigerator. There were a few bottles of diet soda, a package wrapped in saran wrap that looked as if it contained some sort of lunch meat, and a couple cans of beer. I walked over to the cupboards, opened them. There were a few dishes and cups in one, but the rest were empty. The Keurig coffeemaker had a mug sitting on it, but the water reservoir was empty.

Apparently cooking wasn't one of her skills. It seemed Julia had taken most, if not all, of her meals out.

We continued down the long hall into the bedroom. The bed was huge, a California king, and took up most of the space, slicked with what appeared to be genuine satin sheets the color of ripe cherries. A baby pink comforter was folded neatly at the edge of the bed. There was a dresser along the opposite wall. Its lacquered top was bare. I walked over, opened the top drawer. Several pairs of silk pants and thongs lay neatly folded, and a few bras. I opened the second drawer and found two nightshirts. The closet was next. It held several pairs of pants, blouses, and dresses, all on satin hangers. The floor was covered with shoe boxes, all bearing designer labels. I picked one up, opened it. Inside lay a pair of black Yves Saint Laurent Tribtoo suede pumps. I'd seen a similar pair in *Glamour* magazine not long ago. They cost over $400 easily. I set that box down, picked up another. These Dolce & Gabbana sequined slingbacks were close to $750 a pair.

"Not much on material possessions, but it appears she had a fondness for designer shoes," I observed.

"And luxury bedding." Ollie sat down on the edge of the bed and let his fingers skim the sheets. "These are satin. Pretty nice. Last time I slept on satin sheets was on my honeymoon, many, many years ago." His grin was rueful. "When you're a lowly PI, you spend a lot of time in low-priced motels.

Satin sheets are hardly a staple. Of course, I'm sure Nick slept on his share of satin."

"So we know she liked expensive sheets and shoes in particular." I pulled out a dress, a simple black sheath, and looked at the label. Dior. "She didn't skimp on dresses, either."

Ollie looked around the room. "Doesn't seem as if there's anything much to find. The police might have been here already. Maybe if there was something of interest, they've taken it."

I reached for another shoe box. "I don't think so. I've been with police when they go through a victim's or a suspect's apartment. Trust me, there's always something out of order." I shook the box, held it up to my forehead. "Okay, what's in this one? There's no designer label on this box. Atwood, Choo, Crew? Wait, I sense a pair of patent leather Louboutins. Only around nine hundred dollars."

Ollie shook his head. "What's the big deal with women and shoes? You spend more money on 'em than I ever did on suits."

"The right shoe can make your legs look lean and long and help reduce butt size. It's a confidence thing." I sat down on the edge of the bed, box between my hands. "According to the box she was a size 7 wide. That's my size. Do you know how hard it is to find good shoes in a wide width?"

His jaw dropped. "You're not seriously thinking of—"

"No, of course not. But it's a tempting thought." I lifted the lid off the box, looked inside, paused, looked again.

Ollie frowned. "What's wrong?"

I reached into the box and pulled out a .38 caliber revolver. "Smith & Wesson Model 10, blued steel," I said. "I knew a cop on the Chicago force, and this was his favorite gun. Odd place to keep it, though. I mean, if she was a cop, why would she have to hide it?"

"Unless," Ollie answered, "this isn't her gun."

"Ah, good point." I sniffed the barrel. "It hasn't been fired, at least not lately." I replaced the gun in the box and knelt back beside the closet. I leaned in as far as I could and burrowed down, selecting a box that had been pushed to the far end behind a tall pair of suede boots. I pulled it out and sat back down on the bed. "I'm almost afraid to look. What do you think? Another gun or Jimmy Choo mules?" I pointed to the description on the side of the box.

"It's a fifty-fifty shot. Go on, open it."

I slid off the lid. On the very top was a manila envelope. Underneath it was a large leather book. I lifted both out of the box.

"Okay, which should we open first?"

Ollie picked up the envelope and slit the flap cleanly with the edge of his nail. He tipped it over, and one lone photograph slid out. I picked it up and frowned. It was a photograph of a sculpture, its two hands suspended in air, holding a face. I felt a niggling sense of familiarity as I looked at it, and another sense, too. Something felt off, but I couldn't quite put my finger on it. I set the photo down and turned my attention to the book. "No title on the cover."

"Maybe it's a diary," offered Ollie. "Maybe she wrote notes in here about what she found out at the gallery, and what's going down there."

I shook my head dubiously. "You think she'd put that in writing?"

"One way to find out."

Still, my hand hesitated over the cover. Ollie said, more

gently, "It's not an invasion of her privacy anymore, Nora. She's dead."

I nodded. "You're right. Besides, if we don't read it, we won't find anything that might help Lacey." I took a deep breath and flicked back the cover of the book.

For a minute neither of us spoke. Then I reached inside the hollowed-out interior and held up the leather case and badge that lay on top. The badge looked achingly familiar. I'd seen one like it not too long ago, on someone else. I opened the leather case and sucked in my breath.

"Julia's last name wasn't Canton," I said. "It was Campbell. And according to this, she's—oh my God, she's—crap, I should have figured it out the minute we knew forgeries were involved. She's—"

"Special Agent Julia Campbell, FBI," said an all-too-familiar voice behind me. "Hello, Nora."

I turned and looked straight into the face I knew all too well. FBI special agent Daniel Corleone. He stood in the doorway of Julia's bedroom, arms folded across his broad, muscular chest.

And, double crap, he wasn't smiling.

NINETEEN

For a minute you could have heard a pin drop in the room. I slid off the bed, plastering what I hoped was a bright smile on my face.

"Daniel. Hey. Fancy meeting you here." I attempted a laugh, which came out sounding more like the yelp of a nervous hyena.

His frown deepened. "What are you doing here?" He paused, let his gaze rake over Ollie. "And you brought reinforcements along."

"Well, that's easy to answer. She's sticking her nose in where it doesn't belong. Still, I might add."

I stifled a gasp as the burly figure of Leroy Samms appeared next to Daniel in the doorway. Samms shook his finger at me. "And here I thought we had an understanding."

Daniel looked from Samms to me. "An understanding?"

"It's no big deal," I began, and then Samms's baritone laugh cut me off.

"True, it's no big deal, Daniel. Just a tiny matter of Ms. Charles, here, impersonating an heiress and a police officer. She told me she'd learned her lesson and was going to leave the detecting to the trained personnel, but—" His tongue clicked against the roof of his mouth. "I knew she'd never keep that promise, even for old times' sake." His gaze fell on my hands. "At least you were considerate enough to wear gloves."

Daniel looked from me to Samms, his expression clearly puzzled. "Old times' sake? Do you two know each other?"

I swallowed. "It's really not even worth mentioning," I said.

Samms turned to Daniel. "She's right; it's no big deal. We both went to U of C, and senior year we worked on the college newspaper."

Daniel's eyebrow rose. "You studied journalism, Lee?"

"English, actually. I thought about being a teacher or a writer." He barked out a laugh. "Life took me in an entirely different direction from Nora."

"Well, well." Daniel trained his gaze on me. "Seems as if you've been giving your old friend a hard time."

"We're not friends," I barked out, a little too quickly. "I mean, we haven't seen each other in years." I glared at Daniel. "You two seem pretty chummy, though."

"We've been working together," Daniel admitted. "Because of Julia."

"Julia? Oh, of course." I slapped my palm against my temple. "How stupid of me. Of course you'd know her. She's FBI." I dangled the badge in the air, then paused as a sudden thought occurred to me. "The case you said you were working on—was this it? The suspected forgeries?"

Daniel shook his head. "No, this was entirely Julia's specialty. She worked the Art Fraud Division. I got involved because she thought she'd found evidence indicating her case was connected to the one I am working on."

I struggled to remember what I knew about the Art Fraud Division. Back in the day, art fraud had traditionally been under the jurisdiction of local law enforcement, but the overflow of other crime—namely, murders, drugs, and other acts of random violence—had meant local law couldn't spend quality time tracking down stolen or forged masterpieces. Enter the FBI, who decided to form a specialized unit dedicated to tracking art and art criminals. It made perfect sense, actually. Stolen and forged art was considered to be the third most profitable international crime, and it was often used to launder drug money and as collateral for arms deals.

I wondered briefly if that was what was going on here. Was the Wilson Galleries a front for drug money, or arms dealings? Either would fall under Daniel's jurisdiction. Another thought struck me at the same time. Was it possible Pitt had discovered something besides a forgery? And could that have contributed to his death?

Samms's voice broke into my thoughts. "So, Nora, we had this place locked up tight. How did you two get in? Did you bribe the landlord? Or have you added walking through walls to your list of talents?"

Ollie opened his mouth to speak, but I clamped my hand down on his arm and squeezed hard. "I have many talents," I said in a purring tone. "You two are the hotshot detective and FBI agent. I'm sure you can figure it out."

The two of them exchanged a look, and then Samms scratched behind one ear. "I guess I can add B and E to the list of charges you're racking up. Getting you into a cell seems to be the best way to keep your nose out of police business."

Daniel crossed over to stand in front of me. "Nora might be a trifle overzealous, shall we say? But past experience has proven she is good at ferreting out clues. As much as I hate to admit it, we'd probably learn more working together."

I narrowed my eyes. "That seems a rather abrupt change of heart."

He shrugged. "Not really. And I do know you have a tendency to do just the opposite of what you're told, so your appearance here isn't all that much of a shock to me. So tell me: Why did the two of you come here? What is it you were hoping to find?"

I clasped my hands together in my lap. "I can tell you what I didn't think I'd find—a badge identifying Julia as an FBI agent. And certainly not that gun."

"Gun?" the two of them said in perfect unison. I got up and went to the closet, picked up the shoe box, and handed it to Daniel without a word. He opened it, looked inside, then closed the box and nodded to Samms.

"It's the gun all right. It fits the description."

"So it's not her gun?" I asked, and got two black looks for my trouble.

"No," Daniel said quietly. "It's not. This gun is evidence in a murder."

"Well, it can't be evidence in Pitt's murder. That would be the knife that conveniently only had my sister's prints on its handle. And this can't be evidence in Julia's because a) she was strangled and b) it would be impossible for her to be hiding her own murder weapon. Ergo, this gun somehow relates to your case, doesn't it, Daniel?"

"You don't need to know that," Samms began, but Daniel held up his hand. Thank God, because I was getting ready to tell Samms what he could do with his "need to know" mantra.

"Yes, it does." His eyes met mine, held. "I have a feeling, Nora, you've found out some things we should know. Like I said, we'd get further along pooling our resources. How about it? Want to share information?"

Samms let out a groan and rubbed his whiskered jaw. "Oh, for the love of—"

"Sounds reasonable to me." I interrupted Samms before he could continue his rant, tossing him a saucy grin. "Go ahead. Share. Whose murder is the gun evidence in?"

"Uh-uh." Daniel wagged his finger. "I'm perfectly willing to the concept of share and share alike, but ladies first. Tell us what you were looking for in Julia's things."

I looked from one to the other and, figuring they weren't going to cave any more, said, "Fine, we'll go first. Ollie and I came here looking for a leather pouch."

Samms and Daniel exchanged glances. "A pouch?" Samms asked.

I nodded. "When I visited Lacey at the jail, she said this girl Jenna Whitt had accused her of taking a leather pouch. Lacey said she seemed very anxious to retrieve it. Lacey mentioned she'd seen Julia with a pouch that looked similar, so I thought it was worth a look. There had to be something in it Jenna wanted back, and I thought maybe . . . it might have been drugs. Tranquilizers, specifically."

"Tranqs, huh? What made you think of that?" Samms asked.

"Because it occurred to me that a man of Pitt's size and strength would never have willingly succumbed to an attack upon his person unless he wasn't able to, of course. Lacey said that when she approached the body, the first thing that hit her was the smell of wine, so I thought perhaps someone might have drugged it. Someone who was familiar with Pitt's ritual of imbibing in the evening."

"Good reasoning," Samms said, "and really quite nice of you to try and lend a helping hand; however, yours wasn't the only brilliant mind thinking along those lines. I had the decanter tested right away. It came up clean. There was only wine in it, nothing else."

"Damn," I swore softly. "What about the body? Any traces of tranquilizers, any needle marks?"

"I'm still waiting on the toxicology report, but I'm betting no. And it's a no to needle marks on the body."

I tapped my finger against my lips. "That doesn't make sense. Even if Pitt knew his attacker, he was a strong man. He should have been able to put up some sort of fight, yet there were no signs of a struggle. Being drugged makes sense. It would have made him unable to fend off an attacker."

"The DA might argue the point that rendering him helpless might not have been necessary if his attacker was a pretty blonde intent on improving her grade by using her feminine charms."

Samms's eyes narrowed. "I also got a tip from Lacey's lawyer regarding parking tickets. I don't suppose you know anything about that?" He didn't wait for me to answer and rushed on. "There was one issued to Mrs. Pitt's vehicle; however, she denies taking her car to the scene of the crime."

I couldn't help my sneer of satisfaction. "Of course she does, because she didn't. It was Taft Michaels. He confessed that to me, just about an hour ago."

Samms rolled his eyes. "And *that* you don't call and tell me?"

I ignored his sarcastic comment and focused on Daniel. "He works at a pub, the Sip 'n Slip. He was working Sunday night, so he's got an alibi for Julia's murder. He's also got witnesses who can testify he had nothing to do with Pitt's murder, even though he was in the building."

Daniel frowned. "The man has lied before. Why should we believe him?"

"I realize his track record isn't the greatest, but I did believe him. He's a pompous, arrogant ass, but I really don't think he's our killer. A cheater, definitely, a forger, maybe, but not a killer."

"Julia suspected Taft might be involved with the forgeries," Daniel said. "She was going to try and persuade him to confess. She'd gotten permission to promise him immunity."

"Hm. That would explain his remark about her death changing everything, wouldn't it? He was upset, though. I could tell. He's confused, unsure of what to do. Maybe if more pressure were put on him . . ."

Daniel flicked a glance at Samms. "Have someone go to that pub and haul Michaels in for questioning if he hasn't already skipped."

"If he has, we know who to thank," said Samms, leveling me with a hard stare.

"Me?" I jumped off the edge of the bed. "It's because of my probing he's in the mood he's in. You should be thanking me, not glaring at me."

"It's because he's in that particular mood he's also susceptible to running off, too. Then we'll really be in a pickle," Samms shot back.

"Be fair. How in heck was I to know he was under suspicion?" I got my face right up in his, my eyebrows drawn together. "Had I known, I might not have said what I did, but, of course, I wasn't on that elite *need to know* basis."

"You haven't changed at all, have you?" Samms hissed. "Still the same stubborn, opinionated . . ."

"Look who's talking!"

Daniel stepped in between us. "Your sniping at each other isn't accomplishing anything here," he began, but I whirled on him, eyes flashing, and jabbed the air under his nose with my finger.

"Okay, I kept my end. I shared. Now it's your turn. Whose murder do you suspect that gun was used in?"

"No one local. Of course, I won't be entirely sure this is the gun used until I've turned the gun over to FBI ballistics, but it matches the description we've gotten from several witnesses."

I folded my arms and glared at him. "You said it yourself: Art forgery isn't your area. So for you to be involved, it's got to be something else, something much bigger. What is it—contraband, drugs?" I gulped. "The mob?"

Daniel gave me a good hard look, then cleared his throat. "Are you familiar with the term 'bling ring'?"

I nodded. "Yes. Hollywood Hills Burglar Bunch aside, they're usually organized jewel thieves from South American countries like Colombia, Ecuador, and Peru."

"Right. They're so well established we've given them a name: South American Theft Groups. About four months ago, one of these groups engineered a heist in France. A security guard was killed. They made off with over a quarter million dollars' worth of gems."

A low whistle involuntarily escaped my lips. "So that's where the gun comes in? You think this is the one used in that robbery? That's what you're hoping a ballistics test will prove?"

He nodded. "We've managed to track down some of the bling ring, and finally we got a clue as to where the remainder was. The gang has a contact here in the States. They've been shipping the booty here to be disposed of, and the money wired into an offshore account."

"Oh my God," I said. "You think the gallery's involved in—"

"Smuggling," Daniel nodded. "Valuable gemstones; specifically, diamonds. Julia thought she'd finally figured out how they had the gems smuggled in, and how they got them to their purchasers. She thought it might have something to do with the forged paintings."

"You mean they created the forgeries in order to smuggle the gems? Is that even possible? I mean, how can you hide gems inside a painting? Unless maybe the frame?"

"They could be secreted in the backing. There have also been cases where the gems were actually covered in oils and embedded in the paintings. It requires a great deal of skill to camouflage them, but it can be done."

"Wow." My eyes widened as a sudden thought occurred to me. "Do you think it could be possible Pitt found diamonds in one of his paintings? Maybe that's the reason he was killed! His wife said he called the gallery the morning of his murder, and she heard him complaining about a flaw. Most likely he was talking about his painting being a forgery, but what if the person he told this to thought he meant something else, like maybe he'd discovered diamonds?"

"It's possible," Daniel admitted.

"Maybe you should take a closer look at those other paintings in his office," I cried, grabbing Ollie's arm. "Maybe we should go there now and—"

Daniel held up his hand. "Hold on. The two of you aren't going anywhere, Nora."

I whirled to face him. "What? But you said we were going to share information. That we were going to work together."

"No," he said firmly, "I said that you might have found out some things we needed to know, and I proposed we share our information. I never said we were going to work together to solve this case."

"That's true," Ollie agreed. "He never said—OW!" He yelped as my elbow made sharp contact with his rib cage.

My eyes narrowed. "That's not playing fair. You lied to me. Finding the answer to these murders is the only way to free Lacey, and you know it."

He leaned over, tucked his thumb under my chin, and raised my face to his. "These people play for keeps, Nora. Samms is right. You're very intuitive, but you're not a trained investigator."

"Ollie is," I said, squeezing his arm again and ignoring the black look he bestowed on me.

"I'm aware of Oliver J. Sampson's reputation. He specializes in missing persons, finding stray animals, taking photos of philandering husbands. An investigation like this is out of his league, and it's out of yours. Do you think I want to see you end up like Julia?"

"I only had one stray animal case," Ollie mumbled. "And the rabbit came home by himself."

I ignored his whining and turned to Daniel. "No," I grumbled. "I don't want me to end up like Julia, either."

Daniel patted my arm. "Good. Now, why don't you take Ollie back to his office and return to Cruz. I'm sure Chantal will be glad to turn the reins of the sandwich shop back to you."

"Chantal is fine," I spat. "And my business won't suffer too much. There's still the little matter of Lacey coming up for trial for a murder she didn't commit, remember? If we can't get a confession out of someone, Lacey's sure to get convicted on that circumstantial evidence."

"I do remember, and you have my word I'm going to do everything I can to find out what Julia discovered and bring Pitt's real murderer to justice. Honest, the best thing you can do is go back home and let us handle things."

"I was planning on staying with my aunt. In case you haven't heard, Lacey's trial has been moved up. I—I need to be here."

Daniel nodded. "I can appreciate that. We'll take you to your aunt's and take Ollie back to his office."

"I've got my own car, thanks."

"I'll take advantage of your offer for a lift, though," Ollie spoke up. "I do have some urgent matters at the office I should attend to."

"Great. One of Samms's men will take you back. I'll follow Nora to her aunt's." He wagged his finger under my nose. "Give me your word you won't do something stupid, or do I need to assign a bodyguard to you?"

"That's not necessary. I promise to behave. Scout's honor." I'd never been a Girl Scout, but what the hey. What Daniel or Samms didn't know wouldn't hurt them.

Daniel, however, was not so easily deterred. "Let me see your hands."

I held them out in front of me. "I promise. See? Nothing's crossed. Do you want me to take my shoes off, too?"

He looked down at my narrow-toed heels and chuckled. "Not necessary. I'll take you at your word. Let's go."

We were halfway out the door when Daniel paused. "Oh, and I do have news for you on another matter. You remember you asked if I could find out anything on Bronson A. Pichard?"

My head snapped up. "Really? You located him? Where is he?"

"It wasn't easy, but you can find him at Greenlawn Heights, in Los Angeles."

"Greenlawn Heights?" I frowned. The name seemed familiar, and not in a good way. Even as I asked the question, I got a creepy-crawly, shivery sensation all along my spine, as if I knew what his answer would be. "What's that, some sort of exclusive residential complex?"

He shook his head. "Of sorts. It's a cemetery. Bronson A. Pichard is dead."

TWENTY

Daniel and Samms walked me down to my SUV, one on each side of me, pressed against me so tight I felt like the filling in one of my sandwiches. I might have actually enjoyed it if the two of them didn't look like they thought I might bolt at any given moment. Once out on the sidewalk, Samms walked Ollie over to a nearby patrol car. I walked right over to my SUV and got in, aware of Daniel's watchful gaze on me as I buckled my seat belt.

"You know, you don't have to treat me like public enemy number one," I said, gripping the wheel with both hands. "I promised to drop investigating, didn't I? Nothing was crossed, remember? Or would you like me to pinky swear?"

"Not necessary. It's not that I don't trust you to keep your word," Daniel said. "But you know as well as I your zeal for solving puzzles often overshadows your better judgment.

Or have you forgotten you were on the receiving end of a .45 recently?"

"Hard to forget that, when people love to keep reminding me," I muttered. "You've made your point. But before we go, tell me what you found out about Pichard, and how he died."

He looked at me for a long moment before he answered. "He'd been living abroad the past year. France, specifically. He died about three months ago, in a train wreck. His body was crushed between two cars. They identified him from the dental records."

I shut my eyes. "Not a pretty way to die." Another question burned on my lips, but I hesitated. Finally, I blurted out, "Was it an accident or not?"

"It was ruled an accidental death, but my contact told me they have their suspicions. Pichard wasn't exactly an up-standing citizen in any country. He was suspected of selling copies of antique originals here. Nothing was ever proven and no criminal charges were ever filed against him, but the police started watching him more closely, particularly after his wife divorced him and he ended up practically penniless. When he couldn't make a go of anything here in the States, he took off across the pond. And while they couldn't find any reports on any shady dealings in Europe, the people he hung around with were . . . questionable at best."

I scratched absently at my ear. "Well, if he's dead, I guess he didn't have anything to do with Nick Atkins's disappearance. Too bad. I thought he was a really good lead."

"He might have been," Daniel said. He reached out, grabbed my hand. "Look, I'm sorry about before. I'm just trying to keep you safe."

I squeezed his hand. "I know you are, but I'm a big girl, Daniel. I can take care of myself."

"I know you can."

I gave him a rueful smile. "You might remind your pal Samms of that."

He gave me a searching look. "As it turns out, Samms is more your pal than mine."

"Not really. I told you, it was one semester a long, long time ago. And we weren't exactly what I'd call . . . friends." *More like two ships that passed in the night.* "I don't think I even remembered what his first name was until lately," I added. "He's always just been . . . Samms."

Daniel reached up, pinched the bridge of his nose. "Sorry. I didn't mean to imply I doubted your word. This investigation is wearing on our nerves. We're so close. If only Julia had lived to tell what she found out, but now we're back to square one."

"I'm sorry. I haven't exactly been a model of cooperation myself. What's eating at me is I don't seem to be able to do a damn thing to help Lacey. I hate the thought of her having to go through the trauma of an actual trial. She tries not to act it, but my sister is really very sensitive. I shudder to think what might happen if she were to be found guilty."

I turned the key in the ignition and the motor hummed to life. "Well, you've got a murderer to find—maybe two— and I've got some catching up to do with Aunt Prudence. I don't want to keep you."

He stepped back from the car and gave me a long, searching look. "You're going to be a good girl, aren't you, Nora? You're going to mind what I said, and leave the investigation to Lee and myself?"

I batted my eyelashes. "Of course. I promised. See?" I wiggled both hands in front of his face. "Nothing's crossed."

He reached into his pocket, pulled out his phone, looked at the screen. "They've got Taft over at the bar. I really need to get there. Do I have your word you'll go straight to Prudence's?"

"Scout's honor." I beamed at him, crossing my ankles as I did so. He nodded and hurried across the street to his car. I waved in a brief salute and made a sharp left onto Main. Then I pushed my foot all the way down on the accelerator and gunned it. The freeway entrance was up ahead about a quarter of a mile, and I was just about to congratulate myself on my swift getaway when I saw flashing lights in my side mirror.

"What the—"

Swearing softly, I pulled over to the side of the road. The police cruiser pulled up beside me. The cop behind the wheel looked like a junior Barney Fife—receding hairline, thick lips, scrawny neck. He exited his vehicle and walked with a slow and steady gait over to me. I sighed and lowered the window.

"What's the problem, Officer?" I gave Barney Junior my brightest smile. "I might have been going a little fast, but well within the city speed limit, I'm sure."

"Oh, you weren't speeding, ma'am. At least you weren't speeding enough to warrant a ticket. You are Nora Charles, correct?"

Uh-oh. "Yes?"

"Good. I've got orders from Detective Leroy Samms to follow you to your place of residence and make sure you don't leave. If you'd be so kind as to just wait for me to get back into my vehicle, I'll be escorting you home."

Heck, did I have a choice? Apparently Samms was even more of a butinsky than I remembered. I smiled sweetly. "Why of course, Officer."

"Good." He walked back around to his car, got in, and then motioned for me to pull away. I did so, seething, and pounded my fist lightly against the wheel. Men! But if they thought a little thing like a police escort would deter me, they had better think again.

When I made the turn onto Prudence's street the first thing I noticed was the sleek black sedan parked diagonally across from her house. Slouched across the wheel was a man, apparently engrossed in reading a newspaper. The cruiser pulled up next to the car, and the officer got out, walked over, and leaned inside the driver's window. The officer pointed to my car, said a few more words, and then got back in the police car and pulled away. The other man glanced up as I exited the car. He gave me a quick once-over and then returned to his reading, apparently unconcerned.

Well, well. Either one of Samms's men or one of Daniel's. Take your pick. I guessed Daniel's, since Samms's men all seemed to resemble sixties' sitcom personas.

I hurried up the steps of the house without a backward glance. Irene had the door open before my hand could touch the knob. She reached out, grabbed my arm, and pulled me inside, then bustled over to the window and stood behind the curtain, peering out from around the side.

"He's been out there for over an hour," she hissed.

I felt my jaw drop slightly. "An hour? Irene, are you sure?"

She bobbed her head up and down. "I think he might

be—what is it robbers do? Oh yes. 'Casing the joint.' Should I call the police?"

Out in the kitchen I heard a faint squawk, and then, "Police! Police!" Apparently Jumanji had super hearing.

"No, Irene. I'm pretty sure he *is* the police." I said this through gritted teeth because, if Irene was correct about the timeline, which she most likely was, then Daniel and/or Samms must have arranged it earlier. "How do you like that?" I muttered under my breath. "They didn't trust that I'd just come home and stay out of it. They made sure somoene was here to watch me."

Irene was still peering out from around the edge of the curtain. "Do you think they're here on account of Lacey?"

"No, it's a long story, Irene. But you can feel safe. He's definitely not a robber."

She still looked dubious. "You're sure?"

I pulled a grimace. "Unfortunately, yes."

"All right then." She let the curtain fall back into place and stood for a minute, hands on hips. "Your aunt isn't here. She went to the market. We're having a roast for dinner. Think you can stick around?"

"At this point, it's a very real possibility."

I trudged up the stairs and entered my room. I tossed my purse on the chair and flopped onto the bed, where I rubbed at my forehead with the tips of my fingers. "Something isn't right," I mumbled. I felt the bed shake, and then soft fur swatted my nose—Nick's tail.

I pulled him onto my lap, all twenty pounds, and rubbed his ruff. "Ever get that feeling that something's floating around in your brain, but you just can't put your finger on it? That's how I feel. Something's bothered me ever since I saw that photo earlier."

Nick blinked at me and I laughed. "Oh, of course. You don't know what photo I mean." I grabbed my purse and whipped out the photo of the sculpture that had been in the manila envelope. "I managed to sneak this into my purse when Daniel and Samms weren't giving me the evil eye." I laid it on the bed and then went over to my dresser to retrieve the bit of plaster from the burlap sack in the warehouse. "Sculptures can be made of plaster," I murmured. "You know, it wouldn't be a big deal for an expert to substitute a plaster cast for a more expensive one. Those grooves in that bit of plaster looked big enough to hide gems inside. And if they stuffed it with enough stones, well, it'd be pretty heavy, right?"

Nick arranged himself, sphinxlike, on the bed and cocked his head.

"Jenna Whitt said her specialty was sculpture," I continued. "And she was pretty upset over losing that pouch. She told Lacey it was because it contained some friend's tranquilizers—but what if she were lying. What if it contained something else? Something infinitely more valuable?

"What if it contained diamonds?"

I got up and started to pace to and fro under Nick's watchful gaze. "I bet that pouch was full of diamonds. Maybe it was her payoff, or maybe she was supposed to put them into a sculpture to be shipped out and she misplaced the pouch. Maybe Julia did find it after all. Dammit, if only Ollie and I had more time to search we might have found it."

The more I thought about it, the more sense it made. Pitt's death might not be connected to a forged painting or a jealous mistress at all. What if he'd gotten the wrong sculpture by accident, one of the casts containing jewels? He'd surely have noticed, being the consummate expert. That could have been the flaw his wife heard him mention on the phone. He'd told Julia he'd discussed the situation with the person in charge, which had to have been Wilson. Maybe some remark of his had led Wilson to think he'd discovered the hiding place for the diamonds.

I stopped pacing and jabbed my finger at Nick. "A nice theory, right? But I need proof. Damn, I wish I could get inside Pitt's office again. I'd like another look at that sculpture. I'll bet anything if I turned it around, there'd be a slight crack in it. And who knows, maybe diamonds inside."

My laptop chirped suddenly, and I walked over, noticed that I had a new mail message from Louis with an attachment. I opened the missive and read:

Hey—I managed to download a few pix from the police server. Thought maybe they'd be a help. Don't lose this copy, because I'm deleting the original and all traces of my being in their system. You can reward me with an exclusive article on Pitt's murder for the next issue of *Noir*.

I had to admit I was impressed with Louis's hacking skills, and maybe just a tad frightened, too. I opened the attachment, and a second later photo images floated across my laptop screen.

I examined each of the photos closely. None of them stirred anything in my brain, until the last row. I clicked on the last picture and enlarged the image. I leaned forward to study it and then let out a squeal of excitement, startling Nick, who'd jumped up and arranged his portly body next to the laptop.

"See." I pointed at the screen and then snatched up the photo I'd purloined from Julia's apartment. I held the photo next to the one on-screen. "They're different. The sculptures. The one in the crime scene photo has the mask in the hand on the right, like this photo. That's what bothered me. When I was in Pitt's office that day the sculpture I saw had the mask in the *left* hand. Someone switched the sculptures."

I stopped, frowning. Said switch would have had to be done after the murder, which meant there had to be another way into that office. Whoever switched sculptures could also have gotten rid of the drugged wine at that point, as well.

I heard a light clicking sound and looked down. Nick was using his claws to push some of his favorite Scrabble tiles along the polished hardwood floor. I rolled my eyes. I wasn't even going to attempt to guess how he'd gotten his paws on them.

"Whatcha got there, buddy?" I leaned down and scooped up the tiles. A P, an L, an E, an A, and an N. Put them all together and they spelled . . .

"PANEL!" I breathed. I'd read enough Nancy Drew and Hardy Boys mysteries growing up to remember they used to be chock-full of old houses with secret panels, usually behind walls, and that they made a clicking sound when they slid into place. I shuddered. It would explain the sound, and also how the murderer could have gotten away so quickly without anyone seeing him—or her.

Nick's upper lip curled back, exposing his sharp fangs. He shuffled over to the wall. He rubbed his furry body against it.

I leaned over to give Nick's head a pat. "Good theory, boy. But how can I prove it?"

I walked over to the window and nudged the curtain aside. The unmarked car still sat there, parked at a vantage point where it could see both the front and side entrances. "The easiest way would be to check out Pitt's office again, but that won't happen while Big Brother is watching."

I frowned. From the way the car was parked, he'd surely see me even if I snuck out the back way. Dammit. Where was a teleportation device when you needed it? I stepped back from the window and glanced down at Nick. His tail was a black furry bush, his ears flat against his skull.

"Nick? What's wrong?"

I paused as a sound, very faint, came to my ears—a slight whir. I stared in amazement as the left wall of my room started to move slowly inward. A moment later Irene stepped through the opening, a bunch of freshly laundered towels in her arms. "Sorry." She tapped her ear. "I left my hearing aid downstairs. I didn't realize you were still in your room." She patted her bundle. "I was just going to drop off a load of fresh towels."

I looked over her shoulder at the half-open wall and the inky blackness beyond. "Is that—is that a secret passageway?"

"Eh, what was that? Did you ask about Joel McCrea? I didn't think a gal your age would remember him. Great actor. He's been dead for . . . oh gosh, I don't know. Longer than I care to remember."

"No, no. I didn't say Joel McCrea." I raised my voice a few decibels and pointed at the open wall. "Is that a secret passageway?"

She chuckled. "Sure is. Your aunt doesn't use it much,

but I like to when I stay here. The stairs aren't as steep. This one leads straight from here down into the basement and the laundry room. This house was built back during the Mexican-American War, you know. Lots of homes around here were. They had passageways like this to hide stuff like gold and firearms."

"Do tell. Lots of homes in this area, you say? Would the Pitt Institute happen to be one of them?"

"Oh, honey." She waved her hand. "Of course it was. I'll tell you something else, too. I happened to find it out from the former owner—met him one day at a tea at the library: The Pitt school is a larger version of this house." She stuck her chest out proudly. "They were built by the same architect. Why, there are probably dozens more of these secret passageways networked throughout that old building. Probably in all the same places, too. Isn't that interesting?" She chuckled. "Your aunt never uses this. She thinks it's spooky. Me, I think it's a time-saver."

"Extremely." I closed my eyes and did some quick calculating. If I remembered correctly, Pitt's office was in the west corner of the top floor—same as my room. If the buildings were similar in construction, that would put the secret passage behind the far wall next to the bar. The same one with the bookshelves bearing the sculptures.

"There's a whole network of secret passageways running through this house," Irene continued. "Secret panels, too. Good for hiding stuff. See!"

She walked over to the wall next to the entryway and tapped along the bottom molding. A few seconds later, a bit of it shot out, revealing a small three-by-four crevice. Irene reached inside and pulled out a small necklace.

"Your aunt does use these. She hides stuff all over the place." She chuckled. "Beats paying the fee on a bank vault."

I was studying the aperture. "Are there more secret panels like this in the house?"

"Every room has at least three, as far as I know. Some are in the walls, some are under the floorboards." She crossed to the bed, moved the braided rug, tapped again, and a small opening appeared in the floor. This one looked large enough to fit Nick inside—or maybe a decanter of wine?

I turned to Irene and, keeping my tone loud, said, "I got some good news and some bad news today, Irene. The good news is, I'm very close to proving Lacey didn't kill Pitt."

Irene laid the towels on the bed and cocked her brow at me. "Really? Well that's great. Your aunt will be thrilled when she hears." Her eyes narrowed. "You said you had bad news, too?"

"Yes. I may not have enough time to prove her innocence. They've moved Lacey's trial up to tomorrow."

"Really? Your aunt will be devastated if your sister is found guilty, and frankly, with the evidence as it is now . . ."

"I agree." I took a step closer to Irene. "There's something I can do, though, that can break this case wide open, that can prove Lacey had nothing to do with it, but in order to get it done, I need help. And I think you, Irene, could provide it."

Her stance relaxed a bit. "I could? Well, your aunt would want me to help in any way I can, so . . . tell me just what it is you think I can do. How can I help you prove Lacey's innocent?"

I pressed my lips close to her ear, so she'd be certain to understand me. "Just how loud can you scream?"

TWENTY-ONE

Twenty minutes later I slid my SUV into a space about a block away from the Pitt Institute. I got out of the car, locked it, and then hurried toward the school. I was going to have to take back everything negative I'd thought about Irene. The woman should be on the stage.

I felt something warm and furry brush my leg, and I looked down. "How did I know you'd be here?" I said to Nick, who blinked twice and then fell into step beside me. "Just stay close."

We reached the rear entrance of the school, and I immediately zeroed in on a flight of stone steps leading down. If Irene's theory was correct, and this was built like Aunt Prudence's house, then these steps would lead to the laundry room. Or, in this case, the basement, aka school archives. Fortunately, the door at the bottom of the stairs was unlocked. The basement was one endemic to old edifices, complete with the traditional cobweb-laden low ceiling and beams with nails poking out every which way, waiting to stick a tall person forgetting to duck. I stood a minute to let my eyes adjust to the inky blackness, when suddenly, the room was flooded with dim light. I whirled and saw that Nick had jumped up on a stack of boxes, right next to an old-fashioned light switch. I mouthed thanks at him and took a swift look around. The entire left side of the basement was filled with old, battered filing cabinets that had definitely seen better days. Off to the right stood an antique washer and dryer, and a creaking boiler occupied space in the very back of the room. I noticed one file cabinet in the far corner had a drawer partially open. I walked over and peered at the label. The word PLANS was printed in large capital letters. I pulled the drawer all the way out and sucked in a breath. From the looks of things, I wasn't the only person to rummage in here. Sets of blueprints were jammed in the drawer, some in manila folders, some not. I thumbed through them quickly. There appeared to be one for every floor of the old building except, surprise, surprise, for the third floor. I shut the drawer and turned toward a small archway that looked as if it led further into the edifice's subterranean bowels. The room beyond was inky black, and I felt along the wall, frowning as I realized there was no light switch for what lay beyond.

I heard a scraping sound behind me, and out of the corner of my eye I saw Nick push a large lantern forward with his nose. I snatched it up. It worked, although the battery was pretty weak. I hoped there'd be enough juice left to take us where we wanted to go: Pitt's office. I swept the light over the dirt floor and the curved brick walls, stopping at a large opening in the wall farthest away. A flight of stone steps led upward. I started climbing, Nick at my heels. At last we reached the top step. In front of us stretched a long wall.

"Hm. Now let's see," I mused. "How did Nancy open all those secret panels?"

I stepped forward and started rapping lightly against it with my knuckles. Nothing. I crossed to the middle, laid both my palms flat, and pressed. Still nothing. I shifted my position to a bit lower down, and then stopped as a faint click reached my ears. I splayed my hands, set my feet apart, and pushed harder. The wall suddenly caved inward, and in my peripheral vision I saw Nick jump backward into the shadows as I spilled forward into Pitt's office. My purse slid off my arm and tumbled to the floor, its contents spilling out, but that was the least of my worries. Apparently my sudden presence had startled the woman who stood behind his desk, the drawers pulled out, papers strewn all over the thick carpeting. Her hand came up like lightning, and I suddenly found myself looking once again down the barrel of a .45.

"So, Nora," Jenna Whitt said calmly. "Mind telling me what the hell you're doing here?"

I struggled to my feet and found my voice at the same time. "Me? I could ask you the same thing. This room is still sealed."

She looked at me pointedly, the gun still aimed at my mid-section. "You're in here." She gave a tight little laugh. "So you figured it out. About the secret panel, I mean. Not bad."

"That's not all I've figured out," I said boldly. "Pitt found diamonds in the sculpture; that's why he was killed, right? To prevent him exposing your scheme?"

"You just can't help being snoopy, can you?" Jenna sneered. "Lacey used to talk about you, all the awards you won, and how smart you were, but frankly, I used to think she was exaggerating." She cocked her head to one side. "Your sister's nothing like you. She can be a real hothead, acting without thinking. When she blew up at Pitt that morning, I knew she'd be the perfect patsy."

"So you'd already planned to kill Pitt."

"Pitt was a pompous ass. Trust me, no one shed any tears over his death. He fancied himself a patron of the arts. He hated defacement of art in any form. He called my brother that morning, complaining he'd discovered the 'dirty little secret' in the artwork he sold him, and unless he settled the matter to his satisfaction, he'd report him to the authorities." Her tongue snaked out, licked at her bottom lip. "How in hell were we to know he meant the forged Engeldrumm and not the sculpture?"

My eyes widened. "Pitt meant the painting? He never found the diamonds?"

She shook her head. "We assumed he meant the sculpture, because when we checked the records, we discovered that Taft had delivered the wrong one to Pitt. He should have delivered the sculpture with the left hand holding the mask. The right-hand ones have the gems inside." She tapped her chest proudly. "I do them, and they're damn good, if I do say so myself. It isn't easy to get those diamonds down far enough in the plaster so no lumps show. And I use a lead-based paint, to deter detection by X-ray." A deep sigh escaped her full lips. "Now that the feds are onto us, though, tonight will be our last shipment. Tomorrow, the gallery will be closed and we'll be gone, back to Europe, with new identities, looking for our next score. Your sister will take the rap for Pitt's murder, and poor Julia's death will remain unsolved, unless we can find some way to pin it on Taft. He wasn't good for much, anyway," she spat. "Sure, he painted the forgeries, and that was a nice little side venture, but our real cash came from the gems."

"That would be difficult," I said stiffly, "considering he was working at a bar at the time of her murder."

"Don't worry, we'll find a way. Taft is remarkably stupid. I'm sure we can convince someone at the bar that night to say he left for approximately forty minutes." She gestured with her gun for me to sit in Pitt's chair. I lowered myself and, as I did so, cast a quick glance at the entryway.

Nick was nowhere to be seen.

I looked at Jenna. "I know you didn't work alone. You have a partner."

She angled her jaw. "Sure do."

I turned. Armand Foxworthy was standing in the entryway, also leveling at gun at me. But he looked much different than he had on the two other occasions I'd seen him. Gone were the battered jeans, shirt open to the navel, and greasy gray ponytail. Now he wore a three-piece blue pin-striped suit with a light blue shirt and blue and yellow tie. He still wore the dark sunglasses, but the ponytail was gone. Now he had thick black hair, shot through with gray, cut in a sort of Elvis style. He moved all the way into the room and went behind the desk, slipped an arm around Jenna. He gestured toward the mess on the floor. "Nothing?"

She shook her head. "Nope. Julia didn't hide 'em here. I've been through everything, Foxy," Jenna said. "I might have to search her place again."

He shook his head. "Julia would never have left them in her apartment. She would think it would be the first place someone would look for them. Besides, the FBI and Miss Charles have already searched there, am I right?"

As I stared at Foxworthy, something suddenly clicked in my head. "You fled to Europe," I said in a tight voice. "You went there when your schemes here were exposed, but something must have happened over there, too . . . something really, really bad, for you to need to fake your own death."

Jenna looked at Foxworthy, puzzled. "What is she talking about, Foxy?"

"She doesn't know?" I asked. "And as for your allergy, that's bogus, too, right? You're no more allergic to fluorescent lighting than I am. It's all catching up to you; you might as well admit it."

Jenna stamped her foot. "What's going on, Foxy? What should you admit?"

He chuckled. "It would seem, my dear, that my rather inglorious past has caught up with me."

He whipped off his glasses in a single motion, and I stared straight into eyes that belonged to a living corpse: one sky blue, one mud brown.

The eyes of Bronson A. Pichard.

TWENTY-TWO

Armand Foxworthy, aka Bronson A. Pichard, made a little bow in my direction. "My dear Ms. Charles, I'm truly impressed. I had no idea my fame extended this far." He tapped the dark glasses against his wrist. "No one's ever suspected I wasn't who I said I was until now."

"I should have guessed your real identity," I muttered. "I saw in the file the university has on you that your middle name was Armand."

One eyebrow rose. "File? You saw a file on me?"

"It was a journal, actually." I swallowed, my heart thudding double time in my chest. "Very copious notes taken by one Nick Atkins. You remember him, don't you?"

He lowered the gun, just a fraction. "Nick Atkins. Now there's a name I haven't heard in a long time." He stepped forward to peer at me more closely. "You and he are friends, you say? That's surprising? You hardly seem his type." He flicked his thumb in Jenna's direction. "He'd more likely be attracted to Jenna. Nick liked 'em rough and slutty. Well, most of his women, anyway."

Jenna's lower lip thrust forward. "Hey!"

I ignored her and remained focused on Foxworthy. Calling him Pichard would take some getting used to. "He's the one who got the evidence of you cheating so your ex-wife could divorce you. He's also the one who tipped off the authorities to your shady dealings at your gallery. You considered him responsible for ruining your life, and you wanted revenge on him." I paused. "Is that why Nick's gone MIA? Because of you?"

"Ex-wife?" Jenna's eyes shot sparks and she glared at Foxworthy. "You were married?"

Foxworthy ignored Jenna's remark and continued to stare at me. "Nick's missing?"

"For quite a while now. A witness saw a shadowy figure fire a gun at him, and he hasn't been seen since." I pointed an accusing finger at him. "Did you kill him? Or have him killed?"

His bicolored eyes flashed. "I won't deny I'd have loved to be the one to pull the trigger, but if Nick Atkins is dead, which I seriously doubt, by the way, it was someone other than myself who did it. And make no mistake, there are lots of someone elses who'd also like the pleasure of putting a bullet in his brain."

"Fine, let's say you didn't kill him. Maybe he's in hiding. I don't know. But I think you do."

He slipped his dark glasses back on. Lowering his weapon, he leaned forward and jerked me to my feet.

"Enough playing around. I know nothing about the whereabouts or possible demise of Nick Atkins, but one thing I do know. This is the end of the line for you, Ms. Charles. I can't take the chance of you blabbing all this to your friends at the FBI and revealing my true identity to Interpol. I know you'd take advantage of the very first opportunity to do just that. We're taking a little trip." He poked the gun into my ribs. "And no funny stuff. I promise you, your end will be swift."

"Like Nick's?"

He ignored my remark but asked, "Just how do you know Nick, may I ask? Did he do PI work for you? Or did he help you with reporting on a case?"

"Neither. I never met the man, actually. I adopted his cat, or rather, the cat adopted me."

He peered at me over the rims of his glasses. "You adopted his cat? And that gives you what? Some sort of karmic connection?"

I lifted my chin. "You could say Nick is our common bond." I paused at his blank look. "The cat. I named him Nick, even before I was aware it was his owner's name."

"I have no time to waste with this confusing nonsense," he growled. "Nick Atkins, Nick Atkins's cat, it all means less than nothing to me. I do know Nick couldn't stand any animal when he was alive, especially cats. Dogs and birds he could tolerate, maybe. And only then if he thought it'd earn him points with some chick."

"Well, he was fond of this cat. Little Nick is very special. He has amazing deductive powers."

Foxworthy's lips twisted into a sneer. "Now I know you are lying. No animal is that smart."

"You'd be surprised. Why, it's because of Little Nick I figured out the secret panel."

"You, my dear, are slightly deranged, I fear. Your years of investigative reporting have caught up with you, I'm afraid. They are affecting your good sense." He turned to Jenna. "Is the shipment ready to go?"

She nodded. "Kurt has all the paperwork in order. He's got the passports, too. All we have to do is meet him at the warehouse."

"Good. As much as I regret leaving those missing diamonds behind, we can't waste precious time searching for them. If Nora Charles managed to figure this out, no doubt that insufferable detective will as well. Let's go." He snapped the slide closed on his pistol and held it up to my face. "You know, Ms. Charles, in spite of your babbling about Nick Atkins and cats, I find you quite interesting. Another time, another place, who knows what might have been? Alas, though, now it's time to go."

His arm reached toward me, but Jenna grabbed it in mid-air. She inclined her head toward my purse and its spilled contents. "She should pick all that up, Foxy. What if the police come here again and find it? We don't want to leave them any hints as to what may or may not have happened to her."

"You're right." He pushed me down on the floor. "Gather it up, and make it snappy. We're on a timetable."

I gathered up the articles that had fallen out of my purse—all except the Wilson Galleries card. I pushed the card halfway under the desk, slung my bag over my shoulder, and rose shakily to my feet. Foxworthy's fingers bit cruelly into my forearm.

"Come along, Ms. Charles. Don't look so sad. It'll all be over soon."

We went back down the passageway, Jenna leading, me in the middle, Foxworthy bringing up the rear, his gun jabbing right into the small of my back. Out in the back courtyard was a black SUV. Jenna opened up the rear door and shoved me unceremoniously in. Then she crawled in the back with me, keeping her gun leveled at my chest, while Foxworthy sped the vehicle out of there.

"No tricks," she warned me, waving the gun in front of my face. "I know how to use this, and believe me, I've got no qualms about shooting you dead to save our hides."

I scooted toward her a bit, but the warning look in her eye made me stop. She definitely wasn't bluffing. I tried the calm voice of reason. "Jenna, you know, there's still a chance for you. You haven't killed anyone yet. The most they can get you on is aiding and abetting."

"And forgery and smuggling," she sniffed. "Do you think I'm stupid? I'd still get fifteen years if I'm lucky." She waved her free hand up and down her body. "Do you think I want to waste the best years of my life in a prison cell? I'd be an old hag when I got out. No one would find me attractive."

I doubted anyone but a psychopath would find her attractive now, but I kept that to myself. "They'll catch you, you know," I said. "They always do. And if you help them kill me, then it'll be worse for you."

Her lip curled. "They won't catch us. That's just wishful thinking on your part, Nora. By the time they find your body, we'll be in Europe doing our disappearing act. We've spent lots of time planning it."

We'd reached the Billings Warehouse. Foxworthy pulled straight into the loading dock. Out the rear window I could see at least a dozen boxes lying there, ready to go. Kurt Wilson was leaning on one of them, a manila envelope clutched in one hand. His beady eyes widened as the rear door opened and I climbed out, Jenna close behind me. I winced as the blued steel of the revolver bit into my ribs.

"What the—" he said, looking from me to Jenna to Foxworthy and then back to me again. "How—what is Ms. St. Clair doing here?"

"Ah, let me bring you up to speed, Kurt." Armand Foxworthy laughed. "This is not Abigail St. Clair; this is Nora Charles, the sister of Lacey, the girl we framed for Pitt's murder."

"Ah." Kurt appeared to be very uncomfortable. "What are we going to do with her?"

Foxworthy gave a giant sigh. "What do you think?"

"Not another murder?" Kurt frowned. "You know, I never really understood why we had to go that far. I didn't like it when you shot that guard in Paris, and I liked it less when you killed Pitt and Julia. Especially Julia."

"Now, now. You know why they had to die." He jammed the gun into my ribs. "Inside, Ms. Charles. Quickly, now."

I moved inside the warehouse. Foxworthy was right behind me, Kurt beside him, still ·yammering. "Pitt's death was all a misunderstanding," Kurt spat. "And as for Julia, I just don't see why we can't tie this girl up and leave her in the underground tunnel. We should have done that with Julia. At least if they were dead by the time anyone found them it wouldn't be as if we actually pulled the trigger."

"That's a good one," sneered Foxworthy. "You don't mind deaths as long as you don't actually kill the person hands on. Well, guess what?" He shoved the gun in Kurt's face. "Maybe I'll make you pull the trigger this time. How do you like that?"

Kurt jumped back as if he'd been stung. "I don't like it," he whined. "I don't want to actually shoot anyone, Armand. It's just not in me."

Foxworthy whirled, fire in his eyes. "Well, you'd better get it in you. This girl's gonna die, and you're gonna do it."

Armand shoved Kurt. Kurt shoved Armand. Then the two of them started shoving and shouting at each other. Jenna stepped in to try and pull them apart, and they shoved her back, too. Then Jenna, eyes flashing, lunged at her brother. Soon they were all dancing around the dock in a crazy sort of rhythm. They'd all forgotten about me, just standing there, with no gun pointed at me. They hadn't even bothered to tie me up or blindfold me.

I mentally blessed stupid, overconfident criminals, turned on my heel, and started running toward the nearest exit.

Behind me, I heard a loud whoop: "Holy shit, she's getting away!" A few more stupids were tossed back and forth, and then in the stillness of the warehouse, I heard the distinct click of a safety being turned back.

The next instant a bullet whizzed past my cheek.

I kept running.

Another bullet narrowly missed my left calf.

"I'm just toying with you, Ms. Charles," Foxworthy shouted. "I advise you to stop now, or you'll meet your end in a much messier fashion than I'd planned."

The exit from the loading dock was about three feet from me. I inhaled deeply and kept on running. And then—

I felt a searing pain in my left shoulder. Glancing over, I saw a dark red stain marring the crisp whiteness of my blouse. Stars danced in front of my eyes, and I felt shock creep through every bone in my body. I sank, panting, to the warehouse floor. My vision was starting to dim—out of the corner of one eye, I saw Foxworthy approach, gun in hand. He raised his arm, the gun pointed straight at my heart. "Say hello to Nick for me—if the two of you end up in the same place, that is."

"FFT-FFT. Ma-ROW! Ma-ROW!"

A black blur came hurtling out of the shadows and hit Foxworthy squarely in the chest. The gun went flying, and Foxworthy went down, Nick's teeth clamped firmly on his wrist.

"What the—where'd this beast come from?" Foxworthy shouted. "Get him off me!" he yelled. "Shoot him."

Kurt just stood there, jaw agape. Jenna started to scramble for the gun, but at that moment three police cars with flashing lights skidded to a stop just outside the bay. A swarm of policemen, guns drawn, jumped from the cars, leveling their weapons at the three crooks.

"Put your hands in the air and step forward," one shouted through a megaphone.

Jenna and Kurt complied at once. Foxworthy writhed on the ground, Nick's teeth still in his flesh.

"Nick," I whispered. "Let him go."

Nick released Foxworthy just as two officers came up. They hauled Foxworthy to his feet, spun him around, clamped handcuffs on him.

I struggled to a sitting position. Nick came over, gave my arm a head butt, then circled twice and settled himself in the crook of my hip. His rough tongue darted out, licked the back of my hand. I pulled him closer just as the policemen passed, Foxworthy between them. He paused and looked down at me, at Nick, and slowly shook his head.

Behind me I heard a shout.

"Nora! Nora, dammit, I told you to stay out of this!"

Daniel raced to my side and knelt down. He gingerly touched my shoulder, and I winced.

"Flesh wound?" I asked.

"Looks that way, but you've still lost a lot of blood. We'd better get you to a hospital and fast."

Another shadow loomed over me, and I looked up to see Samms's unsmiling face. I gave him a two-fingered wave. "Thanks for showing up."

"Actually, we went to your aunt Prudence's," Samms said. "I got the toxicology report back from the autopsy—no tranqs."

I cut him off with a moan. "No? I was so certain—"

"Let me finish. No tranqs, but there was a very, very slight trace of aconite. Not enough to be fatal, but enough to incapacitate. You were gone by the time we got to Pitt's office, but we found the card you dropped—the Wilson Galleries card—so we figured we'd better hightail it here."

Daniel finished putting a tourniquet on my upper arm, and I winced as a bolt of pain shot through me. Gritting my teeth I said, "Thank God you did, but how did you know to go to Pitt's office in the first place?"

Samms and Daniel exchanged puzzled looks. "Don't you remember? You dialed my number," Samms said. "When I answered I heard you talking with Jenna and Foxworthy. I'm still amazed at how you did that, 'cause it sure sounded like they had a gun on you the whole time."

"Wha—my cell phone?"

Geez, they were right. Now that I thought about it, I hadn't seen my cell when I'd bent to retrieve the contents of my bag. Which meant . . .

I glanced over at Nick, who sat calmly, licking his paws into an ebony sheen.

"Are you sure you're not part human?" I whispered, and then I couldn't help it. I passed out.

TWENTY-THREE

I woke up to a Winter Wonderland of white, white, white . . . ceiling, light in my face, tile walls, and the sheen of an oxygen mask covering my face.

"Anyone there?" I tried to speak, and my voice came out a breathy whisper, more strangled than sexy. I lifted the mask off my face, and the door popped open and a stern-faced nurse bustled in.

"You need to keep this on, Ms. Charles," she said. "You've lost a lot of blood."

"I can breathe, thanks."

The door opened again, and Daniel and Samms both walked in. Daniel gave me a tight smile, and Samms led in with a "Hmpf. You look like hell."

I sat up, leaning against the pillows. "Gee, thanks. How long have I been here?"

"Only less than a day," Daniel answered. "That wound

ended up being penetrating, not perforating. They removed the bullet, but you did lose a lot of blood. The doctor wants you to stay here at least another day to get built back up."

"Oh. Well, it could have been worse." I gave them a small smile. "I guess Foxworthy wasn't the great shot he claimed to be." My fingers fisted in the thin blanket. "Lacey?"

"Freed," said Samms. "The DA didn't give us a problem, once we had Foxworthy's confession, or should I say Pichard's."

"We had a suspicion he might still be alive," said Daniel. "When you asked me about him, I hoped you weren't after a story, or getting mixed up in that mess. But I couldn't say a word about it to you. Not my call, sorry. The directive came from another division."

"It's okay." I waved my hand. "I think the three of them—Foxworthy, Wilson, and Jenna—thought they'd planned the perfect crime. Although if I had to guess, I'd peg Wilson as the weak link in the chain."

"And you'd be right," admitted Daniel. "Wilson caved first, actually. Once he did, I guess Foxworthy realized he had no choice but to come clean."

"What happened?"

"Well, it all started with Pichard. After his divorce he had a run of bad luck, mainly because the local authorities had received a tip on his shady dealings and were watching him very closely. He fled the States for Europe, where he wasted no time getting involved with some pretty unsavory characters, and soon he was in over his head again. It wasn't long before an enterprising reporter exposed his involvement in art smuggling. At that point, he came up with the idea of faking his death, which he did, and did a pretty good job, by the way. He almost had Interpol fooled. He took on the identity of Armand Foxworthy, and that's how he became involved with the Wilsons, who, by the way, are brother and sister. The W in Jenna's name stands for Whitley, their mother's maiden name. She just shortened it for an alias."

"The Wilsons were down on their luck, too." Samms took up the gauntlet. "They were petty jewel thieves who left the US for Europe, doing small scams, but never really hitting the big time. When Jenna met Foxworthy, everything just clicked. They connected with a 'bling ring' masterminded by a South American group and executed the theft that netted them half a million in rare gems. Foxworthy, who apparently has an itchy trigger finger, killed the guard in the ensuing melee, much to Kurt's chagrin, and that's when they all decided to relocate back to the States. They settled on California, set up shop as the Wilson Galleries. It wasn't long after that they ingratiated themselves with the Pitt Institute, which provided them with the perfect front for selling the gems to the highest bidders and shipping them out."

"They had a pretty slick operation," Daniel admitted. "Jenna was the brains behind that. She used her talent to secret the gems inside sculptures and send them out to their contacts. Kurt chatted up Pitt to give the gallery an air of respectability, and Foxworthy, well, as Pichard he did have a degree in Art, so it was a simple matter to fake diplomas and get hired as an instructor, which he did to keep an eye on his sister, whom he suspected of fooling around with Pitt. Pitt's art collection was an added bonus. When they met Kurt and found out about his talent for copying they hit upon the forgery scheme as a supplement. Foxworthy's long-range plans, once all the gems were disposed of, included duplicating the portraits Pitt had in his collection, substituting the dupes, and selling the originals."

"A very enterprising fellow, wasn't he?" I observed. "But plans changed when they thought Pitt found out what they were doing."

"Yes." Daniel nodded. "Their first mistake was selling Pitt a forgery. The Engeldrumm was hot, passed to them as payment for one of the gem shipments, and they couldn't take the chance of losing the original. Then to compound matters, Taft delivered the wrong sculpture to Pitt. A natural mistake on Taft's part since he wasn't involved with the diamonds. When Pitt unwrapped the painting to give it to his son, he noticed right away it was a forgery, and he called Wilson complaining about the flaw, but he meant the portrait. They automatically assumed he meant the sculpture, since the ones containing gems do have a slight crack in the back of the head. Foxworthy, afraid Pitt would turn them in, decided he had to be silenced. When Jenna told him about Lacey's argument with Pitt, he knew just what to do.

"Jenna put the poison in Pitt's wine. She knew just how much, because she was pretty well versed on the subject. Taft picked up that bit of knowledge listening to her. She knew Pitt kept his office unlocked during the day, so she went in at lunchtime, knowing he wouldn't take any wine until the evening. When she saw the sculpture missing, she naturally thought Pitt might have discovered the diamonds. Actually, he'd taken it to show to Julia. Imagine Foxworthy's surprise when he stepped in that night to kill Pitt and saw the sculpture back on the shelf. He couldn't do anything about it then, though. Lacey came too quickly. He'd found the plans in the file cabinet downstairs, so he and Jenna both knew all the secret labyrinths. He went in later to dispose of the wine and switch the sculpture." Daniel chuckled. "He never figured on Nora's eagle eye noticing the difference in the hands."

"So he was still in the room when Lacey arrived." I shuddered. "My sister is lucky. He could have killed her."

"He could indeed," Samms agreed. "But then she wouldn't have been able to take the fall for the murder, as he planned. And oddly enough, Pitt didn't notice the crack in the sculpture. Julia did. That was what started her thinking. She went on a little quest of her own and discovered the sculptures in the storeroom, along with some bits of broken plaster. She put two and two together, and that was what she was going to tell me in the warehouse that night. Unfortunately, Taft saw her poking around the boxes and told Wilson, who told Foxworthy, who then figured she had to be either police or feds, so he followed her to the warehouse and strangled her." Samms shook his head. "Just all in a day's work for the bastard. He strangled her, had himself a relaxing smoke, and then took off. You didn't miss him by much."

"Like Lacey, I had a close call. I'm sure he wouldn't have hesitated to strangle me as well." I slumped back against the pillows. "What happened to the diamonds in the pouch Julia found?"

"Jenna left the pouch on her worktable, and Julia accidentally knocked it over. When she saw the diamonds inside she figured she'd hide them in a safe place until she could report to us—and to her, the safest place was Pitt's office. As a federal agent, she was able to come and go as she pleased into the room."

"And I'll bet I can guess just where she hid them. In some molding along the side of the wall."

"Ah, you found the secret panel in your own room," Samms laughed. "See, I knew you were a junior Nancy Drew."

"Taft's agreed to the deal Julia wanted to cut for him," said Daniel. "His testimony will go a long way toward making sure these three rot in prison where they belong. We're hopeful this experience has taught him a valuable lesson."

"So Giselle, Althea, and Philip had nothing to do with any of this," I said. "I didn't think they did, although that parking ticket had me going for a while."

"Yeah, me, too," said Samms. "Althea Pitt admitted to me that she'd gone to the school that night. She wanted to talk to her husband about why he pulled the plug on giving Philip that portrait, but when she saw Giselle's car she just kept on driving."

"Ah, that's why she thought Giselle might have had a hand in Pitt's murder. She didn't know that it was Taft using Giselle's car to cheat on her." I smiled thinly. "Looks like Giselle's only crime was being a gold digger, just like Althea and Philip suspected."

"Yep, so everything's resolved." Daniel covered my hand with his. "Lacey's outside, along with your aunt. Feel up to a visit?"

I smiled weakly. "Sure."

"Great. We'll give you some privacy."

Samms leaned over the bed. His fingers twisted in the thin sheet as he said gruffly, "Well, I guess, I mean, I suppose you were a big help here, at the end."

I perked up and put a hand to my ear. "What? Was that an actual compliment I heard come out of your mouth?"

"Let's not get carried away. You did some stupid things, too, like going back to the scene of the crime without notifying us of your theory, but your reasoning did go a long way toward the end result."

"Not lavish praise, but I'll take what I can get."

His lips twigged upward. "Compliments from me have to be earned, remember?"

Oh, I did indeed. But before I could think of an answer, Daniel stuck his head in the doorway and called impatiently, "Come on, Lee. There are a few others who want to say hello to Nora."

Samms gave my hand a quick squeeze. "Take care, Red."

I eyed him. "I HATE that nickname and you know it."

"I don't know why but it suits you to a tee." He let his lips curve upward. "Who knows, maybe our paths will cross again someday." Before I could fathom how to respond to *that* statement, he was gone, and I found myself besieged by Lacey and Aunt Prudence enveloping me as best they could with hugs and kisses.

"Thank you, thank you, for getting me out of this mess. I'll never fight with you again," Lacey whispered. "Or at least, not for the next six months. Pinky swear."

I grinned at her. "Are you coming back to Cruz? Want to stay with me?"

"Actually, I thought I might finish up at the Institute. I've only got a bit more to go and then—" Did my sister actually giggle? "Peter said he had a friend in the design department of a small company here who might need a good artist. So, I think I might stay with Aunt Prudence for a while, at least."

"Uh-huh." I took in her flushed face and sparkling eyes. "I don't suppose Peter Dobbs figures into this equation at all?"

"We're just good friends," she smiled wickedly. "Like you and that Daniel." She shook her head and rolled her eyes. "What a hunk! And so is the cop who arrested me. Boy, do the two of them think pretty highly of you. I don't know how you're gonna decide between them. They're so *hot!*"

I blanched. "What do you mean, decide between them? There's nothing to decide, no sirree."

"My turn. Don't hog your sister."

Lacey moved back so Aunt Prudence could brush a light kiss across my forehead. "You just can't help yourself, can you?" She wagged her finger under my nose. "Somehow I think you'll always find time for a good mystery, even with all your duties at Hot Bread. Oh, and speaking of that! We've got another surprise for you. Are you up for it?"

Before I could answer, the door burst open and Chantal rushed in to smother me with a bearlike hug. "*Chérie! Mon Dieu!* I did a reading, and the Tower kept coming up. I was so worried. I called Rick, and he called Daniel. As a matter of fact, Rick drove me up as soon as we heard what happened." She patted my shoulder. "Don't worry, Lance is watching Hot Bread. And we are going back first thing tomorrow." She gave my hand a tight squeeze. "I just had to make sure you were still in one piece. Nicky, too, of course."

"I should be out of here by tomorrow. But I thought I'd stay an extra day or two, if you don't mind. Have a real visit with Lacey and Aunt Prudence." I grinned. "I need to get Irene a thank-you gift, too. If she hadn't told me about the secret corridor, I might still be banging my head against a brick wall, the crooks would have gotten off scot-free, and Lacey'd be on trial for murder."

"So all's well that ends well. And I see you have found both Kings—Wands and Swords." Her eyes flashed. "Daniel introduced me to Detective Samms."

I felt my cheeks start to flame as Lacey poked Chantal's shoulder. "Aren't they hot! And to think they're both after my sister!"

"They most certainly are not," I sputtered. "Daniel and I are just getting to know each other. As for Samms . . ." I waved my hand dismissively. "Well, we don't get on very well."

"So I gather." Chantal gave me an odd look then bent close to me and whispered, "The card that turned up in my reading—the Lovers. That person from the past is him, isn't it? This Samms?"

I squirmed a bit and leaned back against the pillows. "Well, sorta. I mean, there is a bit of history there, but it's irrelevant, really. I mean, he's here in St. Leo, we're in Cruz. We'll probably never see Samms again."

Chantal put a finger to her lips. "I would not bet on that. I have a feeling this isn't the last you're going to see of him." She leaned in closer and whispered, "One day soon, *chérie*, you are going to have to share the details with me. And I mean *all* of them."

Oh, swell. What's that old saying? Your past comes back to haunt you?

"Speaking of your men, there is one more. Wait." Chantal hurried out the door and came back a few minutes later with Nick clasped in her arms. She set him down on the bed next to me. "We can't stay long. The nurse will have a fit, but Daniel charmed her."

I riffled Nick's fur. "Saved me again, didn't you?" I whispered into his ruff.

Nick blinked and meowed softly.

Chantal leaned over and plucked Nick up. "We'd better go. We'll be waiting for you at your aunt's. Daniel is going to try and get you released a little early."

"Great."

Lacey leaned over and gave me a swift kiss on the forehead. "Yeah, sis, hurry up and get out of here. I can't wait to tell you all my plans and grill you about your past with Samms. Hoo-wee!"

Chantal's grin stretched ear to ear. "Yes, hoo-wee, indeed!"

I sighed. No way I could fight both of them. I'd have to pray for divine intervention. They were halfway out the door when Chantal suddenly turned and made a beeline back to my bed. "I almost forget, *chérie*," she said. She hefted Nick off to one side and whipped a white envelope out of her purse. *Nora Charles* was scrawled in almost illegible script across it. "Daniel wanted me to give you this. He said to tell you it was from Foxworthy."

I took the envelope. "Foxworthy? Really? Thanks." Once they'd left, I slit it open and a single sheet of lined paper and a twenty-dollar bill fell out. I unfolded it and read:

Dear Ms. Charles:

Please accept my congratulations on solving a very complex case. I must say, I am impressed beyond words by your detective prowess. Why, you might even be a better detective than our friend Nick, although, trust me, that blowhard would never admit to that.

And speaking of Nick, I was sincere when I told you I know nothing about what might have happened to him. The only thing I can tell you is that like the proverbial cat, Atkins has nine lives, and I fully believe he hasn't expended a one of them. He's like a bad penny. Atkins will turn up again, mark my words, when you least expect it. He was always big on drama, that Nick. But, if you are determined to find out more about him, there is one person I can think of who might be able to lend a hand.

Ask Nick's former partner about Angelique. That's all I can say. But if there is anyone who can tell you what might have happened to Atkins—if he is just missing or truly dead—then Angelique's your girl.

And when Nick does turn up, dead or alive, tell him I always liked him, deep down, even if I still hold him responsible for all that's happened to me. Oh, and buy that lifesaving cat of his a bit of extra kibble, or whatever he's eating these days. From the looks of him, I'd say he enjoys a good steak—or maybe two?

Deepest Regards,
Bronson A. Pichard

I tapped the sheet of paper thoughtfully against the tip of my chin before setting it down on top of the twenty. I closed my eyes. The phone at my bedside rang. I reached over and picked up the receiver. "Hello?"

"Hey, Nora." Ollie's anxious voice floated over the wire. "I heard you're on the mend."

"Yep. Pichard's arrested, and I should be out of here by

tomorrow." I hesitated, unsure of whether or not to broach the topic of Angelique, but Ollie's next words drove all cohesive thought from my mind.

"Good. Rest up, because something's happened that leads me to think . . ."

"Think what, Ollie? What's wrong?" I asked as the silence grew so thick you could cut it with a knife.

"I don't really know what to say," he admitted. "I can hardly believe it myself, but something's happened that makes me believe . . . that there could be a chance . . . aw, heck, I'll just come out and say it. I guess you might have been right all along.

"Nick Atkins might be alive!"

FROM NORA'S RECIPE BOOK

PETER DOBBS PANINI

Sub roll or Italian bread
2 tablespoons olive oil
2 teaspoons anchovy paste
2 slices fresh mozzarella cheese
2 slices fresh tomato
Salt and pepper to taste

Brush the inside of a split sub roll or sliced Italian bread with olive oil. Spread on anchovy paste. Fill with 2 slices each of fresh mozzarella and tomato; season with salt and pepper. Put into panini press and cook until golden.

GEORGE FOREMAN GRILLER

1½ pounds ground chuck (80 percent lean) or ground turkey
(90 percent lean)
Salt and freshly ground black pepper

4 slices cheese
Sliced onion
4 whole wheat or spinach wraps
Ketchup
Toasted burger buns

Divide the meat into 4 equal portions (about 6 ounces each). Form each portion loosely into a ¾-inch-thick burger. Season both sides of each burger with salt and pepper. Cover with cheese and onion. Place on grill until done, then fold into wrap, smother with ketchup, and enjoy!

BRAD PITT ALL-AMERICAN HERO

Long hero roll
2 tablespoons mayo
6 slices Virginia ham
6 slices bologna
6 slices cheddar cheese
Hot peppers
4 slices of tomato
Shredded lettuce
Oil and vinegar

Slice long roll; spread liberally with mayo. Cover with a layer of Virginia ham, then a layer of bologna, then cheddar cheese. Garnish with hot peppers, tomato, and shredded lettuce. Sprinkle with oil and vinegar.

ANDY GARCIA CUBAN SPECIAL

Panini bread (or long roll, if desired)
2 tablespoons mayo
3 tablespoons each of oil and vinegar
Spicy mustard
6 slices of turkey
6 slices of Italian speck
6 slices of Colby-Jack cheese
Sliced dill pickles
Olive oil

Mix the mayo and oil and vinegar and spread liberally on panini bread (or roll if preferred). Place layers of turkey, speck, and Colby-Jack cheese, spreading spicy mustard in between each layer. Place sliced dill pickles on top; spread top of bread or roll liberally with spicy mustard. Close sandwich, brush top of bread lightly with olive oil. Place under press or grill until cheese is melted. Slice and serve hot.

A Preview of the Next Nick and Nora Mystery

OF CRIME AND CATNIP

"I declare, Nora, with food like this the museum's annual gala can't help but be a success."

I smiled politely at the speaker as I rose to refill my mother's good bone china bowl with tortilla chips. Nandalea Webb, the Cruz Museum's curator, was a no-nonsense type of gal and as feisty as the Australian meaning of her given name implied. She waved a red-lacquered hand in the air, leaned back in her chair, and reached for one of the deviled eggs on the tray in the middle of the table. She took a bite and batted lashes heavy with several coats of Lash Plus mascara.

"Heaven," she murmured, dabbing at her salmon-tinted lips with the edge of a napkin. "I can't tell you how much the committee appreciates your stepping in to cater this year's fund-raiser on such short notice."

"My pleasure," I assured her, reaching for a chip myself. "Not only would my mother have encouraged me, I consider it an honor. Anyway, I've catered events on less notice. Mac Davies's retirement from Cruz Detective Squad, for example. I had about twelve hours' notice for that."

"True, dear, but that wasn't of the magnitude this is." Nan's teeth flashed in her version of a smile. "This will be a real challenge for you."

"Well, we Charles women always love a challenge. Plus, I can definitely use the extra income." I set the newly refilled bowl of chips in front of her. She took one, plunked it in my spinach dip (actually, I can't claim credit for that; the recipe is my Aunt Prudence's), and popped it into her mouth. "My mother was always a staunch supporter of the museum. I know she would be proud."

"Indeed she would be."

I turned my attention to the other speaker. Violet Crenshaw was a lifelong resident of our little town of Cruz, California, with all the "old money" that usually accompanied such an honor. A senior member of the museum's board of directors, probably the most senior, at age seventy-one, she was extremely well preserved. Slight of frame, her clothes fit her like a runway model. Today she had on a dress of lightweight fire-engine red wool that screamed "expensive designer." It was definitely a dress I'd have killed for, if the color didn't clash with my hair. Violet's own lavender-tinted hair was done in a becoming upsweep that set off her high cheekbones and delicate bone structure to advantage. I could see why the women made such an effective team. Where Nan was outgoing and effusive, Violet was the more laid-back of the two, but just like the old saying, still waters ran deep. Violet might tread softly, but she carried a big stick, just like her idol, Teddy Roosevelt.

On this late autumn afternoon we were seated in the back room of Hot Bread, the sandwich shop I'd inherited from my mother a few months ago, to discuss my catering their annual fund-raiser. The Cruz Museum fund-raisers were always a big deal; expertly planned to raise a great deal of money, they were always successful, plus they paid very well. The firm they usually used to cater their events had shut their doors abruptly a week ago. One of the owners had been diagnosed with a heart murmur, prompting the momentous decision to retire in Palm Springs and reap the fruits of their years of successful labor, and so I'd been approached for the job, not only because no other caterer in a twelve-mile radius wanted the responsibility or pressure of catering a gala for two hundred people on two days' notice, but also because my late mother, in addition to being a museum patron, had also been a friend to both Nandalea and Violet.

Violet helped herself to one of the finger sandwiches I'd prepared and eyed me with a steely gaze over the rims of her Ben Franklin–style glasses. "Your mother was an excellent cook, Nora. She put her all into Hot Bread. I always felt bad we had that long-standing contract with Mike Rodgers. She would have enjoyed catering our affairs."

Nan's dark brown pageboy bobbed up and down in agreement. "Yes, she always supported our cause with generous donations. She loved Cruz and its history, and she loved the museum."

"It's very gratifying to see you taking over where she left off, following the family tradition." Violet coughed lightly then added, "Family is so important. Sometimes one doesn't realize how much."

I caught the wistful note in the older woman's voice and smiled. "I couldn't agree more."

"*Er-owl!*"

We all jumped. The large (although portly might be a better word) black-and-white tuxedo cat sprawled across Hot Bread's kitchen floor pushed himself upright to regard us with wide golden eyes. His ears flattened against his skull as his mouth opened, revealing a row of sharp, pointed teeth. He waved one forepaw in the air in an imperious manner.

"Ah," Nan laughed. "I see your cat agrees family is important. What's his name again?"

"Nick."

The two women burst out laughing. "What else? Of course you'd name him after *The Thin Man*." Nan chuckled. "Your mother loved those old movies. For that matter, so did I. Who didn't love William Powell? This younger generation has no idea what they've missed." Her gaze swept the cat up and down. "He looks well cared for. What shelter did you get him from?"

"No shelter, although I do think that's a marvelous way to adopt a pet. He just appeared on my doorstep one night, waltzed inside, and that was that. Honestly, I blame Chantal. She talked me into keeping him, although I've never regretted it." I laughed. "It's hard to tell sometimes who owns who."

"One never owns a cat, dear. They own you," Nan said with a wise nod.

Nick sat up on his haunches and pawed at the air, his head bobbing up and down.

Nan leaned over. "So you agree, do you, big fella?"

Nick rolled over on his back and wiggled all four paws in the air.

Violet peered at the cat over the rims of her glasses. "He's quite the little ham, isn't he?"

I suppressed a chuckle. "You don't know the half of it."

Nick sat up, wrapped his tail around his forelegs, cocked his head to one side as if studying the women. Then he got up, trotted over to the fleece bed in the corner, swiped his paw underneath the cushion, and reappeared a moment later with a catnip mouse. He dropped it at the foot of Nan's chair and looked up expectantly; then he squatted down and proceeded to attack the mouse with his teeth and claws.

"Oh, how cute," Nan gushed. "He seems quite intelligent, and he certainly likes his catnip." She grinned as Nick flopped over again, mouse clenched firmly between his paws, and wiggled his hind legs. Quite a sight.

"Believe it or not, he likes the Scrabble tile set more."

"What, he can spell?"

Both women started to laugh at Nan's outburst, but I wasn't kidding. Nick's penchant for spelling words had helped me solve two mysteries; however, I didn't feel like sharing those details. Instead I just shrugged. "It's not as far-fetched as it sounds. Dogs can be trained, right? So why not cats? For my money, they're the most intelligent animal around."

"Spoken with no prejudice whatsoever," laughed Nan. "I've always been a dog person, myself, but you know what? I think your cat could change my mind."

"Mine, too," agreed Violet. "I mean, look at him. He actually looks as if he wants to speak."

Nick sat erect, his teeth visible in what I termed his "shit-eating kitty grin." I was convinced that if cats could talk, he would undoubtedly have lots to say.

"It wouldn't surprise me. He's very smart. My biggest

fear is Nick will show up one day out of the blue and want his cat back."

Violet turned her questioning gaze on me. "I'm sorry. I'm a bit confused. I thought Nick was the cat's name?"

"It is, and coincidentally, it's also the name of his former owner. Nick Atkins."

"Nick Atkins?" Violet's gaze swept upward to my face, her lips forming a perfect O of surprise. "You're kidding! He owned a cat? *This* cat?"

"Yes. Did you know him?" I asked, wondering how on earth the stately Violet would ever have connected with a character like the hard-boiled PI. Talk about an odd couple!

Violet's gaze darted from the cat to me back to the cat again. It seemed as if she were unsure how to answer the question. The next minute, however, her hesitation became moot as the unlikely strains of "California Gurls" chirped from the depths of her purse.

"Excuse me." She fished the phone out, glanced at the number, then snapped it open with a brisk, "Yes, Daisy. What's the matter?" She listened intently for a few minutes then sighed audibly. "Tell him we'll be back shortly and to wait until we get there. Surely twenty minutes won't make a monumental difference in their schedule." She snapped the phone shut, slid it back into her bag, and turned to me with an apologetic smile. "So sorry for the interruption. Where were we?"

Nan smiled over the rim of her coffee cup. "I believe we were about to discuss the pros and cons of a sit-down dinner versus a buffet."

"I don't think much discussion is necessary," Violet cut in. "After all, it's a costume ball. Formal dinners are lovely, but who wants to bother with all that at a masquerade?" She gave her head an emphatic shake. "We want our patrons loose and happy so they'll whip out their checkbooks and give generously. After all, the happier the patron, the bigger the contribution, am I right?"

"Oh, listen to her. She's so wise," Nan whispered.

"Hmpf. Wise has nothing to do with it. It's common sense," Violet snorted. "Just like a big part of keeping 'em happy is getting 'em plastered."

"Violet!" Nan's jaw dropped and she looked at me. "She's blunt as a knife sometimes."

"Well, it's true." The older woman chuckled. "The more they drink, the happier and looser they get, and then out come the checkbooks, and better yet, the zeros on the checks!" Her smile was wide as she turned to me and closed one eye in a broad wink. "We spring for complimentary wine and soda, but the real proceeds flow from the cash bar. Which reminds me: Our old caterer also provided the bartender. Nora, do you know where we can find a good bartender? The position pays quite well." She named a figure that made my eyes pop, and I thought immediately of Lance Reynolds. He ran the only tavern in Cruz, the Poker Face. I'd known him for years, dated him in high school. I was positive he'd agree; not only could he use the money the museum would pay, but it would be great publicity for his own bar. I mentioned his name, and Violet nodded solemnly.

"I'm ashamed I didn't think of him right off," she said, reaching in her purse. She pulled out a notebook and made a swift notation. "I'll have Daisy get right on this."

I arched a brow at the second mention of the unfamiliar name. "Daisy? Is she a new employee?"

"She's my new assistant," Violet said crisply. "Maude Frickert up and retired on us, can you believe it? Went to live in the Carolinas with her daughter. Didn't give us a lot of notice, either."

"Now, now, don't be like that, Violet. She did give us a week," interjected Nan. "We were very fortunate Daisy happened along just when she did. It was really a case of being in the right place at the right time. She happened to be in the museum and overheard us talking about finding a replacement. It's a great opportunity for her. She just moved back to the States after studying abroad in London and was going to start looking for a job. What do you call it again, when events intersect just so?"

"Fate," I answered, sliding a glance Violet's way. "I guess I always assumed that when Maude finally retired, Nellie would take her place." Nellie Blanchard was a part-time docent who'd worked at the museum forever. It was no secret the woman aspired to an office position.

"So did Nellie," Violet sighed. "Don't get me wrong, she's done a fine job as a docent, but office work is different. She wouldn't have the freedom she does now. I'm not all that sure she'd be able to adapt to a nine-to-five regimen."

I nodded. That much was true, and Nellie'd never made any bones about the fact she enjoyed being able to set her own hours. Still, she'd always hinted that when Maude went, she should be the next in line, and no one could really dispute her claim. She had the background and the experience, if not the formal education.

As if she'd read my thoughts, Violet said quickly, "Nellie's got the background and experience, and she's very familiar with the museum and our patrons. It wasn't an easy decision, but I think it was the right one. Daisy's rather young, but her references were excellent. You'll like her, I'm sure. So then"—Violet clasped her hands together—"are we in agreement on the menu? Buffet style?"

I nodded. "I have quite a few ideas on what can be done. I'll outline a menu and get it to you tonight."

"You are such a dear to do this for us on such short notice. Now, don't forget we'll need to have some of your dishes named in line with our theme."

I looked at the two of them blankly. "Theme?"

"Yes. We want the flavor of the ball to reflect the exhibit that debuts the following week." She cast an irritated glance in Nan's direction. "Didn't you mention that when you brought over the contract?"

Nan hung her head. "My fault entirely. I was remiss. I take full responsibility. It simply slipped my mind, what with all we had going on."

Violet's jaw shot forward, and before the older woman could make a disparaging remark, I said, "It shouldn't be a problem. What's the theme?"

They both answered at the same time. "The Arthurian Era."

"You mean King Arthur? As in Knights of the Round Table King Arthur? He's a fictional character, right?"

"Well, that's debatable." Nan pushed back a bit in her chair. "The historical basis for the King Arthur legend has long been a point of controversy among scholars. One school of thought sees him as a genuine historical figure, a leader who fought against the invading Anglo-Saxons sometime in the late fifth to early sixth century. Then others . . ."

"Argue Arthur was originally a fictional hero of folklore—or even a half-forgotten Celtic deity—whom they credited with real deeds in the distant past," finished Violet. "There is no concrete evidence proving or disproving either theory, but Sir Rodney Meecham, a collector from England, has assembled quite a collection of Arthurian artifacts and memorabilia, which he claims supports the former." She leaned in a bit closer to me, her voice now a hushed whisper. "Recently, he was able to acquire a very, very rare artifact. It will be shown for the very first time in the United States at our exhibit the night of the gala. That's why it's imperative everything be just perfect."

"I see," I said slowly. "And just what is this artifact, might I ask?"

Once again they answered in unison. "The grimoire of Morgan LeFay!"

As the two of them beamed at me, I frantically tried to remember everything I'd ever read or seen in the movies and on television about King Arthur and his legendary Knights of the Round Table. I nibbled at my lower lip as I thought, and finally shook my head.

"Sorry. I do remember Lancelot and Guinevere but I can't quite place Morgan LeFay."

"She's a powerful sorceress in the Arthurian legend. Even though early works describe her character as more of a magician, she became much more prominent in later prose works as an antagonist to Arthur and Guinevere. She is said to be the daughter of Arthur's mother, the Lady Igraine, and her first husband, the Duke of Cornwall. Arthur is her half brother. Oh, she was quite the troublemaker." Nan rolled her eyes skyward.

"And the grimoire?" I asked. "I'm not familiar with that term."

"A grimoire is an ancient book of spells. A witch's

textbook, if you will," Violet answered. "Morgan LeFay's is supposed to contain the blackest spells in all the world. The jewels that encrust its cover are supposed to act as conduits to her power. Legend or truth? It's one of those mysteries that make the study of the Arthurian era so interesting. Was Morgan LeFay real or not, and if so, was she truly a sorceress of that magnitude?" Violet paused and let her gaze bore into mine. "There are many people who would love an answer to those questions, including yours truly."

"Regardless, it's an important piece of the legend of Arthur, to be sure, and of interest to many historians," Nan added. "We're counting on it to attract fresh blood to the museum."

Violet leaned forward and brushed her hand against mine. "We've already contacted the Cruz Police Force about stepping up the security detail for the length of the exhibit, and the gala, of course."

"Yes, so you needn't worry about anything, Nora, other than preparing your excellent food," Nan remarked.

"I can name some of the sandwiches and main dishes after the more popular characters in Arthurian mythology. I'll just need to do some research."

"Splendid!" Nan clasped her hands in front of her. "And several food critics will be there. They're patrons of the museum, so it will be a wonderful opportunity for your shop, Nora. Why, you might generate more business than you can handle."

"That would be welcome, believe me."

Violet glanced at her watch and rose. "We'd best get going. The exhibit manager is waiting for us back at the museum. Apparently there are many cases to unload. We may have to give the exhibit the Red Room."

Nan was shrugging into her fleece jacket. "We'll give you a key to the kitchen, so you can just stop in anytime to look it over or whatever. You can pick it up later tonight, and do let me know if there's anything you'll need."

Nan bustled out the door, Violet trailing at a slower pace. She paused to lay her hand on my shoulder. "I hear you've become quite the sleuth. I heard what you did for your sister, and I read the account of the Grainger case. Very impressive. Like that sort of work, do you?"

"I enjoyed tracking down leads when I was a true crime reporter, so I guess it's really not that much of a stretch."

She nodded. "Well, then, when you've got a bit of time to spare, stop by my office. There's a matter I'd like to discuss with you that the sleuth in you should find quite a challenge."

Her hawklike gaze pinned me, and I thought I'd drop over at her next words.

"It's a matter that might even involve . . . a murder."

FOR THE LATEST IN PRIME CRIME AND OBSIDIAN MYSTERIES, VISIT

berkleyobsidianmysteries.com

- *See what's new*
- *Find author appearances*
- *Win fantastic prizes*
- *Get reading recommendations*
- *Sign up for the mystery newsletter*
- *Chat with authors and other fans*
- *Read interviews with authors you love*

berkleyobsidianmysteries.com

WELL-CRAFTED MYSTERIES
FROM BERKLEY PRIME CRIME

- **Earlene Fowler** Don't miss these Agatha Award–winning quilting mysteries featuring Benni Harper.

- **Monica Ferris** These *USA Today* bestselling Needlecraft Mysteries include free knitting patterns.

- **Laura Childs** Her Scrapbooking Mysteries offer tips to satisfy the most die-hard crafters.

- **Maggie Sefton** These popular Knitting Mysteries come with knitting patterns and recipes.

- **Lucy Lawrence** These brilliant Decoupage Mysteries involve cutouts, glue, and varnish.

- **Elizabeth Lynn Casey** The Southern Sewing Circle Mysteries are filled with friends, southern charm—and murder.

penguin.com

M5G0610